The Other
Edie Trimmer

The Other Edie Trimmer

JACQUELINE WILSON

Illustrated by Rachael Dean

PUFFIN

PUFFIN BOOKS

UK | USA | Canada | Ireland | Australia
India | New Zealand | South Africa

Puffin Books is part of the Penguin Random House group of companies
whose addresses can be found at global.penguinrandomhouse.com.
www.penguin.co.uk
www.puffin.co.uk
www.ladybird.co.uk

First published 2023
001

Text copyright © Jacqueline Wilson, 2023
Illustrations copyright © Rachael Dean, 2023

.The moral right of the author and illustrator has been asserted

Set in 12.5/20pt Baskerville MT Pro
Typeset by Jouve (UK), Milton Keynes
Printed and bound in Great Britain by Clays Ltd, Elcograf S.p.A.

The authorized representative in the EEA is Penguin Random House Ireland,
Morrison Chambers, 32 Nassau Street, Dublin D02 YH68

A CIP catalogue record for this book is available from the British Library

HARDBACK ISBN: 978–0–241–56718–0

INTERNATIONAL PAPERBACK ISBN: 978–0–241–56719–7

All correspondence to:
Puffin Books
Penguin Random House Children's
One Embassy Gardens,
8 Viaduct Gardens,
London SW11 7BW

To 'Dreezel' and her generous mum

Chapter One

My name is Edie Trimmer. I've wanted to be an actress ever since I was taken to see *Mary Poppins* on the stage when I was five. I acted it out in my bedroom for days afterwards. I pretended to be Mary and borrowed Mum's big bag and Dad's umbrella and made two of my Barbies be Jane and Michael in the nursery, though I'd never seen children with big chests and pointy toes.

It started to seem so real I believed I *was* Mary and launched myself off my bed, hoping I'd fly. I ended up in hospital, having ten stitches in my forehead because I cut my head badly on the end of my bedpost. Mum and Dad said I wasn't allowed to play Mary Poppins ever again.

My best friend Alexandra has always wanted to be an actress too. We act out all sorts of plays together, sometimes making up our own version. We were especially fond of *The Sound of Music* and watched it practically every day during the summer holidays last year. We pretended the Von Trapp family had twin girls called Dreezel and Teezel who were very naughty and pranked their brothers and sisters and played wicked tricks on Maria, the ex-nun who came to look after everyone. Sometimes we even used these names as nicknames for each other! Alex was Dreezel and I was Teezel. It's so great to have a best friend like Alex. She's so funny and kind and we both love art and writing stories – but we especially love drama.

We started going to Evelyn Day's stage school last autumn. It's not an actual school you go to every day. We go once a week on Saturdays, but it's very serious – it's not like Drama Club at school, where you mostly mess about. We do singing and dancing and act out scenes from plays and also do impro. Alex likes singing best. She's got a lovely voice, much better than mine. I like impro most. I'm good at making things up on the spot.

Everyone got very excited this spring, because the Pavilion Theatre on the seafront was putting on *Oliver!* as a summer

show for six whole weeks. Alex and I have seen it on television heaps of times. It's based on a brilliant book by Charles Dickens, a Victorian writer – we learned about him in English last term at school. They had TV soap stars playing Fagin and Bill Sykes, and the singer Maddie Spark playing Nancy – but the Pavilion producer wanted to come to our stage school to find children to play the workhouse kids, including Oliver himself!

'Imagine if we get chosen!' said Alex. 'Wouldn't it be incredible!'

'You and me in a real professional musical!' I said.

We talked non-stop about acting as the orphans in the workhouse.

'I don't think they're given names – well, apart from the Artful Dodger and Oliver himself. So we could make up our own names and our back story to make our acting more interesting. We could even be orphan twins like Dreezel and Teezel,' I said.

'That would be fantastic – though of course we *could* be chosen for the main parts, Oliver and the Artful Dodger,' said Alex. 'You're much better at acting than me. I bet you'll be picked for Oliver.'

'But you're much better at singing, and it *is* a musical. The Artful Dodger would be a wonderful character role. I'd like to play *him*. I think we'd be much better that way round,' I said. I didn't quite mean it. I desperately wanted to be chosen as Oliver, the leading role. I don't want to boast, but everyone seems to think I'm the best at acting at Miss Evelyn's.

Miss Evelyn started preparing us for the auditions. The boys moaned when the girls took their turn reciting Oliver and the Artful Dodger's lines.

'That's daft! They're boys' parts, aren't they, miss?' one of them shouted indignantly.

'Oliver can easily be played by a girl. Don't be so old-fashioned! Women often play men and men often play women on the professional stage,' said Miss Evelyn. 'When I was a drama student I played Hamlet and I happened to win a medal for my performance.' Miss Evelyn never has any qualms about boasting.

'Yeah, but the girls would still be rubbish pretending to be boys,' Liam insisted. He's twelve and thinks he's *so* cool and good-looking. Well, he is, actually, and lots of girls at our school seem to think that, but Alex and I think he's a royal pain.

Miss Evelyn isn't that keen on him either. 'Oliver sings a beautiful soprano song that's a real tear-jerker. Some of you older boys might well find your voices start to break by the summer,' she said crisply. 'However, you can audition for whomever you choose. I'm very happy if any of you boys want to audition to be orphan girls.'

'OK, then I'll audition for Nancy, miss, seeing as she's the main female part,' said Liam.

'Well, Maddie Spark has already been cast,' said Miss Evelyn, 'so it's hardly likely you'd get the part, Liam, even if you gave the most amazing audition. Now, let's stop wasting time, everyone. Those who want to audition for speaking parts should be word-perfect in a matter of days. Then you must all learn a couple of songs from *Oliver!*, and a lively dance routine.'

'Can we do the song rap style, Miss Evelyn? And do a bit of breakdancing? You did make it plain you don't want us to be old-fashioned,' said Liam.

'You can do that if you wish, Liam, but I don't think it would get you anywhere,' said Miss Evelyn. 'Come along, now! Stop pontificating and prevaricating!' She pronounced every syllable elaborately, her lips stretching this way and that. She's

very elegant but she sometimes sprays a little spit when she talks like that, so it's not a good idea to stand too near her.

We rehearsed and rehearsed and rehearsed. We even met up on weekdays after ordinary school was over. I made out I didn't care too much about getting a part in the play, even to Alex, but inside I still cared desperately. I was starting to find it difficult to get to sleep because the lines kept repeating in my head. I'd wake with a start in the middle of the night and act them out by torchlight in front of my mirror.

Mum heard me muttering in my bedroom and sighed. 'You're getting obsessed, Edie! I think you should be concentrating more on your schoolwork and not this wretched audition,' she said, tucking me back into bed.

Mum wasn't too thrilled about me wanting to be an actress, though she drives me to stage school while Dad goes to the gym. She thinks acting is a very insecure profession where you're often out of work. She's a lawyer and often complains of having too *much* work. She usually goes out before I get up and sometimes isn't home by the time I go to bed. Still, it's a great job and I'm proud of her.

Dad works mostly from home, so he looks after me during the week. He writes lots of different things, even advertising

copy – the words they use on adverts on TV. We often watch adverts together and sing the jingles and rate them out of ten.

If I don't make it as an actress I'd *quite* like to be a copywriter because I'm good at making up little songs. I'd made up a glorious variation of 'My Favourite Things' when Dreezel and I played our *Sound of Music* game.

> 'Toffee on apples and honeycomb Crunchies,
> Haribo sweeties when we get the munchies,
> Running in grass without nettles with stings,
> These are a few of my favourite things.
>
> Banana-split ice cream and lemon meringue,
> Fireworks at night that sparkle and bang,
> Pizza and chips and baked beans on toast,
> These are the things that we really love most!'

Dad helped me just a little bit, but it was mostly me. I let Alex believe I'd thought of it all, and she said I was a genius.

I am *not* a genius, but it's great that Alex thinks I am. Mum seems to think I'm quite clever too. She thinks I could be a lawyer like her if I put my mind to it.

'You're good at writing essays and *very* good at winning arguments!' she said. 'But you should work much harder at your maths. It will help you develop logic, analysis and problem-solving – key issues when you study law.'

'Mum! I'm rubbish at maths,' I said truthfully enough. 'I want to be an *actress*.'

It would be so wonderful if I got the part of Oliver. It would prove to Mum and Dad that I had a bit of talent.

I got myself in such a state that I couldn't keep still the Friday we had the actual audition. Mum had deliberately booked a day off work to take me but her case overran and she had to go to court.

'Oh darling, I feel I'm letting you down,' she said, looking so sorry as she gave me a good-luck hug early that morning.

'No probs, Mum. Dad'll take me,' I said.

'Oh no, have I got to sit with the pushy mums?' said Dad, pulling a face.

We took Alex to the auditions at the Pavilion too because both her parents were out at work. Dad had to sit in the stalls between two mums he didn't know, but when I peeped out from the wings he seemed to be chatting away happily to them. One of them was Liam's mum. She actually cheered when

Liam came on stage to do his audition piece, which made him cringe. Still, he *did* do a bit of rapping for his Dodger speech. Miss Evelyn frowned, but it made the producer and the director laugh.

We auditioned in strict alphabetical order, so Alex went before me.

'I'm so nervous!' she said. 'Look, I'm shivering!'

When I squeezed her hand it was freezing cold. 'Good luck, Alex! You'll knock them dead!' I said.

We hooked little fingers, and then she took a deep breath and ran on stage into the spotlight. She looked very small and anxious, nibbling her bottom lip. Miss Evelyn had drummed it into us that we should march confidently on stage with a smile on our face.

'Smile, Alex, smile!' I mouthed at her – but she couldn't see me.

They asked for her name and she stuttered a little, and I practically died for her. Still, she managed her Oliver speech perfectly. She didn't quite remember all the gestures Miss Evelyn had taught us but she looked very sweet. She came into her own when she sang Oliver's solo about love. Her voice was a little quavery for the first couple of lines, but then it soared.

I could see the producer and director sit back, clearly impressed. Then she performed the dance routine very gracefully, finishing with a curtsy at the end.

'Well *done*, Alexandra!' they called out.

It was so difficult waiting until almost the end. I wished I didn't have Trimmer for a surname. I was second to last, before Jamie Underwood. He was a lovely boy but already way taller than anyone else and not that great at acting either. I couldn't help tingling all over. I was sure I was in with a chance!

'Next!' they called.

It was me. I walked on stage confidently, grinning from ear to ear.

'My name is Edie Trimmer!' I announced, and then I launched into Oliver's speech. I put in as much expression as I could, trying to show what it would really be like to be a hungry little orphan in a grim workhouse. I remembered every gesture – and at the end I hung my head.

Then I did my song, singing loudly to show them that people sitting right at the back of the Pavilion would be able to hear every word. Perhaps I wobbled once during my dance, but I didn't let it put me off, and when I finished I stayed in

character and bowed instead of curtsying.

'Well *done*, Edie!' said the producer and director – but perhaps with slightly more emphasis than before.

I joined the row of Miss Evelyn's children sitting onstage, glowing. I looked along the row at Alex, and she grinned at me and mouthed, 'Brilliant!' I craned round to see Dad and he gave me a thumbs-up sign. After Jamie skittered around on stage like a daddy longlegs and received his 'Well *done*, Jamie, we were all told to give ourselves a clap.

'We're going to confer with Miss Evelyn now and then we'll have a careful think. I'm afraid you'll have to wait a little while before we reach our final decision, and we might ask some of you back for another audition. But we'll let you know our choices as soon as possible, I promise,' said the producer.

'Please don't be downhearted if you don't get chosen. You might be an outstanding performer, but just not quite right for this particular show. You've all done your very best, and I'm sure you've made Miss Evelyn very proud,' said the director. 'Off you go now!'

I pushed my way to Alex and we had a big hug.

'You were incredible, Edie,' she said.

'So were you!' I said firmly.

'No, I was rubbish. I was so scared!' she said.

'So was I,' I said, but the moment I'd stepped on the stage I'd lost my nerves. I'd felt marvellous.

Dad made a big fuss of both of us and took us to the ice-cream parlour over the road from the pier. We had banana splits and they were heavenly.

Mum managed to come home early and asked straight away how the audition had gone.

'You see before you Master Oliver Twist,' said Dad.

'Really?' said Mum. 'Have they made up their minds already then?'

'Not yet – but it's obvious. She was outstanding. Little Alex was great too, but not a patch on our Edie,' said Dad.

'Dad! That's not true!' I said modestly, though I was thrilled. 'I think Alex should be chosen for Oliver.' I'm ashamed to say I didn't really mean it.

We had to wait a fortnight. Alex actually had to do another audition, which was a bit worrying. Maybe they thought she was too shy to act professionally? She wasn't usually quiet at all; she was generally very bubbly and bouncy.

Miss Evelyn wasn't giving anything away the next Saturday.

'You'll just have to wait patiently,' she said.

'But they must have given you a little hint, Miss Evelyn,' I said.

'Edie, my lips are sealed,' she said, and pretended she couldn't speak when I went on badgering her.

But the Saturday after, we knew as soon as we saw her that the Pavilion people had made their decision. Her eyes were sparkling and her usually chalk-white face was flushed pink. She clapped her hands for us to be quiet and then gestured us towards her. She was holding her phone.

'I've heard from the Pavilion management, my dears. They emailed last night. Now, don't get too upset if I don't read your name out. Money is tight and they can't have the large cast they'd ideally like. Only ten of you have been chosen – eight as orphans, chorus and general extras. And two for the speaking parts, obviously: the Artful Dodger and Oliver Twist.'

Alex and I held hands, squeezing tight. Her hand was very cold again. Mine was hot. I hoped it wasn't too sweaty – but Alex was too kind to complain.

'So, I'll put you out of your misery and announce the two major parts first. The Artful Dodger is Liam!'

'Yes!' he cried out and punched the air.

Liam! I so wanted it to be Alex! I squeezed her cold little hand harder in sympathy. It would have been fantastic acting together. It would be a nightmare acting with Liam. He'd muck about and do his best to grab all the attention. Why *Liam*? Miss Evelyn obviously thought likewise, but she was doing her best to look enthusiastic.

'They took a real shine to you, Liam. They thought you were made for the part. And it seems they were rather taken by your rapping,' said Miss Evelyn.

'Oh wow! Fantastic! So who's going to be Oliver then?' Liam asked.

Miss Evelyn swallowed. Her eyes flickered in my direction. My heart was thumping so hard I felt it was about to burst through my T-shirt.

'It's Alexandra!' said Miss Evelyn.

For an instant I thought she'd simply got us mixed up and said the wrong name. But she was smiling at her now and giving her a little clap, her bangles jingling.

Alex gasped. 'But – but there must be a mistake!' she said.

'No mistake, Alexandra dear. They were absolutely certain. You look perfect for little Oliver – and you sing like an angel.

Well done! You're a credit to my stage school,' she said.

I pulled myself together. 'Yes, well done, Alex! Fantastic! I'm so happy for you!' I said.

I *was* happy too. I meant every word. If I couldn't be Oliver then it was marvellous that my best friend Alex had the part. But it was such a shock. I was *sure* I'd be chosen. So now I wouldn't have any speaking part at all. I'd only be an unnamed orphan.

It was actually worse than that. Miss Evelyn read out eight names – and none of them was mine. Even Jamie Underwood had been chosen! He seemed as stunned as I was.

'Are you *sure* they picked me, Miss Evelyn?' he said, wrinkling his nose. 'Aren't I too big for an orphan?'

'Well, I did wonder, Jamie, but they said it would look great on stage if they had one very tall orphan with clothes much too small. And they really liked you!'

'Great!' said Jamie. 'My mum won't half be pleased.'

It would be agony telling Mum and Dad that *I* hadn't been chosen for anything. They knew how much it mattered to me. Alex knew too. She went boldly up to Miss Evelyn.

'Excuse me, Miss Evelyn, but I think there's been a mistake,' she said. 'I think our names have got mixed up.

I can't be Oliver!'

'No, you're definitely Oliver, dear – I promise you,' she reassured her.

'But it should be Edie. It's so unfair,' said Alex.

'Oh Alex!' I said, rushing up to her, feeling my cheeks flaming. 'It's OK. I know we can't all be picked. It wasn't a mistake, was it, Miss Evelyn?'

'No, I'm afraid it wasn't,' she said gently, putting her arm round me. I wished she wouldn't. I didn't want to burst into tears in front of the whole class.

'But Edie's the best at acting, everyone knows that. They must be crazy not to choose her!' Alex said fiercely.

'I thought they'd pick Edie too,' Miss Evelyn said.

'Then why didn't they?' Alex demanded.

Miss Evelyn looked at me carefully. 'Do you want a little feedback, Edie – or do you just want to forget about it right now?' she said, sensing I was near to tears.

I took a deep breath. 'I'd like to have the feedback, please,' I said.

'Sensible girl! All actors must learn to take suggestions. Well, they felt you were very accomplished, almost too much, in fact. They said you were a great little actress, but

you seemed rather too sure of yourself, whereas Oliver Twist is a timid little lad. You're a good dancer, and didn't let it bother you when you wobbled, which is great – and you have a nice singing voice, though, again, almost too strong – suitable for an anthem with a rousing chorus, not a soft melancholy little air,' she said. 'Don't be downhearted, Edie. They're going to put on a pantomime at Christmas and they'll need lots of child performers then, so your time will come.'

It was so difficult to hold back the tears now. Pantomime! I wanted to be a *serious* actress!

'Oh, I love pantos,' said Alex. 'In fact, I love everything about Christmas. It will be great if we're both in it together, Edie. I shall hate being in *Oliver!* without you!'

I gave her a hug, and then I thanked Miss Evelyn for being honest with me.

'You're such a sensible girl, Edie. Like any true actress, you're ready to take things on the chin and chalk it up to experience,' she said.

I nodded and sniffed hard, quickly wiping my eyes with the back of my hand. All that long day, I managed to act as if I didn't really mind. I even stayed relatively calm when I told

Mum. I talked non-stop about Alex and how fantastic it was –
but when we'd taken her home and I was alone in the car with
Mum I started howling.

There was a special celebratory tea because Mum and
Dad had been so certain I'd be picked. We ate it anyway. In
fact, I gobbled mine down, determined to try and make myself
feel better. It didn't work. I was violently sick not long
afterwards. Then I sat on the sofa between Mum and Dad
while they did their best to comfort me.

'Never you mind, darling. We know you'd have been
magnificent as Oliver,' said Dad.

'And all great actresses have had parts snatched away from
them,' said Mum. 'I think this will make you even more
determined. Good for you!' she said, though I knew she didn't
want me to be an actress at all.

Well, I didn't want to be an actress now. Ever, ever, ever!

Chapter Two

I tried so hard to pretend to everyone that I didn't really care – but of course I did. Not being in *Oliver!* changed everything. I didn't see much of Alex that summer term. We sat together at school, and went round with linked arms in the playground, but I hardly ever went over to her house to play after school, and she could rarely come over to mine. She was too busy rehearsing. She had her part to learn, plus most of the songs, and several complicated dances. Miss Evelyn gave her special lessons after school sometimes – with Liam.

'You poor thing,' I said. '*Liam!* He's such a show-off!'

'Yes, he is,' said Alex, but then she added, 'though he can be quite funny, actually. And surprisingly kind too, sometimes. I kept forgetting stuff in one of my speeches and it was driving me bananas, and Miss Evelyn got a bit cross and said I wasn't concentrating when I *was*, and I started crying like a fool, and Liam put his arm round me and said he was rubbish at learning lines too.'

'He put his *arm* round you?' I said. 'What, like he's going to be your boyfriend or something?'

'Of course not!' said Alex, but she didn't quite look me in the eye.

Saturday stage school was entirely different too. Everyone in *Oliver!* was being coached by Miss Evelyn. We leftovers had her assistant, Sophie, who worked with the little ones, teaching bunny hops and pointy toes and how to sing 'I'm a Little Teapot'. We didn't have to do *that*, thank goodness. Sophie let us make up our own play so that we had something to rehearse too, and I was quite good at getting ideas and helping with funny lines – but it wasn't as if it was a proper play that was going to be acted in front of paying customers.

We still mixed together at lunchtime and Alex always came dashing over so we could swap sandwiches and share the same

apple, and play catching yoghurt almonds in our mouths like seals the way we always did. Liam didn't come near her then – he just mucked around with the other boys as usual. But after a while Laura O'Neil came to sit with us too.

I didn't even know her last name before the whole *Oliver!* catastrophe. She was a small, pale girl with a ponytail scraped back fiercely, making her forehead look enormous. She was the littlest orphan – and she'd also been chosen as an understudy for Oliver.

I could accept Alex playing Oliver because she was my best friend for ever and I loved her – but I couldn't help having a grudge against Laura. She seemed to think Alex was *her* friend now, and wanted to talk non-stop about being in the play. Alex was tactful enough to keep quiet about it most of the time, but Laura nattered on relentlessly, and kept practising her lines and trilling the *Oliver!* songs.

'I wish you wouldn't go on and on about it,' I said, exasperated. 'It's as if you're secretly hoping Alex is going to fall over and break her leg so that you can go on stage instead of her.'

'No, I'm not! Though I might well have to play Oliver if Alex wants to go on holiday, see,' she said, swishing her ponytail.

'We're not actually going on holiday now, not in the summer,' said Alex.

'Oh good, then we can see each other every day!' I said. 'You're only acting in the evening, aren't you, Alex?'

'Well, I think we have to do regular singing and dancing classes during the day – and then there are the matinees,' Alex said apologetically. 'But I'm sure we'll see each other *sometimes*.'

'*We'll* be seeing each other every day, won't we, Alex?' said Laura – and I wanted to slap her.

I went to the first night of *Oliver!*, of course. I gave Alex a special good luck present I'd made myself. Dad took me to one of those pottery places where you can choose a mug or bowl to decorate. I chose to paint a bowl. I painted it blue and wrote two words on it: *More Gruel!* Oliver Twist is so hungry he dares say to the workhouse man, 'Please, sir, I want some more!' Gruel is a weird kind of porridge that poor people ate in Victorian times. Charles Dickens wrote all about it in his book.

Alex laughed when she saw it and gave me the biggest hug ever.

'Good luck, Alex! You'll be brilliant, I just know it!' I said.

The audience loved her right from the start. When she sang her sad little song about wanting to be loved, nearly everyone was in tears, including me. She'd stopped being Alex and was poor little Oliver now, the star of the show.

I felt almost in awe of her when we went backstage to congratulate her. She'd been my best friend since the Infants and yet here she was, still dressed as Oliver, her face made up with white greasepaint, her eyes outlined to look sad and vulnerable. I didn't even know what to say to her. She was looking at me anxiously.

'Was I all right?' she asked.

'You smashed it!' I said, hugging her. I got smears of her make-up over my own face which made us both laugh. I managed to be almost as happy for her as I would have been for myself if *I'd* played Oliver.

I went on being happy for Alex too – but it was so lonely being without her during the holidays. We hardly got to see each other. She was generally so hyped up after the evening performance that she didn't get to sleep till way gone midnight, so she slept most of the morning. Then, as she'd warned me, she had matinees and dancing practice and extra singing lessons, so we didn't have time to do ordinary fun things together.

We managed to go to the beach a couple of times, but people recognized her and kept wanting to talk to her and get her autograph and have a selfie with her. It was like she was really famous. Well, she *was*, now. There was a huge photo on the billboard outside the Pavilion, with a quote from the glowing review in the local paper, and half the town seemed to have come to the show as well as the holidaymakers.

She wasn't my Alex any more. She was the local child star. It looked as if she'd stay a star too. She was too tactful to tell me, but I read in the papers that some producer at CBBC had been in touch, and they wanted her to have a part in a long-running series. She didn't wish she could be an actress any more. She *was* one.

Mum and Dad tried hard to make a fuss of me. Mum managed to hand one of her law cases to someone else and we went away on holiday to Venice, the three of us. It was like a fairy-tale city, without any roads, only canals, and it was great fun going on the water buses, though the water itself smelled a bit because it was so hot. Still, it was cooler in the churches and art galleries, and I was allowed to have *two* ice creams every day, so it was one of the best holidays I'd ever had. Mum and Dad bought me a little blue glass bird as a holiday souvenir.

It was a beautiful bright blue, with a yellow beak and delicate black legs with little orange claws.

'It's a bluebird of happiness,' said the friendly glassblower who had made it.

It was a whole holiday of happiness. I could forget about *Oliver!* But then we went back home. Mum went back to work. Dad kept me company at home. Sometimes we went swimming. Sometimes we walked along the cliff. Sometimes we stayed home and did some cooking together. It was fun a lot of the time. But not always. Sometimes I didn't feel like doing anything at all when Dad was concentrating on a project or making a Zoom call. I just flopped around on the sofa, staring into space.

'Come on, Edie, stir yourself,' said Dad. 'Why don't you read one of your Victoria Rose books?'

They used to be my absolute favourite stories, about a Victorian girl living in a three-storey house with white steps – a bit like *our* house, but we don't have a maid to clean the steps! The first few books are about Victoria Rose when she's a little girl, but the last story ends when she's getting married and going for a grand tour of Europe on her honeymoon. I had all ten books in the series, and a DVD of the TV adaptation.

'I've read every one at least three times. I'm bored of reading,' I said.

'Well, why don't you get your paints out and do a picture?' Dad suggested.

'I'm bored of painting too,' I said, sighing.

'OK. Then how about watching one of your favourite films?' Dad asked.

'I'm bored of them.' I yawned.

Dad sighed too. 'Well, I'm bored of you being bored. If you can't think of anything to do while I'm busy, then go and tidy your room, OK?' Dad very rarely gets cross with me, but it sounded as if he was now.

'It's not OK. Nothing's OK any more!' I said. 'I feel like my life is over! I don't see the point of anything.'

'Well, I don't see the point of trying to please you when you're acting like a spoilt brat,' said Dad. 'Just go to your room.'

I sighed once more for dramatic effect and then slouched out of the living room, slammed the door and stamped upstairs to my bedroom. It was a bit of a tip but I ignored the shoes kicked on the floor, the dressing-up clothes draped over my chair and the jumbled make-up on my dressing table from

when I'd borrowed some of Mum's old stuff to see what it looked like on me.

I went over to my windowsill and flicked at my old Sylvanian Families so they all tipped over onto their backs, their big feet in the air. One of the rabbits skittered sideways, barging right into my bluebird of happiness. It wobbled on its delicate claws.

I reached out to catch it but I wasn't quick enough. It fell over too. The bird wasn't anywhere near as sturdy as the Sylvanians. One of its legs snapped right off, *and* the tip of its blue glass wing.

'Oh no!' I couldn't bear it. I'd ruined my beautiful little glass bird. I cradled it in my hand and burst into tears. And then I couldn't stop.

'Edie?' Dad knocked at my door, and then came in anyway. 'Oh Edie, I'm sorry. I didn't mean to snap at you,' he said.

'I'm sorry too!' I wept. 'I don't think I can ever be happy again!'

'Now then,' said Dad, putting his arm round me. 'That's being a bit melodramatic, isn't it?'

'It's true!' I said and showed him my poor mangled little bird. 'Look what's happened to my bluebird of happiness!

It fell over and it was all my fault!'

'Oh dear, oh dear,' said Dad. We sat down on my bed together while he looked carefully at the little glass bird.

'Do you think we can mend it?' I sniffed.

'Well, we can give it a go. But I'm not sure it's going to work. I think it might show, even if we manage to glue it together. It's so delicate,' Dad said sadly.

'I'm so so sorry!' I said. 'I love that bird!'

'I know,' said Dad.

'And I really am a spoilt brat,' I said.

'Yep,' said Dad, but he gave me another hug.

'It's just . . . I wish *I* was playing Oliver and not Alex,' I mumbled.

'I know,' said Dad.

'Does that make me a truly bad person?'

'No, it makes you human. We all get a bit jealous at times. And I know how much you wanted that part,' said Dad. 'You'd have been a wonderful Oliver.'

'No, I wouldn't. Not as good as Alex. I can see that now. I'm no good at real acting. I don't know what I want to be instead though,' I said wretchedly.

'Why don't you wait and find out when you're older?' said

Dad. 'When I was your age I was desperate to be a rock star.'

'A rock star?' I thought of Dad singing in the shower.

'I know. I've always been rubbish at singing. I didn't dream that one day I'd be a copywriter. I don't think I even knew what it was. But I love my job now. And I'm good at it. When I get the chance to do my work,' said Dad.

'Ouch!'

'Give me another hour or so, just to get this bit done. And then we'll have some lunch – and then we'll go over to Appleton and see if Peter and Gordon can somehow fix your bluebird,' said Dad.

'Oh yes!'

If anyone could mend the bluebird, Peter and Gordon could. They had an antique shop in Appleton, five miles away. We all liked to go there. Mum admired their jewellery, Dad was intrigued by their vintage gadgets – and I loved their little trinkets cabinet. Peter and Gordon often sold me things half price so I could buy something with my pocket money.

I've started my own trinkets cabinet at home. So far I've got a Victorian glass bottle with a stopper that used to contain medicine; a pinchbeck pocket watch that looks very grand, though it doesn't work any more; and a little china

doll not much bigger than my longest finger. She had a nearly identical twin. I gave her to Alex for her birthday present last year.

We called them Dreezel and Teezel, of course. Alex likes Peter and Gordon's shop too.

Peter is the older one – he's really tall, with very short hair. He's very clever but he likes to lark about a lot. Gordon is small with dark curly hair, and he wears a lot of rings and brooches. He's very artistic and kind.

I carefully wrapped my poor little bluebird and his little wing-tip and foot in tissue paper and bubble wrap while Dad made cheese crêpes for our lunch. Then we drove to Appleton.

'*Hello*, Edie!' said Peter.

'Edie!' said Gordon.

'Well, how's it going?' Peter asked eagerly.

I'd told them about auditioning for *Oliver!* the last time we'd been to the shop. I glanced round at Dad. He was shaking his head and pulling a face. Peter and Gordon caught on at once.

'Are you having a lovely day out with Dad?' Peter asked quickly.

'Come and have a good look at my new costumes,' said Gordon hurriedly.

I took a deep breath.

'It's OK. You don't have to be tactful. I didn't get chosen as Oliver – or anyone else actually. But my best friend, Alex, did. She's brilliant at acting,' I said.

Dad gently squeezed my shoulder to show he was pleased with me.

'Bad luck, Edie,' said Peter. 'But good luck too, because now you've got the whole summer to have fun in.'

'And especially good luck for us because hopefully you can pop into our shop more often. I might even give you another sewing lesson!' said Gordon. He had tried to show me how to stitch a neat seam but I'd been a pretty hopeless pupil.

'Is that a threat or a promise?' I said.

'Edie, don't be cheeky!' said Dad.

'I was wondering if there was any way you could fix this?' I said, unwrapping my poor little bluebird of happiness. 'Mum and Dad only just bought it for me when we were in Venice and now it's been broken.'

I held the little bird out on the palm of my hand, with the blue tip of his wing and one orange foot.

'Oh dear!' said Peter.

'Poor little thing,' said Gordon.

They peered at it carefully.

'It's going to be very tricky as hand-blown glass is so delicate,' said Peter.

'But we'll have a go,' said Gordon. 'You can get special glue for mending glass. You have to leave it to dry slowly for days, and the join might still show a little bit – but I'm sure we'll be able to fix him back together again.'

'You're both so kind,' I said. 'It was all my fault he got broken. I was a bit careless.'

'Don't worry – we sometimes break things too,' said Peter.

'Have a little look round while you're here. And try any of the clothes on. I've got quite a lot of new stock,' said Gordon.

I wandered around peering at everything. Dad did too.

'You've got a barometer!' he said delightedly.

'What's that?' I asked.

'People used to have them in their hallways. It's a scientific instrument that measures the air pressure, so it can tell if there are any changes in the weather. My grandad used to have one. He would look every morning to see if he needed to take an umbrella to work,' said Dad. 'This one's exactly like it!'

'It's a mercury barometer, polished walnut, late Victorian,' said Peter.

'Oh dear – it says *showery*,' said Dad.

'Well, we've got several very fine umbrellas in the stand,' said Peter.

'You haven't got one with a parrot head for a handle, have you?' I asked eagerly.

'A *stuffed* parrot?' Dad asked, appalled.

'A carved one. Like Mary Poppins had, remember?' I said.

'Oh yes – I've tried to forget! Edie used to pretend she was Mary Poppins after we took her to see the play, and she thought she could fly too. She fell down off her bed and cut her head open. It gave us a terrible shock!' said Dad.

'Dad! I was only little then,' I said, squirming, not wanting

Peter and Gordon to laugh at me.

'Perhaps it's just as well we *don't* have an umbrella with a parrot head,' said Peter.

I wandered over to the clothes. There were gloves on a shelf too, arranged with empty clasped fingers as if they were waiting patiently to be bought. Some of the hats were set at a jaunty angle on white featureless manikin heads, some facing each other as if they were having a soundless conversation. The head right at the end wore a strange unbecoming bonnet. Gordon had drawn a downturned mouth in beige lipstick on the face, to give it a haunting look.

'Why have you made this one look so sad?' I asked.

'Oh, that's a genuine workhouse cap,' he said.

'A workhouse? Like in *Oliver!*?' I wondered. They were long-ago horrible institutions where poor people had to work really hard and didn't get enough to eat.

'Sorry, Edie,' said Gordon, trying to whisk the head and its bonnet away to his workroom at the side.

'No, don't take it away! Can I try it on?' I said.

'Sure. But I don't think it will be very flattering.' He set the bonnet on my head. 'Oh dear! You do look a poor little orphan girl,' he said.

I stared at myself in his mirror. He was right. It looked so weird on me. I touched it doubtfully.

'It's OK. I've boiled it thoroughly and starched it. It was only a little grey rag when we found it,' said Gordon.

'Dad, look at me!' I said.

He was deep in conversation with Peter about the barometer. He looked up and blinked at me.

'Ugh, take it off, Edie! You look such a waif in it!' he said.

'I know,' I said, sucking in my cheeks and trying to look downcast.

'I think you look way too convincing, like a real workhouse child in that,' said Dad. 'Where on earth did you guys get it?'

'A London auction. Builders were converting an old nursing home into luxury flats. Various trunks were found in the basement, left over from when the building was a workhouse. We thought they could be interesting and put in a bid for them,' said Peter.

'Oh wow!' I said. 'Did you find anything really exciting?'

'Not really. A lot of the garments were in shreds, but they're still fascinating,' said Gordon. 'How does it feel being a little workhouse girl, Edie?'

'I'm not sure I like it!' I said, taking the bonnet off quickly.

'This was in one of the trunks too,' said Peter. He picked up an old wooden box, worn and scratched. It had a lock and a key that didn't look right, too big and ornate for the box's simple design. 'The real key was missing, but we keep a whole drawerful of spare keys, and this one just about fits if you twist it around a bit,' Peter explained.

He turned the key and jiggled it in the box's lock.

'So what's inside?' said Dad. 'Old bank notes? Diamond necklaces? Ruby rings?'

'We wish!' said Gordon. 'But it is quite interesting.'

Peter managed to get the key at exactly the right angle to make it turn. There was a little click and then he opened the box with a flourish. We peered inside. There was a quill pen with a sharpened nib and a little pot of ink, though it had dried into dark brown powder at the bottom of the inkwell. And there were several manuscript books with faded marbled covers.

Peter carefully opened the one on top. It was a register, with long lists of names and ages written in small pinched copperplate. Old-fashioned names: Ebenezer Turner 56, Arthur George Black 19, Frederick Driscoll 27, Silas Mackenzie, Alfred Luke Manning 42, Nathaniel Stark 71, Emanuel Edwards, Josiah Butterworth 28, Male . . .

'Why do some have their ages, and others don't?' I asked, squinting at the lists, page after page of them.

'Maybe some of them simply had no idea how old they were,' said Peter. 'And clearly one poor man didn't even know his name. He might have had learning difficulties. It was a very inadequate system in those days – people with all kinds of needs jumbled up together.'

'Just men?' I asked.

'No, this book is for women,' said Peter, showing me another manuscript book. 'Ida Elizabeth Jeffries, twenty-two, Rebekah May James, seventeen, Jane Brown, fifty-three, Phyllida Gotham, thirty one, Mary-Jane Butterworth, twenty-seven . . .'

'Do you think Mary-Jane was Josiah's wife?' I asked.

'Probably. They would have been kept strictly apart, men in one wing of the workhouse, women in the other, even married couples,' said Peter.

'That's so mean to split them up,' I said. 'What happened if they had children?'

'They were kept separately too,' said Gordon. 'Look, this one's the most heartbreaking.'

He delved in the box and showed me the third manuscript book, shaking his head sadly.

'Adelaide Barnstable, ten, Norah Jane Wickering, nine, Sarah Ann Wickering, seven, Stephen Robert Smithson, three, Barnaby Smithson, one, Baby Smithson, newborn,' he read out. 'That poor little mite doesn't even have a name.'

'But little children can't work!' I said.

'I think the babies lived in some grim nursery-type affair – but the older ones were considered suitable for labour. You'd be expected to work a full day, Edie!' said Peter.

'Seriously?' I said. 'What sort of work?'

'Not quite sure,' said Gordon. 'People in prison picked oakum – whatever that is. Something to do with oak wood?'

'You crack me up sometimes, Gordie!' said Peter. 'It's a kind of rope, and prisoners were expected to unravel it.'

'That doesn't sound *too* bad. I quite like unravelling old jumpers,' I said. Mum had let me unravel some of hers last year when I'd decided I wanted wool so I could knit a scarf with alternate stripes of colour. The unravelling had been easier than the knitting!

'I think they had to pick at it with their fingers. It must have felt horribly sore,' said Peter. 'They were probably dripping blood by the end of the day.'

I stared at my own hands, imagining.

'Perhaps we'd better put these books away, guys,' Dad said briskly. 'I don't want Edie to have nightmares.'

'No, do go on!' I said. 'This is fascinating! We'll be doing Crime and Punishment as our topic next year, Dad. Maybe I could write about workhouses for my special project!'

'Really?' said Dad, wavering. He always thinks schoolwork is very important.

'The other manuscript books are empty,' said Peter, peering at them. 'This one at the bottom's got water damage, though it's long dried out.' He held it out to me. 'Would you like it, Edie? You could write a story in it for school about a workhouse girl.'

'Oh, yes *please*!' I said.

'Let's give her the ink bottle and the pen too,' said Gordon. 'Then she can make it look really authentic.'

'Wow!' I said, clapping my hands.

'Well, you must let me pay for them,' said Dad. 'Surely they're quite valuable?'

'We'll keep the box with the registers, but we don't even know if the ink and pen came with them. I think they were chucked in the trunk willy-nilly,' said Gordon. 'You have fun with them, Edie.'

He wrapped them carefully in tissue paper, put them in a piece of old cloth, tied the little parcel with blue ribbon and put it in one of their special carrier bags stamped with *Peter and Gordon, Antiques and Curios.*

'It's very kind of you. You're a lucky girl, Edie,' said Dad. He was looking over at the barometer again. 'Just a second,' he murmured, and went to peer at it. He looked at the price ticket.

Peter winked at me. 'I think your dad's very tempted,' he whispered to me.

I wasn't so sure. I'd heard Mum and Dad talking about cutting down on buying stuff. Dad had been particularly insistent that we needed to spend less. However, he looked as if he was wavering now.

'I think maybe I'll take the barometer,' he said, getting out his wallet.

'Dad!' I said. I'd read the price label and seen how much it cost.

Dad looked sheepish but offered his credit card to Peter.

'That's a lovely choice, Mr Trimmer. It's beautifully made and in perfect condition,' Peter said. 'And because you're Edie's father, I'm happy to knock twenty per cent off the price.'

I felt my heart thump with pride. Dad looked pretty grateful too.

I gave Peter and Gordon a big hug each. It took a while for Peter to take the barometer off the wall and wrap it up very carefully. Dad held his big parcel as if it was a precious baby as we walked back to the car. I swung my carrier bag, peeping inside occasionally.

'Well, we've got some lovely treats,' said Dad.

'And mine didn't even cost anything,' I said.

He looked furtive. 'I hope you're not going to tell Mum exactly how much my barometer cost, even with the discount.'

'Of course I won't,' I promised him.

Dad wrapped his barometer in the car rug and put it in the boot. I sat clutching my carrier bag to my chest, feeling the hard edges of my manuscript book. I loved the idea of writing a story about a workhouse child. I could maybe add a little water to the brown dust at the bottom of the inkwell and use the quill pen. Perhaps I could disguise my usual round handwriting and attempt a sloping copperplate like the register entries in the other manuscript books.

I hugged my knees and gave a little shiver of anticipation. I knew exactly how I was going to start: *My name is Edie Trimmer . . .*

Chapter Three

Dad unwrapped his barometer carefully when we got back and walked up and down the hall with it, wondering where to hang it.

'What's Mum going to say?' I asked.

'She probably won't even notice it,' said Dad hopefully.

I helped him find the perfect place between two paintings, above the old umbrella stand.

'So if it says it's going to rain, I can take my umbrella as I go out,' Dad said, though he didn't actually ever bother with an umbrella even when it was pouring.

I was dying to start my workhouse story, but before I could

even take it out of the carrier bag, Alex and her mum paid a surprise visit.

'There's no matinee today, and no classes this afternoon either, so Alex begged to come round,' said her mum.

'I've got so much to tell you!' said Alex. She'd had a new haircut to make her look more like a little Victorian orphan and it looked very cute. She was wearing a T-shirt with an *Oliver!* logo and new shorts and cool boots. She didn't really look like old Alex at all.

It was crazy, but I felt almost shy with her. We went up to my bedroom and sprawled on my bed, and she chattered excitedly about theatre stuff. I tried to look as if I was interested. Apparently, the man playing scary Bill Sykes was actually having an affair with the singer playing Nancy, and Alex had seen them kissing in the wings.

We giggled a bit about that because we knew that Nancy was a Lady of the Night. 'That means she's a prostitute – everyone knows that,' I said.

Alex tittered even more. 'We're not supposed to say that word,' she said.

'It's in the Bible, though,' I said, pleased to have the last word.

She told me some of the funny things that had happened too. Once, the woman playing the matron had flung back her head to sing and her cap and her wig had fallen off, and when she placed them on again, they were back to front and everyone collapsed with laughter. Liam had decided to turn a couple of cartwheels in the middle of a performance and had ended up cartwheeling right off the stage, though he wasn't actually hurt and the audience thought it was all part of the act.

'Typical Liam!' Alex said, shaking her head. Then she stopped, looking stricken.

'What is it?' I asked.

'I'm being so boring, going on and on about the theatre!' she said.

'That's OK. It's really interesting,' I said flatly.

'No, tell me what *you've* been doing, Edie,' she said, sitting up expectantly.

'Well, we had a lovely time in Italy,' I said. I started on about the places we'd seen, but I sounded like a travelogue and my voice petered out.

'Go on!' said Alex. 'What flavour ice cream did you like the best? I like the cherry sort most! And did you have a ride on a gondola? What was it like?'

I knew Alex had been to Venice herself and was probably just being polite.

'I liked the nutty chocolate flavour best. The gondolas were too expensive, but we went on the *traghetto* ferry once, which was almost as good. And Mum and Dad bought me a little glass bluebird,' I said.

'Oh, you lucky thing!'

'Yes, but it got broken this morning.'

'Oh dear!'

'But Dad took me to see Peter and Gordon, and they're going to try and fix it for me. And look what they gave me as a present!' I said, and unwrapped the manuscript book and the pen and inkwell.

Alex watched expectantly. She tried very hard, but she couldn't help looking disappointed when she saw them. I could see them through her eyes. The pen was a plain wooden one with a rusty nib, the inkwell had a chip in it, and the manuscript book was very stained.

'Oh, how lovely!' she said nevertheless.

'I know they look a bit tatty, but they're from an actual Victorian workhouse,' I said. 'And I'm going to write a story in it about a workhouse girl.'

It sounded a bit feeble when Alex was acting in a proper play about a workhouse boy but she tried to look suitably impressed.

'You're so good at making up stories,' she said.

'You don't have to keep trying to be nice to me,' I said. 'I'm OK, really. Go on about the theatre. What else has Liam been up to? Only please don't tell me he's your boyfriend now!'

'As if!' said Alex. 'Though some of the other girls follow him round and giggle hysterically whenever he talks to them. Particularly Laura.'

We went on chatting until Alex's mum called up to her that it was time to set off for the theatre. It felt a bit lonely when she was gone.

'Come and help me cook supper,' said Dad.

'In a bit,' I said, and went to look at my manuscript book again. I gave it a little stroke on its worn cover. The back was so blurred with damp that it had lost its colour and pattern, but the front still had visible navy-and-maroon marbling, though very faded. I followed the whirly shapes with my finger while I worked out the beginning of my story.

I examined the pen. The nib was stained, but the point looked reasonably straight. I'd never used a dipping pen

before but it seemed simple enough. I'd probably need blotting paper and I didn't have any – but hopefully the tissue paper might do instead. I peered at the inkwell and the little grains of ink still clinging to the insides of the glass. I carefully tipped a little water from my drinking glass onto the dried ink and stirred it around with the end of the pen. Nothing much happened at first, but I went on stirring, and slowly the water turned pale brown and thickened. It looked rather sludgy and I'd have to be careful of blots, but I might actually be able to write with it.

I opened the manuscript book at the first page – and then stared. There was already writing on the top line. I blinked at it, thinking I must be mistaken. But it was there, right in front of me, perfectly clear.

My name is Edie Trimmer.

It was what *I* was going to write – but I hadn't even dipped my pen in the ink yet! It was similar to my own handwriting but much neater with little twirly bits so that it looked very fancy. It looked exactly as if I'd written it – but I hadn't!

I touched the lettering. It wasn't wet. It had been dry since

Victorian times. Some long-ago girl had written it. A long-ago girl with my name.

I touched the *Edie* on the top line and my finger tingled strangely. For a split second the room seemed to slip sideways and I was somewhere else entirely, somewhere dark and bleak and cold. I took a step backwards and then I was back in my room, and it was light and colourful and the sun was shining through my window.

'What do you fancy for pudding?' Dad called.

I picked up the manuscript book and went running to the kitchen. Dad was sitting at the table, flicking through a recipe book.

'What's up, Edie?' he asked.

'Look!' I said, holding the manuscript book in front of him.

Dad wrinkled his nose. 'It smells ever so fusty. I know Peter and Gordon meant well, but maybe we should just chuck it out?'

'We can't do that! It's an antique!' I protested. 'And look at the first page, Dad!'

Dad glanced at it. 'Ah, I see you've started your story already.'

'But I didn't write it, Dad! It was there already, on the first

page. Some long-ago girl wrote it – but it's my name, see!'

I pointed at the line of handwriting.

Dad peered at it. 'That's quite good, Edie,' he said. 'It looks almost authentic.'

'It *is*!' I cried. '*I* didn't write it. It was there already! Isn't that the most astonishing coincidence in the whole world? It's kind of creepy, isn't it?'

Dad didn't look astonished. He seemed amused.

'Aren't you amazed?' I said.

'Nice try,' he laughed. 'You almost convinced me. Now, puddings. Shall we have frozen fruit with white chocolate sauce?'

'You don't understand!' I said. 'I truly didn't write the sentence. I swear to you I didn't!'

'Hey hey, you funny sausage,' said Dad. 'Don't forget I know Peter and Gordon gave you the pen and ink as well as the manuscript book.'

'Yes, but I didn't use them. Don't you believe me?' I said, starting to get really upset.

'I believe you've got a vivid imagination, sweetheart,' said Dad.

'I'm *not* imagining it!' I shouted. 'It's true, honestly!'

'All right, all right! There's no need to get in such a state,' said Dad. 'OK, let's see the pen and inkwell.'

'I didn't write anything myself – I *didn't*!' I said – but when I fetched them, Dad shook his head.

'Oh Edie, it's obvious you've already used the pen and ink yourself!' he said. 'You've watered the ink, and the pen nib's stained, look! Come on, darling, let's stop this nonsense and get on with supper.'

'I feel a bit sick. I don't really want to think about supper at the moment,' I said. 'I think I'll go and have a lie-down for a bit.'

I flopped down on my bed, clutching my manuscript book. I hated it that Dad didn't believe me. I suppose I must have nodded off to sleep. I woke when I heard the door downstairs and Mum's voice. I sat up and looked at the first page: *My name is Edie Trimmer.*

I felt weirdly dizzy. I knew it was written by a long-ago Edie, but there was no way I could prove it. I ran my finger over the line.

'My name is Edie Trimmer too,' I said, looking in my mirror. I seemed to be seeing double. I saw two Edies instead of one – but they weren't the same. We were both dark-haired

with blue eyes, but one was much bigger than the other. One had rosy cheeks, and one was sallow and her cheekbones stuck out sharply. I turned round, but there was no one else in the room. The two girls peered back at me anxiously from the mirror. The most frightening thing was that I couldn't work out which one was me.

I ran out of my bedroom, blinking hard, trying to get rid of the image. I could hear Mum and Dad talking about me in the kitchen.

'Edie seemed so upset,' Dad was saying. 'Maybe I should have pretended to believe her.'

'It's such a strange thing for her to make up though. Perhaps she's more upset about this whole *Oliver!* thing than we realized,' said Mum.

'Well, I suppose it didn't help that Alex came round this afternoon. Perhaps poor old Edie felt left out and sorry for herself,' said Dad.

'Maybe she's saying all this stuff about some other Edie writing in her book to draw attention to herself?' Mum said.

I burned with humiliation. How could they think that of me? I went into the kitchen, still holding the manuscript book.

'Stop talking about me like that!' I said.

They both looked stricken.

'Darling, we do understand,' said Mum.

'No you don't! And now something really weird just happened,' I said, and I realized I was trembling.

'Something weird?' Mum asked.

'Can I show you?' I mumbled.

'Yes. Yes, of course, darling,' Mum said. I took her hand and led her upstairs to my room.

'Tell me, pet,' Mum said gently.

'It happened when I looked in the mirror,' I said.

'What?'

I dared look in the mirror again. I saw one girl. Clearly myself. I went weak with relief.

'Oh, thank goodness! She's not there any more! I saw this other girl – it was like I was seeing double,' I said, blinking quickly, making sure she was really gone.

'Don't do that, darling, you'll give yourself a twitch. Perhaps it's eye strain. Maybe you need glasses? I'll see if I can make an appointment for you at the opticians' before you go back to school,' said Mum.

'Oh Mum!' I suddenly gave her a hug. She made everything seem so *normal*. She always had a rational explanation for

everything – even though she could be wrong sometimes.

'Now, let's see this manuscript book of yours,' she said.

She pulled a face when she saw it. 'It's a really manky old thing! I think we should get you another notebook for this story,' she said. 'Peter and Gordon usually have such lovely things, but this is only fit for the bin.'

She opened it up and saw the writing. *My name is Edie Trimmer.*

'I didn't write it, Mum, truly. I might fib a bit sometimes, but I don't tell whacking great lies!' I said.

'I know you don't.' Mum was looking at the writing carefully. Then she smiled. 'I know what! I think Peter or Gordon wrote in it themselves, to give you a surprise!'

'Oh! Maybe!' It was the sort of thing they might do. It was such a relief to think of it – and yet a disappointment too. It had been so exciting to believe there really was a long-ago Edie who had written it herself.

We went back downstairs. 'Mum thinks Peter and Gordon wrote in it!' I told Dad.

'Of course! Why didn't I think of that?' said Dad, smacking the side of his head with the palm of his hand. 'It's obvious now! I'm so sorry I doubted you, Edie.'

'Why don't we give them a ring just to make sure?' said Mum.

'Won't their shop be closed now?' said Dad.

'They won't mind. They're friends. They're probably waiting to find out if Edie's seen it yet,' said Mum, looking up their number on her mobile. She handed it to me when it started ringing.

I waited impatiently. It rang for a long time. Then at last Peter answered.

'It's Edie here, Peter,' I said.

'Oh hello, Edie. We'll have to be quick, sweetheart. I'm in the middle of making hollandaise sauce and it's threatening to turn into scrambled egg. There's not a problem, is there? Your dad's still happy with his barometer? Has he got it up on the wall and working properly?'

'Oh, it's fine. He loves it. No, it's about my manuscript book. Can you tell me honestly – did you write in it?'

'There wasn't any writing. It was the empty one at the bottom of the box,' said Peter.

'It wasn't completely empty. There was only one line. *My name is Edie Trimmer.* You wrote it, didn't you? Or Gordon?'

'Well, I certainly didn't,' said Peter. He sounded utterly convincing. 'Hey, Gordie, did you write Edie's name in that

workhouse manuscript book?' He waited. 'He's shaking his head, looking puzzled.'

'Truly? You're not still teasing me?' I persisted.

'No, I promise. Why?' said Peter.

'Because when I opened it at the front page there was a sentence already written there, in a slanted Victorian hand. *My name is Edie Trimmer.*'

'Ah! Spooky!' said Peter. He paused. 'Are you sure *you're* not teasing *us*?'

'No, I'm not. Honestly,' I said. I knew it was useless to persist, and I heard Peter swear softly at his special sauce. 'Oh well, sorry to have bothered you,' I said, and rang off.

'No joy?' said Dad.

'Peter said it absolutely wasn't them. And he asked if there was a problem with your barometer.'

'Your *what*?' Mum asked. She had obviously walked straight past it when she came home.

I left them in the hall, discussing the barometer. Mum asked how much it cost and I heard Dad saying it was only half what he'd actually paid for it. *He* was the fibber, not me. I went back to my room and looked inside the manuscript book yet again, peering at those five mysterious words.

It really did look like my own handwriting, just sloping more than usual. I looked at the watery ink in the inkwell. It was the exact same shade of pale brown. I looked at the stained nib. *Had* I written those words myself and then somehow forgotten I'd done it? It sounded impossible, but sometimes I got a bit daydreamy and forgot whether I'd cleaned my teeth or done my homework. Maybe no one was playing games with me. Maybe I was playing a game on myself without realizing it.

What about the girl beside me in the mirror? Perhaps that had been a trick of the light. Or I simply needed glasses, as Mum suggested. Or maybe I'd made the girl up. I'd often made up imaginary friends when I was little, and was puzzled when Mum and Dad couldn't see them.

I went back to Mum and Dad in the hall.

'The barometer does look lovely, doesn't it, Mum?' I said. Dad flashed me a grateful look. 'And we'll be able to see what the weather's going to do whenever we go out.'

'I suppose,' said Mum. 'But it's much easier and cheaper to look at the weather app on your phone.'

'But this is much more fun,' said Dad. 'Give the barometer a little tap, Edie.'

'How does that make it work?' I asked.

'There's a little bellows inside. It fills up with air and makes the mercury respond to the temperature of the air. Go on, give it a go.'

I tapped. I thought it would take a minute or so, like when you take your own temperature, but immediately the liquid shot right up to the top of the glass, and the little pointer quivered dramatically, spinning from *fair* to *rain* and back again, until it made your eyes blink.

'It can't seem to make up its mind,' I said. 'Should it do that?'

'Oh dear. No, it shouldn't. Not as violently. Something seems to have gone wrong with the mechanism,' said Dad, sighing. 'Yet it looked in perfect working order in the shop. Maybe it simply won't work on this wall. Perhaps I'll have to put it right beside the window.'

He unhooked it carefully and carried it to the window wall. It calmed down at once and accurately indicated that it was sunny and fair, though when I got near it to check for myself it started spinning madly again, indicating every weather condition in rapid succession. It eventually settled on the word *changes*, though it quivered violently every now and then.

'That's strange,' said Dad. 'It doesn't seem to like you, Edie!'

I knew he was just joking. I wasn't daft enough to think that a barometer could have feelings. Yet it felt horrible that a piece of polished wood had taken against me.

'Well, I don't like *it*,' I said. The word *changes* echoed in my head ominously. *What* changes?

Chapter Four

I went back to my bedroom and put the manuscript book on my desk, open at the first page. I dipped the pen into the strange sludgy ink. I took a deep breath and then started writing straight after it. I whispered the words as I wrote, copying the sloping style:

I am going to tell you

It was an exact match. I stared at my little addition, chewing on my lip. I carried on:

about my life.

I looked at the last word. I stared at my sentence and the words danced up and down on the line so that I could barely read them. I tried pointing underneath them, like a child in Year One learning to read, but my finger wavered too. It was getting very dark. Perhaps the barometer was right, and the weather was changing dramatically. I could hear distant rumblings, almost like thunder.

It grew darker still, as black as night. My bedroom started shaking violently until I fell off my chair. I cried out for Mum and Dad, trying to get up and run to them, but the floor wasn't there. I was falling, falling, falling through the darkness.

I landed flat on something soft, squelchy and disgusting. I tried to scrabble up but something – someone? – held me fast by my ankle.

'Let me go!' I cried, spluttering. I tried to wipe the filthy mud from my face and realized I was holding something hard in one of my hands. It was a small glass bottle with a label stuck on it.

It was exactly like the pale green glass bottle I'd bought from Peter and Gordon with my pocket money. It had been empty, of course – but this bottle seemed to be full of liquid and had a cork in the top. Somehow I knew this was medicine

for Mother. *Mother?* Was Mum ill? What was the matter with her? And where was Dad? Was I in some sort of dream? Where *was* I?

Then a hand clapped itself over mine, trying to prise my fingers away from the bottle.

'Don't you dare steal Mother's medicine!' I screamed. I found the strength to get free and have a proper look at this thief.

It was only a child, much smaller than me, a little boy half naked. He was wearing a shred of shirt and a ragged pair of trousers that were far too big, tied with string to stay round his skinny waist. They were caked with mud too – he was completely covered in it. His skin was browny-grey and his hair thick with it, sticking straight up. And he smelled – oh, he smelled so dreadful.

He threw himself at me, still trying to grab the bottle, but I pushed his chest and he tottered backwards, his bare feet slipping in the mud. He fell right over and knocked his head on an old brick half buried in the sludge. A trickle of blood coloured his filthy forehead.

'I didn't mean to hurt you! But I couldn't let you take the medicine – my poor mother's so sick,' I said. *What?* I couldn't

mean *my* mum, could I? 'Oh goodness, you're bleeding!'

The little boy put his hand to his forehead and gave it a cursory wipe with his shred of shirt. 'That's nothing,' he said, though he winced.

'Where's your own mother?' I asked. 'I'll take you to her.'

'Ain't got one,' he said.

'Then your father?' I tried.

'Ain't got one of them either,' he said.

'Oh goodness, I'm so sorry,' I said. 'So who looks after you?'

'No one. I looks after myself,' he said.

'But you're only about . . . *five*?' I gasped.

The boy shrugged. 'Maybe.'

'You don't *know*?'

'You don't know nothing neither or you wouldn't work on this patch. Digger owns it, and he won't let no one else here. Only me. Because I'm his mate, see,' he said, jutting out his chin proudly.

'Well, go and ask him to wash your face and put a plaster on that cut,' I said.

He stared at me incredulously, and then burst out laughing. 'Ask Digger?' he said. 'Are you mad?'

'Why is that funny?' I said, trying to brush some of the mud off my dress. It wasn't *my* dress. It was tartan, the red and blue squares faded. The hem had been turned down so there was a brighter edge at the bottom. I was wearing black stockings, darned many times. My black patent boots – really old-looking – were much too tight and hurt my feet. I must have been wearing them for *years*.

'You try asking him and you'll get a thump,' he said. He hit his own head, demonstrating.

'He sounds horrible if he hits a little boy like you,' I said. 'What's your name?'

'Boy,' he said.

'Yes, I know you're a boy, but what's your name? I'm Edie,' I said. I *was* Edie. The real Edie inside, even though I was wearing strange clothes and struggling in the mud on a filthy river shore at low tide. Like I was doing impro for real! But . . . impro? What was that? It seemed like a dream now, like an old memory fading and disappearing. I looked up at the old rotting buildings along the bank, warehouses and tumbledown homes. Not *my* home. This was a city, not the seaside. The air was so thick with fumes I could hardly breathe.

'I'm Boy,' the boy insisted. 'Ain't got no other name.'

I stared at him, trying to imagine not having a proper name. His forehead had stopped bleeding, but he was so dirty I was worried he'd get some awful infection from the open wound.

'I'll clean it for you,' I said. 'Are there any toilets round here?'

'What?' he said.

'You know,' I said, though he obviously didn't. 'Places where you go to have a wee, and then you wash your hands in a basin?'

He still looked blank. I pointed to the crotch of his ragged trousers and made a little gesture, blushing.

'Oh! I pees in the river,' he said.

No wonder everywhere smelled so awful if this was the custom here. Where *was* 'here'?

'Where are we?' I asked, though if he didn't know his own name it seemed unlikely that he'd know.

'We're in Lunnon,' he said. He tapped the side of his head with his finger and nodded at me, as if *I* was the fool.

'Lunnon?' Then I realized. 'London?'

'Like I said.'

Somewhere deep inside, I knew that I'd been to London to
see plays at Christmas, and Alex's family had once taken me
there to a concert. I'd been shopping in Selfridges and Harrods
and Liberty's with Mum. Dad had brought me to the museums
in South Kensington. We'd gone on a boat trip to Greenwich
along the River Thames.

This river? It was more like a dreadful sewer. I peered at
the disgusting water and then saw something floating along. A
dog of some sort, long dead. I gasped in horror – and the boy
snatched the bottle from my hand and started running.

'Come back! You little thief!' I yelled and started running
after him.

It was impossible to run properly in the thick grey mud. I
slipped this way and that, unable to get a proper footing in my
tight boots. The mud spattered everywhere, spraying my dress
and petticoat, even splashing up into my face. The boy was
hampered by the trailing hems of his too-large trousers, but he
was making much better progress barefoot.

He turned round and crowed with laughter when he saw
me floundering. He waved the bottle like a trophy. It was a
fatal mistake. He waved too wildly and toppled sideways,
staggering but unable to stop himself falling. He landed in the

mud with a splat, but instinct made him hold the bottle up so it didn't smash.

I lumbered forward and snatched it back before he could get to his feet again. I stuffed it down the neck of my dress for safety. The waist was so tight I knew it couldn't fall out.

'How dare you try to steal it again! Especially when I was trying to help you!' I shouted.

'Well, I've got to have a go, haven't I? And you was standing there so gormless, staring at that rotten old dog,' he said, totally unabashed.

'How can you be so heartless!' I said, horrified.

'No point fussing about a drownded dog. You see them every day,' he said. 'And folk too, floating along like boats.'

'Stop it!' I said. 'What are you *doing* here, scrabbling around in the mud?'

He stared at me incredulously. 'I'm a mudlark, ain't I,' he said. 'It's what I do, every low tide. I looks and I gathers and I takes it to Digger and he gives me my grub – or a good hiding if I haven't found nothing.'

'What are you looking for?'

'Anything what's fallen in the river. Coal off a barge. Hats.

Umbrellys. Nails. Copper ones are best, but we're too far away from the boatyard on this patch,' he said.

'But what do you want them for?'

'Digger sells them!' said the boy, shaking his head at my ignorance. 'Coals fetch a penny a pot. We takes the other stuff to the rag shops. We got a whole shilling once, but mostly it's pennies. You don't know nothing, do you?'

'Not about this mudlarking. You do it every day, even when it's cold?' I asked.

'Yep,' he said.

'But don't *you* get cold?' I asked.

He stared at me pityingly. 'Course I do. Last winter was perishing. Me feet went purple and I got the shakes. Even Digger was bad with it.'

'But isn't there anywhere you can go where they'd look after you?' I asked.

'Nah,' he said. 'Digger looks after me anyways.'

'But you say he hits you sometimes?'

'Yes, but it's my fault, because it's when I haven't found nothing,' said the boy, as if it was perfectly reasonable.

'Well, what about the workhouse?' I said. 'They look after children, don't they?' I had a vague sense that someone had

been talking about workhouses only the other day.

'What?' He tapped his head again. 'Not never going there! Digger was there once, and he said they whip you every day and feed you vomit.'

'No they don't! I bet he was just saying that to frighten you. They might be a bit strict, but they'd give you proper clothes and keep you warm and give you regular meals,' I said.

'What grub would they give me?' he asked.

'They give you gruel,' I said.

The boy pulled a face. 'I like a plate of stew and a flagon of beer,' he said.

'You don't drink beer, silly! You're only little,' I said.

'Yes I do! Digger gives me my own rations, see. I've got to drink!' he said indignantly.

'But not beer! You should drink . . . milk?' I suggested uncertainly.

'Where would I get milk from?' he asked.

'Well, a shop,' I said.

'Ain't got no money.'

'Then drink water,' I said.

He stared at me incredulously. 'Drink *water*?' he said, looking at the filthy river.

'Not river water, silly. Water from a tap.'

'Ain't got no tap neither,' he said. The blood on his forehead was starting to trickle again, and he swiped at it impatiently.

'Don't do that! We need water now, clean water. Where do you wash?' I realized it was a stupid question. It was clear from the state of him that he never washed.

'Digger washes when he sees his girl,' the boy said surprisingly. 'Under the pump.'

'Ah! Then let's take you to the pump and get you cleaned up,' I said.

'Can't take the time. Got to go looking. I ain't found nothing yet. Apart from the bottle, and you took it off of me,' he said resentfully.

'It's mine! For Mother. She's ill.' It was the one thing I was certain about, though everything else was so muddled. 'And you'll get ill too if you don't get your head cleaned up. You don't want to end up in hospital, do you?'

He looked at me fearfully. 'Not going to no hospital. You don't come out. They kill you off in hospital, everyone knows that.'

'No, they make you better there,' I said, but he shook his head violently.

'Digger's boy before me went to hospital with a spike in his foot and he was deaded in a week,' he said.

'Then let's get you to this pump,' I said. 'Show me where it is.'

I wasn't totally sure what a pump looked like. Dad pumped up the tyres of the car, but that little machine didn't produce any water. I had a vague memory of an old nursery rhyme book with a picture of a village green. Mum read me the rhyme and we looked at the picture together. I pointed to each object in the picture and Mum told me the name. 'Pump!' she said, and I repeated 'Pump-pump-pump-pump!', laughing because it sounded so funny.

My mum wasn't the mother who was ill, was she? I suddenly felt sick with fear. If I was Edie still, having this weird dream or whatever it was, then maybe she was my own mum. I fingered the shape of the bottle down my bodice. What sort of medicine was it? Would it really make her better?

'Quick, we'll get you washed and then I must go to Mother,' I said, taking the boy's grubby hand.

He came with me without protesting, frightened by the very idea of hospital. He led me up some rotting wooden steps

to the bank, and then dived down a narrow passage between two ancient warehouses, both leaning precariously as if about to tumble down. The passage was as filthy as the river, and I heard awful squeaking and scuffling at my feet.

'What's that?' I asked fearfully, trying to see in the dark.

'Only the rats,' said the boy. 'You just kick out at them and they goes away, mostly.'

'Rats!' I said, terrified. I clung to his hand and we stumbled on. Then it grew lighter and we walked out into a communal backyard. The terraced dwellings looked even more unstable from the back. One was a total ruin, blackened with fire, and most of the roof was missing.

'What happened to that one?' I asked.

'The folk was burning wood and rags in the fireplace, and a spark flew out and they burned themselves dead,' said the boy matter-of-factly.

'How terrible! You must have been so frightened,' I said.

He shrugged his skinny little shoulders. I tried putting my arm round him but he looked startled and ducked away from me.

'Get off!' he said. He pointed. 'There's the pump.'

It was an old ugly steel contraption, the stone flags

surrounding it orange with rust. There was a handle so I tried to press it down, but it was so heavy it took all my strength.

'Stand underneath while I get the water flowing,' I panted.

'Nah! I'll get wet!' he said, though he was soaking from the river mud already.

It was clearly pointless asking if he had a handkerchief. I bent down and tore a small strip off my petticoat. It was worn threadbare and spattered with mud, but I found a patch that was still relatively clean. I held it under the trickle of water I achieved after a second attempt and then advanced on the boy.

'Don't you hurt me or I'll get Digger on you!' he said.

'I'm not going to hurt you, I'm going to help,' I said, though I looked a little anxiously up at the buildings. I imagined Digger as some towering thug, happy to hit a small child whenever he felt like it. Perhaps he was nicknamed Digger because he had huge hands like shovels as he dug his way through the river mud.

'Hold still now, Boy,' I said, and I wiped his dirty face as carefully as I could. The cut on his forehead wasn't as bad as I'd feared, and after I'd pressed the petticoat scrap against the wound for a couple of minutes it stopped bleeding altogether. I turned the material over and carried on washing the rest of his face.

He looked younger as I cleaned him up, and when I'd
wiped the caked mud off his eyelashes I saw his eyes were
actually beautiful, a deep green with long curling lashes. But
they were looking at the bulge of the medicine bottle inside my
dress and I knew not to trust him an inch.

'There now! You're starting to look lovely. Will you let me
wash the rest of you?' I asked.

'Nah! Think I'm daft? You'll grab my togs and scarper,' he said, folding his arms and pressing his legs together to stop me.

It was so sad that he thought I'd really want his filthy ragged clothes but I could see there was no reasoning with him.

'All right then. Look, I'll wash this scrap clean again, and then you keep it and clean that cut with it if it starts bleeding again,' I said.

He accepted it, tucking it into his armpit for safe keeping. He was eyeing the torn hem of my petticoat.

'You've spoilt it now. I reckon you've got another at home. Let me have the torn one, eh?' he said. He shivered dramatically. 'Reckon it'll keep me warm and dry if I wind it round me like a little cape.'

'I think you just want to sell it!' I said.

'Course I do,' he said cheerfully. 'Pity you've torn it though. I'll only get a penny for it now.'

'I tore it to help you!' I said. I was filled with sudden urgency. I was supposed to be helping *Mother*. 'Anyway, I must go now.' I looked back at the dark passage with the rats. 'Is there any other way back to the river?'

'Well, you can go down Harvey's Buildings instead,' he said.

'Is that a bigger passage?' I asked. 'Let's go that way!'

We walked along the backyards. The cobbles hurt through the thin soles of my boots, but the boy danced along them in his bare feet. They were iron black underneath. It looked as if he'd never worn a pair of shoes in his life.

Harvey's Buildings was a factory, in slightly better condition than the other buildings, and the passage beside it was big enough for vehicles, so there was nowhere for the rats to gather. However, I started to wish I'd braved the first alley after all, because the factory smelled terribly, so that I had to hold the hem of my skirt over my nose.

'Whatever does this Harvey make?' I choked.

'Levver,' said the Boy, seemingly unbothered by the smell.

'What on earth is *levver*?' I asked.

'You know. Them boots is levver,' he said, pointing at my feet.

'Oh, you mean *leather*!'

'Yes, like I said,' he replied, raising his eyebrows at me.

'But leather doesn't smell that bad!'

'It's the pure they use to make it soft,' he said.

'What's *pure*?'

He sniggered. 'Dog muck,' he said, laughing.

'You're being silly now,' I said primly.

'No, it's true – I swear it. Digger told me,' he said.

'Pure means something clean and unspoilt,' I said. 'The exact opposite of dog muck!'

'Can't help it. Look, there's some!' said the boy, pointing.

A man was in the factory yard, trundling a wheelbarrow full of something. I peered at it, wrinkling my nose. The boy was right. It was a huge mound of it, some spilling over the rim of the wheelbarrow.

'Ugh! This is *horrible*!'

'Told you so!' said the boy triumphantly. 'Don't pull faces like that. If he sees you doing it he might chuck a lump at you!'

'Stop it! Quick, let's run!' I said, appalled.

'You're soft, you are,' said the boy. 'And you don't know nothing!'

I supposed he was right. Somehow I appeared to be back in Victorian times, but it was so different from the way I'd imagined. I knew there were poor people – but not leading

such dreadful lives. I was this other Edie now, and I was obviously poor myself, because my clothes were worn and my boots far too small, but I was so much more fortunate than this little orphan boy who didn't even have a name. What had happened? If it wasn't a dream, would I be stuck here for ever? My normal life was now vanishing, becoming some kind of misty memory. And this was my new reality . . .

I held his hand and we ran the length of Harvey's Buildings to reach the riverside. There were more mudlarks toiling in the mud near a small shipyard, mostly children, and some bent-over old women, their skirts tucked up, showing their bowed, wrinkled legs. One very frail old lady ducked down to pick something up, lost her footing, and slipped. No one ran to help her to get upright again or even check whether she had hurt herself. They just carried on wading through the mud, peering ahead, intent on finding good pickings for the buckets and bags they dragged along.

'Are you all right?' I shouted, stumbling across the mud to see if she was OK.

She stared at me, startled, and put her arms round her own small bag protectively, as if she thought I was trying to snatch it from her.

'Have you hurt yourself?' I asked, as she struggled wearily to her feet.

'Clear off,' she mumbled indistinctly; she didn't have many teeth.

'I only want to help you,' I said.

'She don't want you to,' said Boy. 'Right, I'm going to scarper. There's Digger over there and he don't want me larking near him. Makes sense to cover more ground, see.'

I stared up and down the riverside curiously, looking for a burly man.

'Oi! You, Boy!' Digger yelled at him, jerking his thumb to move back down river. He wasn't burly – he was thin as a rake. And he wasn't a man. He was probably my age, if that. I started to wade up to him to explain that the boy must keep his head clean until the wound healed. He cut me short almost at once.

'He's *my* boy. You can't nab him!' he said belligerently.

'I don't want to! I only need to explain that he had a bump on his head and—'

'I've told you again and again, watch your footing!' Digger yelled at the boy. 'What am I going to do if you get drownded!'

'Sorry, Digger, sir!' said the boy.

It was so comical I wanted to laugh, and yet so sad that I wanted to cry too.

'Don't be angry with him . . . Digger,' I said. 'It was mostly my fault. Your boy was just helping me on my way.'

'He was helping you, was he?' said Digger, sloshing his way through the shallow water towards me. 'Then what you going to give him for his trouble, eh?'

'What do you mean?' I asked, alarmed.

'You said it was your fault. Did you knock him over?' Digger said. He wasn't quite as tall as me, but his wiry bare arms were well muscled, and his fists were already clenched.

'No! Well, not deliberately. It was because—'

'You felled my poor boy and he bumped his head,' Digger interrupted. 'Yet he escorted you on his way like a little gent. So you owes him, don't you? Act like a little lady and give him his reward.'

'I haven't got anything!' I said. 'I don't have any money on me. I spent every penny on medicine for my mother, truly!'

It was a huge mistake to mention the medicine. The boy's eyes gleamed.

'She's shoved it down her dress, Digger!' he cried.

'Right!' said Digger, and he lunged at me.

I dodged past him and started running. He grabbed at my skirts and pulled so hard that the petticoat ripped and came right off, but I ran on, clutching the medicine bottle inside my bodice, keeping it safe. I climbed out of the mud and ran and ran and ran. Someone threw a stone at me that hit me hard on the back of my head and made me stagger – but I kept on running. I even risked tearing down another dank alleyway, braving any rats. I just knew I had to get away and get that medicine back to Mother – though I didn't even know who she was.

Chapter Five

I'd never been here before and yet I knew where to go now. I turned this way and that, away from the riverbank, down endless small lanes until at last I reached Farthing Terrace. I knew the name before I saw the street sign. I knew which small terraced house to run to. Of course I did – it was my home here, though I had dim memories of living somewhere else in these times in a tall house with scrubbed white steps.

The door of number seven wasn't locked. There was nothing inside worth stealing. I somehow knew most of our furniture had been sold off to pay our debts.

I ran inside and rushed up the bare steps. We didn't even

have a stair carpet any more. I opened the bedroom door cautiously in case Mother had managed to go to sleep – I knew she'd been awake a lot of the night because her coughing was so bad.

She was awake now, trying to sit up.

'Edie!' she said weakly, starting to cough again. She clutched her chest, trying hard to control it. 'You've been gone so long. I thought something had happened to you!'

'I'm so sorry. The pharmacy wouldn't sell me any more medicine at first because we haven't paid our bills. So I went down to the pawnshop near the riverbank and the man there gave me a whole shilling for my locket,' I explained breathlessly. I knew this had happened – my neck still felt strangely airy without the light tug of the chain. Yet I couldn't really *remember* it. My first memory of today seemed to be falling in the mud when Boy tried to steal the medicine, and that must have happened afterwards.

I shook my head, trying to make sense of my muddled thoughts.

'But the laudanum?' Mother said desperately, holding a handkerchief to her lips. 'Where is it?'

'Yes, it's here, still safe, though someone tried to snatch it from me,' I said, bringing it out of my bodice.

I uncorked the bottle and looked for a spoon, but Mother reached for it and took a sip straight from the neck.

'You're not meant to drink it like that! It should be stirred into water – and only a few drops,' I said anxiously.

'I don't care. Just so long as it soothes the cough,' Mother said, lying back on her pillow. 'But it's such a shame you pawned a present from your father. I'm sure it was gold, and worth much more than a shilling.'

'The pawnshop man said it was pinchbeck, and I was lucky to get anything for it,' I said.

Mother sighed and reached for the laudanum bottle again.

'You mustn't have any more!' I said.

'I'm sure this is watered down. It's nowhere near strong enough,' Mother said. 'The bottle's different too. It's not the right mixture. Did you get it from our pharmacy?'

'I didn't want to go back there. That man was so horrid, saying dreadful things about Father,' I said. 'I went to another place near the pawnshop and paid cash.' The words came out of my mouth without thinking. Yet I had no memory at all of going to any pharmacy – was that a chemist? And how did

I know I'd had a pinchbeck locket? I'd become this other Edie now. And so was this mother *my* mother?

Of course she wasn't. This mother looked much older than Mum. She was as pale as the sheets, her arms so thin they looked as if they would snap any moment. Her poor face had hollow cheeks, and her eyes were sunken, with dark smudges like bruises underneath. She was nothing like my lovely, glamorous mum with her glossy hair and her rosy face. My mum was very slim, but not emaciated like this poor mother, who looked so ill.

'Oh Edie, you poor darling. I feel so dreadful – my own little daughter haggling in pawnshops to get my medicine,' said Mother, tears welling.

'Don't cry, Mother! It's not your fault you're ill,' I said, trying to soothe her. 'Shall I make you a cup of tea?'

'Yes please, dear – though there's only a little dust left in the caddy,' she said, wiping her eyes.

I smoothed her pillow and pulled the sheet and thin blanket round her neck, then gave her a pat on her shoulder.

'You're such a good girl,' she murmured sleepily.

I went downstairs to the kitchen, knowing exactly where it was – though it was a shock to see it so bare. There were marks

on the floor where a dresser used to be, and just a small hob and a sink with one tap. I filled the kettle with water and put it back on the hob, knowing exactly what to do although it was nothing like our kettle and big stove at home.

I wished with all my heart that I was back there in our own big bright kitchen. This dream was going on much too long. I tried shutting my eyes and then opening them wide, willing myself to wake up. It didn't work.

Was it a dream? When I poured the hot water into the chipped china teapot, a drop or two splashed on my arm and it hurt. Could you feel pain like that in an ordinary dream? Did you even *know* you were dreaming when you were? What if I had hurtled back into the past and become this old Edie for ever? It was such a terrifying thought that I went dizzy and had to sit on one of the two hard chairs left at the table.

My hands were shaking so badly it was hard to pour Mother's tea. I could only find a surprisingly beautiful small set of china: two cups, two saucers and two plates, light and delicate, with a pink, green and deep-blue pattern and a gold rim. I tried to remember if there had once been a full set of crockery, and a big polished table with the right number of chairs in a dining room.

I tried desperately hard and remembered a dining room in a bigger house. It had a dark floral wallpaper and long green velvet curtains. There was a father sitting at the head of the table, a man with curly whiskers and a big moustache and wild hair. He wore a proper suit, and a waistcoat stretched tightly over his big tummy. *My* father? Where was he now? Had he been ill like Mother? Had he *died*?

I picked up the cup of tea, trying to steady my hand. I went upstairs, managing not to spill a drop. The scrapings at the bottom of the caddy had barely coloured the hot water, but at least it still smelled like tea.

I went into the bedroom. Mother was lying back on the pillow, her eyes closed now.

'Here's your cup of tea, Mother,' I said softly.

She didn't stir.

'Mother?' I repeated, going over to the bed.

There was no response. My heart started beating very fast inside my tight bodice. I bent over her. It was a great relief to hear her breathing. She was simply fast asleep. It seemed a shame to wake her now.

I looked at the green medicine bottle. Had she taken another sip? I knew you should never overdose on any kind of

medicine. I took the cork out and sniffed. It had a strange thick, heady smell. It made me feel dizzy. Very dizzy. I wasn't even sure where I was. I jammed the cork back in but the room still seemed to be shifting sideways. I looked again at the poor woman in bed. Was she really my mother? I didn't even know her name! I only knew my *own* name – but it also belonged to this girl in the past.

'*My* name is Edie Trimmer!' I cried, and Mother blurred and disappeared, the house flew apart and I was whirled into the ether.

'Edie? Edie, lovie, wake up!'

I heard the voice before I could see anything through the cloudy mist. I felt hands gently shaking my shoulders and made out Dad's face peering at me anxiously.

'Is it really you, Dad?' I whispered.

'Of course it's me! Who else would it be?' said Dad, his dear, clean-shaven face suddenly clear.

'Oh Dad!' I threw my arms round him and hugged him hard.

'Hey, darling, what is it?' Dad asked anxiously. 'Did you have a bad dream? You were sound asleep at your desk when I looked in on you.'

I was still sitting at my desk now, the manuscript book and pen and ink in front of me. I was truly back in my own room, in my own house, with my own dad.

'Where's Mum?' I asked fearfully.

'Mum's in her study, Zooming a colleague about tomorrow. Do you want her? She's trying to get everything sorted before supper, so we shouldn't really disturb her,' said Dad.

'But she's all right? She's not ill?' I asked.

'She was fine five minutes ago when I took her a cup of coffee. I had to sidle up to her so that I wouldn't be seen on screen!' said Dad. He felt my forehead. 'You're a bit hot. I hope you're not sickening for something. It's not like you to fall fast asleep in the afternoon. Perhaps I *should* go and get Mum.'

'No, it's OK. *I'm* OK.' I looked at the open manuscript. *My name is Edie Trimmer. I am going to tell you about my life.*

Dad looked too. 'Ah! More mysterious writing! Did it just appear out of the blue?' I knew he was gently teasing me.

'I wrote the second sentence,' I said. 'But I truly didn't write the first, like I said.'

'Right,' said Dad, nodding, though I knew he still didn't believe me. I didn't really blame him. The writing in both sentences was identical. And I knew if I tried to explain what

had just happened to me he wouldn't believe that either. He'd simply say I'd had a weird dream.

Maybe it was. I didn't believe in time travel, even though I'd watched lots of old episodes of *Doctor Who*. And I didn't have a Tardis anyway.

'Let's get you a drink of water,' Dad said.

'Or cola?' I said hopefully.

I went downstairs with him, and I took a can of cola out the fridge and Dad grabbed a can of beer. We looked guiltily down the hall towards Mum's closed study door.

'Watch the cricket with me for a bit. I'll explain it to you,' said Dad, pulling me on the sofa with him for a cuddle.

It felt good to be close to Dad as we sipped our drinks, but I soon got bored. I wandered off to the bookcase and pulled down a big fat book about Victorian times. It had very small print inside and was quite hard to read. It would have been difficult to understand though, even if it had been printed in huge capital letters. I leafed through the pages and consulted the index at the back. It seemed full of facts about prime ministers and parliament and wars abroad, but nothing about poor people on the streets, nothing about illness and nothing at all about medicine in green glass bottles.

I heaved the book back on its shelf with a sigh.

'I think it's a bit grown up for you,' said Dad, though he was still watching the cricket intently. 'It's probably a bit too grown up for me too! I think it was your mum's. She did history for one of her A levels.'

Mum came into the living room then, rubbing her eyes and yawning.

'Not another sleepyhead?' said Dad.

'I do hate Zoom calls that go on for ever,' said Mum, stretching. 'Hey, Edie.'

'Hi, Mum,' I said, smiling at her in total relief. She was *my* mum, smart and lively, in her white blouse and navy jacket, though she'd kicked off her high heels and was in her socks, with jeans, as below her waist wouldn't show on the video.

'Are you watching the cricket too, Edie?' Mum asked, looking quizzical.

'Not really,' I said.

'Just having a drink,' said Mum. She frowned, but she wasn't really cross. 'Maybe I'll join you.'

She went into the kitchen and came back with her own can. She clinked it against ours.

'Are we celebrating?' she asked.

'I said Edie could have a cola because she was a bit hot and bothered,' said Dad. 'She was fast asleep when I went to see what she was up to.'

'Really?' said Mum. She reached out and put her hand on my forehead. 'I don't think you've got a temperature. I wonder why you were so sleepy though? Did you stay up late reading when you went to bed last night?' she asked.

'No,' I said truthfully. 'Mum, do you know anything about Victorian medicines?'

'What?'

'The sort that could have been in that green glass bottle I got from Peter and Gordon's,' I explained.

'Ah! Well, it could have been any kind, I suppose. The Victorians took a lot of medicine, not that it really helped them much. They didn't know how to treat most diseases then,' she said. 'You and your Victorians! Have you been writing more of your story in that old manuscript book?' Mum asked, glancing at Dad significantly.

'Only a tiny bit,' I said. 'So if someone swallowed quite a lot of medicine, would it really harm them?' I asked.

'Well, it depends. If it was only honey and lemon to soothe a sore throat then I suppose it wouldn't do much harm,' said

Mum. 'Edie, *you* haven't been secretly taking any medicine, have you? There wasn't anything left *in* that old bottle?'

Dad looked startled. He actually turned the sound down on the remote. 'Is that why you were so sleepy?' he asked, looking at me anxiously.

'No! I promise *I* haven't taken any medicine. I'm not stupid,' I insisted. 'And I've had that bottle for ages. It's because I'm interested in Victorian times. And – and I'm writing about a lady who's sick and she needs this medicine. It's got a funny name. Lord something or other.'

'Laudanum!' said Mum. 'Oh, thank goodness. You can't buy laudanum nowadays.' She looked at Dad and they both breathed a sigh of relief.

'So what *is* laudanum? Is it like our cough mixture?' I asked.

'It's much stronger. It's mostly opium and very addictive,' said Mum. 'Are you writing this story for a school project, darling? I really don't think it's a suitable subject.'

'Not if it's about drug addicts,' said Dad. 'Although didn't Sherlock Holmes take opium?'

'All kinds of people did. I'm not sure they realized how dangerous it was,' said Mum.

'I'm just writing it for me,' I said. 'There's this poor thin, sick lady with this really bad cough, and she's desperate to take her medicine. She says it makes her feel better.'

'Well, I suppose it could give her some relief. Like taking a paracetamol for a splitting headache. So long as she doesn't take an overdose. So what illness does she have?' Mum asked.

'I don't really know what's the matter with her. Could it be Covid?'

'That's a very modern illness. If she's got a bad cough and she's very weak, it sounds more like tuberculosis. So many people suffered from it in Victorian times,' said Mum. 'They didn't know how to treat it then.'

'So how *should* you treat it?' I asked.

'Fresh air, nourishing food, sunlight, warmth. And the right sort of medicines, but they hadn't been invented in Victorian times,' said Mum.

'But they did get better, didn't they?' I asked.

'I suppose a few people did. But mostly they just died,' Mum said.

'Oh no!' I gasped.

'Hey, Edie, don't get so upset!' said Mum. 'This happened long, long ago. Don't be silly. Why don't you turn your story

character into a rich lady in perfect health, with a special friend exactly like your Alex?'

'Alexandra!' said Dad. 'And you're Edith. And you wear long crinolines and go to balls and have a whale of a time.'

They were trying so hard to cheer me up. They didn't understand that I wasn't in charge of this story. It was real and I couldn't change it because it had already happened. Unless . . .

I waited until I went to bed. Both Mum and Dad came to tuck me in as if I was little again, and carried on telling me this ridiculous story about Victorian Edith and her friend Alexandra.

'And then they're both going to meet tall, dark, handsome Victorian gentlemen and get married and have lots of children and live happily ever after,' said Dad.

'No, they're not!' said Mum. 'Edith is going to be a great writer like Charlotte Brontë, and Alexandra can be a great singer like Jenny Lind.'

They were being so sweet. They didn't understand. I wasn't caught up in a story. It wasn't even a dream. When they went downstairs at last, I turned on my desk lamp and picked up my green medicine bottle. I held it up to my nose and had

a big sniff. I was sure I could smell the same sickening sweet smell of laudanum.

I had to go back and see if there was any way I could save Mother for that other Edie. I opened my old cash box and took out my savings, a ten-pound note and a pound coin. I folded the ten-pound note very tightly and slipped the pound inside. I sellotaped it to my left palm several times so that I couldn't possibly drop it when I was whirled back into the past. I was terrified I might get trapped there, but I felt compelled to risk it.

I sat at my desk, opened the first page of the manuscript book, dipped the pen in the inkwell, and started writing.

Chapter Six

My father's business failed and he died of a seizure when I was very young. Our whole life changed. We lost our friends. Mother became ill. We had no money and were forced to move house and sell all our possessions. Then—

Then the room slanted and I started falling in the sudden darkness. Down and down and down until suddenly someone caught hold of my arm as I opened the battered door of 7 Farthing Terrace.

'Where do you think you're going, miss?'

The fogginess cleared and I saw a man with his shirt sleeves rolled up, and a thick brown apron tied about his waist. He was

chewing tobacco, his lips showing his discoloured teeth and a little drool of yellow saliva at the corner of his mouth.

'Let me go! This is my house!' I said indignantly, trying to pull away from him.

'Your house, is it, miss? And how many months' rent do you owe, eh? It's *my* house, and if your wretched ma was still alive, I'd have her in court and sent to the debtors' prison where she belongs,' he said.

'Mother's . . . dead?' I whispered. I was too late! How much time had passed – days, weeks, months?

I hadn't really known this mother back in the past, as I'd only met her once, and yet I was overwhelmed with sorrow. The horrible man blurred as I started weeping.

'That's it, turn on the water tap,' he sneered.

'I won't have you talking about Mother like that! And we won't stay in debt to you. How much do we owe?' I said, wiping my cheek with my right hand. My left hand was still sellotaped. The money was safe!

'I reckon your wretched mother owed me at least ten bob,' he said, turning his head to spit a horrible wad of tobacco onto the pavement.

'Ten bob?' I said. Did that mean ten pounds? 'Very well,

I will clear our debt immediately. And don't you dare call my mother names!'

I pulled the sellotape off my left hand with one painful rip and offered him the ten-pound note. He started to unfold it – and then spat again in contempt.

'Are you playing a joke on me? I don't want your stupid toy money, little girl,' he said, thrusting it back at me. 'That's just worthless paper.'

'No it's not!' I said, snatching it back.

The pound coin fell to the floor.

The man's eyes widened. 'Here, is that a sovereign?'

'What's that?' I asked.

'A gold pound coin, you little numbskull.'

'Yes, then. It's a pound – it says so,' I said, pointing.

'Who's this woman?' he asked, flipping the coin over.

'It's Queen Elizabeth!' I said – and then realized it was actually the wrong queen for these times.

'Think I'm stupid?' he said, but he moved the disgusting wad of tobacco to the side of his mouth, and bit my pound coin.

'You're not meant to *eat* it!' I said.

'I'm testing it – and even though it holds, it don't seem like gold to me. Nah, it's no use to me. I'm laying claim to any

possessions inside of these rooms, so get out of my way.' He pushed me aside and stepped into the house. I put my rejected money into the pocket of my dress and followed him in. I watched in horror as he marched round the half-empty rooms, cursing that we didn't have anything worth taking.

I felt desperate to find anything small of Mother's to keep as a precious memento, but there was so little. The hateful man kicked the table and chairs contemptuously and rifled through the cupboards, but there was hardly anything there. I longed to take one of the beautiful china cups, but he smacked my hand away when I reached out.

Then he went thundering up the stairs to Mother's bedroom. I could hardly bear to look at the poor empty bed. It seemed an outrage that he could ransack her small dressing table and wardrobe and snatch all her personal things. I begged for her cologne bottle, her hair pomade, her tortoiseshell hairbrush, but he wouldn't let me have anything, even though the brush had lost most of its bristles. He took her one remaining decent frock made of pearl-grey wool with a lace trim, and he took her glacé kid boots too, a little scuffed but still beautiful.

He systematically took every little piece that was left of

Mother, pushing me out of the way impatiently as I pleaded with him. I collapsed by the stripped bed, crying helplessly. I heard a little *tick-tick-tick* sound, keeping time with my sobs. It was Mother's pocket watch lying under the bed. It must have fallen out of the sheets. I waited until the man went to the chest of drawers, searching for hidden money or jewels, and then reached out my hand, clasped the watch, and dropped it in my pocket with the money.

I scrambled to my feet and made for the bedroom door – but the man had turned.

'What are you up to? Did you just put something in your pocket? You little varmint!'

He lunged at me, but I dodged and flew down the stairs two at a time. Then was out in the street, running fast. He followed me for a minute or two, but then had to stop with a coughing fit. He'd probably swallowed his own tobacco. I hated him so I almost wished he'd choke to death.

My feet hurt dreadfully because my boots seemed even smaller now. My toes stubbed up against the front, the pain throbbing all the way up my leg. I wondered about taking my boots off altogether, but the buttons looked fiddly and he'd catch me up before I could manage it. I ran on, not realizing

where I was going till I got to the churchyard. I knew Mother wouldn't have been given a proper burial or her own plot so she could lie in peace by herself.

There was an old sexton, sitting on the grass and eating a pie, catching the crumbs on a check handkerchief and enjoying his picnic amongst the gravestones.

'Excuse me, sir, my poor mother must have been buried here recently, but I don't know where to find her,' I said desperately.

'Did she have money, little missy?' he said, his mouth full.

'No, I'm afraid not,' I murmured.

'Paupers' grave, round the back,' he said, indicating with a jerk of his head.

It wasn't a proper grave at all. It was a big ugly mound, away from the proper graves with their marble messages and stone angels and flowers. It looked more like a farmyard dung-heap than a resting place.

I went down on my knees at the edge. I whispered a prayer, holding Mother's watch in my clasped hands, and then I crept furtively to the other well-tended graves and took several roses and lilies and arranged them in a little heart shape at the newly dug edge of the paupers' grave.

'Rest in peace, Mother,' I whispered.

There was a withered bouquet of flowers discarded on the path, still held together by a thin satin ribbon. I undid it, threaded it through the loop at the top of Mother's watch, and tied it round my neck like a precious locket. Then I walked past the sexton, who was still tucking into his pie.

I couldn't help staring at it hungrily. What was I going to do for food? I had Mother's watch, but it was all I had left of her – I couldn't sell it. How was I going to get any money? Was I going to have to live like the mudlark boy, wading through the filthy river at low tide, looking for nuggets of coal and rusty nails to sell for a few pence? I didn't have anyone to look after me now. I had to look after myself.

I knew from Boy that I had to avoid the workhouse. I started walking swiftly, limping now, clasping Mother's pocket watch like a talisman. It was a hot day, the sun still strong though it was late afternoon. People had their sleeves rolled up and collars undone, fanning themselves. Little children ran around barefoot, squealing with laughter. It seemed so jarring to see people happy, when I was feeling so desperately sad and anxious.

I was making for the little market where Mother and I had done our meagre shopping. We bought hot potatoes there

from a cheery man who baked them on a brazier. He had made a fuss of me, calling me Buttercup and picking out the biggest potato he could find amongst his hot coals. Perhaps he might give me a very small one for nothing?

He was there as usual on the edge of the market and gave me a little wave when he saw me approaching. 'Hello there, Buttercup. Haven't seen you in quite a while,' he said. 'How's your ma, eh? You said she was poorly last time I saw you.'

I felt my eyes filling with tears. 'Mother's dead,' I whispered.

'Oh my Lord! I'm so sorry. You poor little mite. So have you got a grandmother or an aunt or anyone else to look after you?' he asked.

I shook my head miserably.

'Well, any time you need a good meal, come and see your Uncle Potato, Buttercup,' he said, picking out a finely baked beauty with his tongs and spearing it on his stand. 'Shall I salt and pepper it for you? And a good dollop of butter?'

'I haven't got any proper money,' I said miserably.

'Don't you worry about cash,' he said. 'I've got a barrelful of potatoes baking here, enough for an army. No one fancies a hot potato when the sun shines. Here you are, my dear. A little

gift.' He wrapped the potato in newspaper and handed it to me. 'Keep your spirits up, girlie. You're a bright little Buttercup. Polite girl like you, you'll be snapped up as a maid when you're a bit bigger.'

'Thank you so much,' I said, giving him a watery smile.

I went to sit on the step of the butter market where it was shady, and nibbled at my potato. It tasted so good that I couldn't help feeling a little comforted. I looked round at the busy market and watched the children working there. Boys clamoured to hold the reins of the carriage horses. Boys served at the stalls. Boys ran around hauling sacks and supplies. Boys swept the gutters clear of rotting fruit and lettuce leaves. Boys played the penny flute and begged for pennies. Boys, boys, boys.

No girls seemed to work here. No, there was one girl wandering listlessly through the crowd carrying a basket of flowers, crying, 'Who'll buy my flowers, penny a bunch, tuppence a fancy bouquet?' She ran the words together in a drawl, so I had to listen to her cry three times to make out what she was saying.

I looked at her flowers. They were wilting already in the hot sun. The girl was wilting too, scarcely able to drag one

boot in front of the other. They were in good enough condition, but much too big and clumsy for her. My boots were dainty, but much too small.

'Hello! I can see your boots are hurting you,' I said politely.

She looked startled. 'Penny a bunch, tuppence a bouquet,' she said.

'Yes, I know. I'd buy some, but my money doesn't work here,' I said.

'Eh?'

I couldn't blame her for looking puzzled.

'Never mind. I can't buy any flowers but I *would* like your boots,' I said. 'I've got bigger since Mother bought me these ones.'

She blinked at me. She only came up to my shoulders, but her face looked older and very pinched. It was obvious she never sold enough flowers to buy herself a decent meal.

'You want to buy my boots?' she said incredulously.

'I want to swap them for mine,' I told her. 'Do you understand? I'll wear your boots and you wear mine.'

She peered at my neat patent boots with their pearl buttons. I saw the flicker in her eyes. I could tell she liked them. 'They're very fancy,' she said. 'Not much good for walking.'

'But you can't walk properly in your own boots because they're too big for you. Why don't you try mine on?' I suggested. 'Take your own boots off and see if mine fit better.'

'It's a trick!' she said. 'You'll grab my boots and make off with them. Think I'm stupid?'

Perhaps she'd been tricked so many times she'd learned to be cautious. 'I'll take mine off first then,' I said, sitting down behind a stall and scrabbling with the buttons on my boots. I'd once had a button hook but all those niceties were gone now. By the time I'd got to the second boot my fingers had learned the knack and I managed more quickly. It was such a relief to get them off. My stockings were worn into holes, exposing my poor bleeding toes. I hid them under my skirts in shame.

'Let's have a proper look at them boots then,' said the girl, setting down her flower basket. She picked them up, examining the soles, peering at the heels, checking the buttons. Then she put a boot on each hand and held them in front of her admiringly, making them walk through the air.

'I *do* like them,' she said.

She stood up – and I worried *she* was going to run off with them, keeping her own boots on. Maybe I was the stupid one. I remembered the mudlark boy. Poor children here were so

desperate they'd snatch and steal from each other given the chance. But I was wrong. She was just standing to kick her own boots off.

'Here you are then,' she said. 'No backsies!'

'No backsies!' I agreed.

I put on her boots. They were very plain and clumpy compared to my patent boots with their pointy toes. But my own poor toes stretched out wide, wonderfully free, and I could stride out without even a twinge of pain.

'Your boots are fantastic!' I said.

'*Your* boots are fine and dandy!' she said, doing a little twirl and then pointing her toes. 'I feel like a lady!' Then she bit her lip. 'I hope my ma won't whack me when she sees what I've been up to. She can be awful fierce. Is your ma fierce too?'

'No.' I could feel my own lip quivering. 'She was sweet and gentle and kind, but she's dead now.'

I started crying and the girl put her arm round me. 'You poor thing,' she said, hugging me. 'And what about your pa?'

'He's dead too, and now I don't know what to do,' I sobbed. 'I haven't got any money for food and I haven't got anywhere to stay.'

'Well, you can't stay with us, because there are ten of us crammed into one room,' she said. 'We ain't got room for a mouse to scratch, let alone another body.'

'*Ten?*'

'Ma and Pa, and my gran who's dottled, and my biggest brother Alf who works on the stalls, and Tommy who's a sweeper in the factory, and my biggest sister Mary-Ann who minds the little ones, then there's Rosie and Johnny and baby Ernest.' She counted them off on her fingers. 'That's only nine! Oh, there's me too. I'm Jenny.'

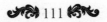

'Goodness. I'm Edie. I don't have any brothers and sisters,' I said miserably.

'You lucky thing!' said Jenny. 'I wish we could swap places as well as boots. I don't rate any of my brothers and sisters. The big ones pick on me, and the little ones pester. Ma just yells at us, and Pa too if we get under his feet. My gran can't talk no more but she can still give you a poke if you get on her nerves.'

I couldn't tell if she was making it up or not. Her family sounded comically dreadful. But I liked Jenny herself. She sighed when she looked at the state of her flowers.

'They look past it, don't they?' she said. 'But I've only sold ten pennies' worth today: eight posies and one bouquet. Ma will be mad at me.'

'But that's a lot here, isn't it?' I said. 'Ten pennies would buy a hot potato for each of you.'

'She has to buy them up Covent Garden though, a shilling a trayful. I haven't made enough money at all. I need another two-pennyworth! Or Ma will whack me something dreadful.' She looked as if she might cry.

It seemed her mother really did hit her, which was horrifying. I had to help her somehow. I stared at the flowers jumbled together in her basket.

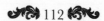

'Perhaps they might sell if we sorted them out a bit to make them look prettier?' I said. I looked at the lettuce leaves in the gutter. 'I know, we could line the basket with green, and then they'd stand out more. And look, someone's spilled a few strawberries. We could dot them about these yellow flowers to make them stand out.'

'But I'm not selling green stuff and fruit – I does flowers,' Jenny protested.

'I know. A penny a posy and tuppence a bouquet. But they'll look prettier if we arrange them properly, and people won't notice they're a bit wilted. Let's try it,' I said.

It worked a treat. Women with a coin or two left over after buying their fruit and vegetables bought a little posy to pin on their bodices. When we walked up and down the streets nearby, gentlemen bought a bouquet for their sweethearts. Then when trade seemed to be drying up I suddenly threw back my head and started singing a song: *'Penny for a posy, pretty, pretty rosie; thruppence for a bouquet, come and buy today!'*

'I don't know that song,' Jenny said doubtfully.

'No one does. I've just made it up,' I said. In the back of my head, I knew I'd done this before. 'Come on, you sing it too.'

Jenny looked at me as if I was mad, but the song was attracting attention, and after I'd repeated it several times, often with silly variations, a little crowd gathered and people actually bought more posies and bouquets. Now Jenny only had a few scattered petals left in her basket, and a pocketful of coins.

'Some of them gents gave me too much and didn't wait for their change,' Jenny said. She jingled the money. 'There's sixpences!' she added, marvelling.

'Perhaps they liked my singing,' I said.

'Did you really make it all up, just like that?' she asked. 'With that tune and them words? You aren't half clever, Edie. Will you sell flowers with me tomorrow?' She picked out one of the sixpences. 'Here, you can have that for wages.'

It wasn't quite fair – she'd earned a lot extra because of me. But it was better than nothing, so I thanked her and popped it in my pocket with my useless modern money.

We walked back to the market. Folk were packing up now. Jenny started skipping.

'Ma will be so pleased with me!' she said. 'I reckon she'll give me a bit of meat with my mash and gravy tonight! I only gets meat on a Sunday usually. It's kept for Pa and my big brother.'

'But that's not fair,' I said.

'They do the heavy work,' said Jenny. 'Course it's fair. Oh well, ta ta, Edie. See you tomorrow.'

'You're going now?' I asked. I'd rather hoped she'd invite me back to supper, meat or no meat, but perhaps her mother didn't allow her to have friends round. She'd made it plain I couldn't sleep over at her place either.

I didn't have anywhere to go. I didn't know what I was going to do. I begged Jenny to stay with me a bit longer, but she looked at me anxiously and backed away. I went looking for the friendly hot potato man, but he'd already packed up and gone home. I clasped the pocket watch hanging from my neck and listened to it tick, trying to calm myself.

Everyone was going home now but I didn't have a home here. I knew there was another Edie Trimmer, one with a lovely home and two parents to look after her. All I had to do was wake up and I'd be there, sitting at my desk, writing in the manuscript book.

I sat back down on the butter market step and tried to assume the position I'd been in at home. I curled my right hand as if I was holding an invisible pen. I made dipping motions with it, as if the ink was there in front of me on my

desk. I imagined I was in my soft comfy pyjamas instead of this tight dress and borrowed boots.

I tried to will myself forward into that time, trying so hard that little beads of sweat burst out on my forehead. Sometimes the market square seemed to tilt a little but when I opened my eyes I was still there, alone now, with the smell of old vegetables strong in my nose.

'Mum! Dad! Wake me up!' I shouted at the top of my voice, but nothing happened.

What if I was stuck here in the past for ever? Would I have to get by selling flowers and begging food and sleeping on steps? What would it be like in the winter? I remembered the tale of the Little Match Girl in my fairy-story book. She'd struck three matches to give her warmth – but then she'd frozen to death.

Is this really what happened to poor orphan children in Victorian times? Or would some scary Child Collector come creeping along and bundle me into his basket and carry me off to the workhouse?

Of course! That was where this Edie *had* ended up. She wrote in the manuscript book that *came* from the workhouse. She must have been taken there as a child . . . and then locked

up there for the rest of her life. If what Boy had told me was right, she'd be shut up in this bleak institution, fed gruel, forced to work every waking hour, and beaten if she rebelled. I didn't want to have to go through all that! Not if I could get back to that other Edie. If I went to sleep in a dream, I wondered, would that mean I would wake up somewhere else?

I started shivering even though the evening was warm. I took shelter at the back of the butter market, squashed into a corner in the shadows where I hoped no one could see me. I huddled into a little ball, my head on my knees. Every now and then I heard the mew of a stray cat or the scrabble of some small rodent, and I looked up in alarm. Each time it was darker, and then it was pitch black.

I nodded off to sleep and then woke with a start. Was I home at last? No, I felt cold stone underneath me. But I wasn't alone now. There were mutterings and stirrings and a sudden curse. I hunched up in my corner, my fists clenched. Someone crept up to me stealthily and put their hands on my neck, but I screamed and kicked out hard with my boots, and they ran off.

I put my hand to my chest to clutch the pocket watch – but it wasn't there. I felt around me in the darkness but it had gone.

Someone had snatched it off my neck, ribbon and all. Rage overcame my fear. I stood up and went rushing into the night.

'Stop, thief!' I yelled. 'How dare you steal Mother's watch! Help, help! Stop that thief!'

I saw the light bobbing in the distance. I ran towards it, still bellowing. As I got nearer I saw it was a lantern, held high by a night watchman in a cloak. He had a wooden baton in his other hand and I stopped running abruptly.

'Who goes there?' he called. 'What's all the shouting?'

'Please, sir, someone's stolen my gold pocket watch!' I gasped, trying to get my breath.

'How come you've got a pocket watch, a little street urchin like you? I think you're the one who's done the stealing!' he said sternly.

'No, sir! It was my mother's watch – I swear it. And I'm not a street urchin, I've been decently brought up!' I said, jutting out my chin.

'What's your name then, and where do you come from?' he demanded.

'My name is Edie Trimmer and – and I lived at . . .'

Then I couldn't remember the address of the little house where Mother had lived. I couldn't remember anything. The

night watchman's lantern was blinding me now. I couldn't see, I couldn't hear, I couldn't keep my footing, I was whirling forward . . .

'Edie? Wake up, darling.'

'Hey, pet. Breakfast's ready!'

I opened my eyes – and Mum and Dad were peering down at me. My mum, my dad, and I was in my own bed in my own room in my own time, back being the right Edie.

'I'm back!' I said, sitting up joyfully. My neck ached so I started rubbing it.

'Have you cricked your neck?' said Mum, sitting down on the bed beside me and rubbing it too. 'We found you sitting up at your desk again, your head lolling forward. No wonder your neck hurts now.'

'You were so sound asleep we couldn't wake you up properly. I had to lift you into bed like a baby,' said Dad.

'So was it you who took the watch?' I ask.

'Your watch? Why would I take it? It's on your bedside table, look!' said Dad.

'No, Mother's *pocket* watch,' I said, and then realized what I was saying.

'I haven't got a pocket watch, darling,' said Mum. 'I've just

got my Apple watch. You're still half asleep. Here, have a sip of tea.'

She put a tray on my lap – a cup of tea in my own old bunny mug, not a gold-rimmed china cup. The tea was strong, with milk. I had toast and honey too, cut into triangles. I started eating it hurriedly, starving hungry.

'This is so good!' I said. 'I didn't have anything to eat yesterday, apart from a potato.'

I saw Mum and Dad look at each other anxiously.

'I mean, I *dreamed* I didn't have anything to eat,' I said. 'I dreamed I was back in the past again.'

'You're having such vivid dreams, Edie. You're not getting a proper restful night's sleep. I wonder if you should see a doctor,' Mum murmured.

'No, I'm fine, really,' I said, gobbling toast. It felt so wonderful to be back being looked after, safe and warm and loved.

It was already getting quite difficult remembering how sad and terrible it had been in the past. All the details were fading. When Mum and Dad went downstairs to have their own breakfast, I sat idly chasing crumbs around my plate, trying hard to get everything sorted out in my head. It was like trying

to remember a dream. Perhaps that was really what it was. Just dreams, and a coincidence or two.

I found I had my hand on my chest, feeling for the pocket watch. No, someone snatched it during the night. I looked over at my trinkets cabinet, and then shot out of bed. There it was, safe behind the glass: the pocket watch I had got from Peter and Gordon months ago. I took it out and held it cupped in my hand. It was Mother's pocket watch!

I looked down at my left hand. It had an outline of grubby marks where the sellotape had been. So where was my money? I looked in my bed, on my desk, inside the cash box. It was missing. All my savings! How could they disappear into a dream?

I was conscious of a small steady sound. The pocket watch in my hand was ticking, though I knew that Peter and Gordon had been unable to get it going again, even with the help of their jeweller friend. *Tick tick tick tick*. It was in full working order.

Chapter Seven

Dad suggested we go for a long walk along the seafront, even though it was a grey cloudy day.

'Can't we just stay in, Dad?' I said. I was busy googling on my iPad. I wanted to find out what happened to poor Victorian orphans. Did they really have to work, even when they were very young?

'No, I think you need to get a bit of fresh air. You're looking very pale,' said Dad. 'I want to see some roses in those cheeks.'

I pinched my cheeks hard. 'There! I bet I've got roses now!' I said. 'Did you know Victorian ladies used to do that on the way to a ball because they didn't have any blusher? Though

Gordon told me some ladies put red rouge on their cheeks, but it was considered vulgar.'

'You and your Victorians,' Dad said. 'You're obsessed. Come on, chop chop. My barometer says it's going to be changeable. I bet the sun will be out soon.'

The weather was changeable, but for the worst. It started raining as soon as we set foot on the esplanade.

'Oh!' I said, pulling a face.

'You look like a little codfish,' said Dad. 'A little bit of rain won't hurt us.'

It wasn't a little bit of rain. The wind blew hard and the rain increased until it was absolutely pouring, drenching us totally.

'We'd better run for the next shelter,' said Dad, but it didn't seem to offer any proper shelter at all. The wind blew the rain in and still soaked us.

'Maybe this wasn't such a good idea after all,' said Dad after five long minutes. 'When the rain stops I'll buy us both a hot chocolate to warm us up. With whipped cream.'

'And marshmallows,' I said.

Dad went to the edge of the shelter and peered out. 'There's hardly a soul in sight. Maybe everyone's been washed

out to sea,' he said, looking both ways. 'Hey, let's go to that little museum in the Martello tower. Perfect for a girl who likes history. We could run there in two minutes . . . and we can't really get any wetter. Shall we?'

'OK,' I said, and we high-fived each other and ran for it.

Alex and I had been taken to the tower once on a school trip. There had been a lot of fossils and bones on display, which were a bit *too* historical for my taste. But this time Dad and I went down the spiral stairs and discovered a lot of other little displays. There was a model Victorian lady dressed in a funny old-fashioned swimming costume, standing on the steps of a bathing hut. Another Victorian lady stood in a haberdashery shop selling beads and buttons and sewing reels. She had an instrument on her counter with a pearl handle and a small hook on the end.

'What on earth's that? Some kind of sewing thing?' asked Dad.

'It's a button hook! It would have come in very useful when I was wearing my boots with the little pearl buttons,' I said without thinking.

'I don't remember you having fancy boots like that,' said Dad.

'Oh! Maybe I dreamed I had some,' I mumbled.

'You and your dreams,' said Dad. He put his arm round me. 'Mum and I are getting a bit worried about you.'

'I'm fine, Dad. Really. I'm not going to keep on dreaming like that any more,' I said resolutely. After all, I had no *need* to go back again.

We wandered round the museum together, and I delighted in explaining Victorian things to Dad as if he was the child and I was the parent.

'This is actually a cracking little museum,' said Dad. 'It's just like stepping back into Victorian times, isn't it?'

It wasn't really like that a bit. The exhibits were genuine, but they were only objects behind glass, and the Victorian ladies were lifeless manikins.

'Do you think they've got a workhouse scene anywhere?' I asked.

'Probably not!' said Dad. 'You're a funny little soul, Edie.'

It had actually stopped raining when we went out of the museum. It was really warm in the sunshine, but Dad kept his promise and we both had delicious hot chocolates.

'Could we possibly have a biscuit too, Dad? Or maybe a cake?' I asked hopefully.

'No, we're having pizza for lunch. And Mum isn't in court this afternoon, so we thought we might go to the zoo if the rain doesn't start again,' said Dad.

'Fantastic!' I said.

I'd lost count of the number of times Alex and I had been to the zoo. They didn't have any big animals that looked unhappy. There were monkeys and meerkats and lemurs, and different kinds of rides and fun things to do, like seeing if you could roar as loud as a gibbon or leap as far as a gazelle. It was a bit strange going round the zoo without her, but Mum and Dad tried hard to make it fun. *They* roared and leaped and even went on the jungle ride with me.

I knew they were making a big fuss of me because they were worried about me. It made me feel guilty, though it wasn't really my fault. I vowed not to worry them any more. When I got home I put on my winter gloves, picked up the pen, the inkwell and the manuscript book, and stowed them on the bottom shelf of my display cabinet, where they were scarcely visible. I didn't want to risk touching them with my bare hands, just in case.

I looked at the glass medicine bottle and the pocket watch, my eyes filling with tears, though I had only spent a small snatch

of time with that poor sick mother. I blinked quickly, and picked up the little Victorian doll instead, little Teezel. She looked back at me with her bright blue eyes. They were fixed in her head, so she could never blink herself. She had a golden wig stuck on top of her head.

I ran my finger over her hair and felt the edges of the china head and then the sudden softness where it stopped. I knew exactly how much glue to put underneath the tiny wig – too little made it insecure and wobble disconcertingly, but too much made it ooze out so that she had ugly brown glue dribbles down her white forehead.

How did I know this? I'd never made a doll like this in my life. In *this* life. Did the other Edie make little dolls? She surely wouldn't do that sort of work in the workhouse. I put the doll back on her shelf carefully, arranging her long nightdress over her bowed legs. My hand cupped round her small body.

Perhaps Edie had kept this one little doll for herself, as a small friend. She might have carried her in the pocket of her dress and stroked her silky hair for comfort.

I wondered if Alex ever played with the twin doll, Dreezel. I texted her, *Have u still got ur doll?* She didn't text back. I sat staring at my phone miserably. She was obviously too busy

getting ready for tonight's show, larking around with Liam and Laura.

I jumped when my phone actually rang.

'Hey there!' said Alex. 'Sorry, we've been having a quick dance class – the director says it's become a bit routine and he wants it more spontaneous. So of course Liam got a bit *too* spontaneous and put us all off, and . . . oh, never mind, sorry – I keep burbling on about the theatre! So, did you mean my little china doll, Dreezel?'

'Sorry, I only wondered. It was a daft text,' I said, embarrassed.

'Of *course* I've still got her! She comes to the theatre with me every night. She's my lucky mascot. I hold her before I go on stage and stroke her hair for luck,' said Alex.

'Really? Oh, that's great!' I said happily.

'It will be so wonderful when *Oliver!* is over and we can get back to hanging out together every day. I'm missing you so!' said Alex.

'I'm missing you too,' I said.

'So, what have you been doing?'

I thought about telling her I'd been transported back to Victorian times – but I knew she'd only think I was making it

up, as though I was pretending I was in the show with her. So I told her about going to the seaside museum and the hot chocolate with whipped cream and marshmallows, and the trip to the zoo. They were lovely treats, but obviously pretty ordinary compared with going on stage every day, the star of the show. I tried to embellish my story a bit, making out that I'd been allowed to feed the penguins and how they looked so cute with their beaks wide open, fighting for fish. Then I said a lemur had jumped right into my arms and I'd been able to give it a cuddle.

I'm not sure Alex believed me, but she laughed and said it sounded fantastic and she couldn't wait till we could go to the zoo together. Then I heard someone talking to her in the background and she sighed.

'Sorry, I've got to start getting ready for the show. Maybe talk tomorrow, properly?' she asked.

'Yes, sure,' I said. 'Bye then.'

I took my own little doll to bed with me that night, hiding her under my pillow when Mum and Dad came to tuck me up. I held onto her, only sleeping in snatches. I kept thinking about the other Edie in the past. I'd left her being interrogated by the night watchman. She told him her name. Our name. *My name is Edie Trimmer.*

That was it! That was the way back! All I had to do was repeat those five words and, no matter what was happening in the past, I could come whirling forward into the present. I'd done it once, I'd done it twice. Did I dare go back just one more time to find out what eventually happened to her and how she ended up in the workhouse? Then I could say, *My name is Edie Trimmer*, and I'd be back safe.

I switched on my desk light, slid out of bed, padded over to the trinkets cabinet and took out the manuscript book. I put the pen and inkwell on my desk, dipped the pen in the ink, and then got carefully into bed, propping myself up comfortably on my pillows. I wasn't going to risk bumping my head on my desk again. I rested the manuscript book on my knees and opened it to the front page. I held the pen poised. I started writing:

I tried to survive by selling flowers but then—

Then the room slipped sideways and I lurched with it, dropping the pen, tumbling out of my bed, tumbling out of myself, down through the darkness, into the other Edie. I wasn't lying on the stone floor of the butter market. I was on a mattress with a blanket over me. It was a thin, lumpy mattress and the blanket was worn and rough, but at least it was a bed of sorts.

How did I end up here? Time had moved on again. Perhaps I shouldn't have risked it. I didn't like the look of this place – or this person standing over me, nudging me with their toe.

'Come on, girl, stir yourself. It's nearly daylight.' It was an old, rather stout woman, wearing a nightcap and a voluminous nightdress. I'd never seen her before in my life – yet I knew her well. She wasn't dear to me. I disliked her thoroughly.

She started battling with the stove, trying to get it to light and cursing it royally.

'Get yourself up this instant or I'll take my ladle to you!' she said, cursing at me too.

I struggled out of bed and stood yawning in my ragged shift. I gave myself a hasty cold wash at the kitchen sink, and then pulled on my old dress. My fingers hurt so much I could barely do up the buttons. I tucked my hands in my armpits, trying to ease the pain before struggling with my boots. One of the soles had started flapping, but Missus didn't give me any money for the cobblers. She didn't give me any money at all, though I slaved all day for her.

I slept on the mattress in the corner of the kitchen. I had to ask permission each time I used the privy in the tiny

backyard. My breakfast was the bowl of watery porridge she was preparing on the stove and a mug of tea. She left me a piece of bread and dripping for my dinner. My supper was a greasy plate of mutton stewed with carrots and potatoes. The stew had to last six days, bulked out with lentils, but on Sundays we had a roast. It was nothing like the roasts I ate when Father was alive and we were rich. It was a shrivelled joint of meat, a spoonful of soggy greens and a few potatoes.

'Right you are, girl,' Missus said. 'Get that porridge down you and get to work.'

The porridge went down in five spoonfuls, the tea in five gulps. I was still swallowing as I dashed out to the privy. It was raining hard but I didn't care. I threw back my head and gulped the raindrops as eagerly as my tea. These necessary trips were my only chance of fresh air.

I stayed outside as long as I dared, waiting until she yelled for me. 'Come inside, you stupid girl, you're getting soaking wet! Into the workroom with you, and stop wasting time,' she said, giving me a cuff on the back of my head as I went.

The workroom was upstairs as it had more light, but on a grey day like this there was little of it. It was sparsely furnished:

only two chairs and a table spread with calico and scissors, thread and needles. There was a basket of heads on a shelf, full of little eyes staring at me.

I stood at the table, flexed my fingers and started drawing round the templates for arms, legs and bodies, and then cutting them out carefully. When I'd done a whole row two of my fingers had started bleeding. I had to bind them up quickly with the calico trimmings. Missus would be angry if I got red spots on the material.

My fingers still hadn't hardened up. I'd been so pleased when Missus took a shine to me in the market, watching me sell flowers with Jenny. I liked pausing at her stall because she sold dolls – little wooden Dutch dolls with shiny black hair and red cheeks, and small china dolls with soft hair and cotton frocks.

'Do you like my little dollies, girls?' she asked.

We both nodded.

'Are you going to give us one then?' Jenny said hopefully.

'Penny for the wooden dolls, thruppence for the little china darlings,' she said.

'We ain't got no pennies, not for us. I have to take every penny of our earnings back to my ma,' said Jenny. 'She ain't

got no ma, so I gives her pennies for her grub,' she added, nodding at me.

'But we would love to buy one of your lovely little dolls if we could,' I said politely.

I remembered an exquisite wax doll I'd been given when Father was alive and sighed. Each time I found myself here, it was easier remembering. It was as if I'd been living this life for ever. This Edie's memories were now *mine*. It was almost as if I'd had two lives: the one before Father's business failed and he had a seizure, when we were so happy and jolly, and this life now with Mother gone too, and me having to fend for myself as best I could.

There was yet another life too – though the memories were getting hazier and hazier. I remembered Mum and Dad and Alex and . . . Peter and Gordon? Were they friends? They'd given me a book once, a manuscript book. I'd written in it – started some sort of story? I kept trying to remember what it was about. I knew it was important. But it was so hard to remember . . .

'What are you doing selling flowers, dearie, when you're quite the little lady?' the doll woman said, fingering the material of my dress.

'I haven't got any choice, madam,' I said. 'I have no family now.'

'I daresay you were taught little niceties at one time, child.' She paused. 'Did you ever sew a sampler, for instance?'

'Oh, I loved sewing my sampler. I did a cross-stitch picture of my house and garden, with little satin-stitch flowers growing in the grass,' I said. 'But that was long ago. I can't even remember the real house properly,' I said.

'So where do you live now, my pretty?' Missus enquired.

'I don't really live anywhere,' I said. 'I sleep where I can.'

'It's awful hard on her,' said Jenny. 'Some bad boy stole her ma's watch off of her one night.'

'Poor little mite,' said Missus, squeezing my shoulders. 'Do you know, the Good Lord says we should help those less fortunate than ourselves. Why don't you come and live along with me in my neat little house, and I'll learn you how to make these pretty dollies. Would you like that, girlie?'

'Oh, I would!' I said.

I thought she'd mother me and I'd have proper meals again, and get new clean clothes and learn to sew a fine seam like Curlylocks. I wondered if this kind doll woman would feed me strawberries, sugar and cream like the girl in the nursery

rhyme. It wouldn't be the same as living with my own dear mother, of course – but it would be so much better than half starving on the streets.

I was wrong in so many ways. She treated me like a skivvy and insisted I call her Missus. Her house was a tumbledown hovel. Her food was horrible, and I had to make do with my own tight dress and borrowed boots. I sewed, of course, making hundreds of small calico bodies and tiny makeshift frocks until my hands bled. She gave me mutton fat to rub into the sores at night, but it only helped a little and I hated the sour smell of it on my fingers.

I had to sit in that airless room day after day after day, sewing and sewing and sewing. My hands hurt, my neck and shoulders hurt, my head hurt, and my eyes watered and I started seeing double. If I hadn't finished ten dolls by the time Missus came back from her stall when the market closed, she'd rail at me. Sometimes she took hold of a walking stick and said she'd beat me with it if I didn't sew any faster. She never actually did it, but the threat was enough. If I tried desperately hard and managed to finish eleven or twelve dolls, she seemed truly pleased with me. She'd give me a barley sugar twist from her own private tin, and sometimes stroke my sore fingers.

'You're a good girlie, really,' she'd say, and chuck me under the chin. 'The best girlie I've ever had.'

I was so starved of any kind of affection now that I worked extra swiftly just for that occasional five-minute fussing. I wondered what had happened to her other sewing girls. Perhaps their hands had swelled into sausages and they could no longer sew a stitch. Did their eyes cloud over from the constant strain until they became completely blind? Or did they simply run away?

I thought long and hard about running away myself but it
was difficult to see when I'd have the opportunity. Missus
locked the workroom door when she went to market, and
although I tried hurling myself at it until I was bruised all over,
the lock would never budge. She left me with a bucket for
emergencies because she hadn't given me access to the privy.
I couldn't make a run for it out the back anyway because the
backyard had a brick wall too high for me to clamber up.

The workroom window was sealed up, and so intricately
leaded there was no possibility of bursting through the glass. I
was a prisoner, kept in solitary confinement. I started talking to
the dolls for company. Their china faces were identical because
they came out of the same mould, but I tried hard to give each a
personality, and made them talk back to me as I fixed their heads
upon their calico shoulders, and glued a little wig on top.

'There now, Louisa,' I'd murmur. 'Don't you look a pretty
girl?'

'Thank you, Edie,' she'd whisper. No one else called me
Edie now. Missus only called me Girlie.

'What a sweet smile, Evangeline,' I'd say.

'I'm smiling at you, Edie,' she'd answer.

'Which colour dress would you like, Clementine?' I'd ask.

'How about blue to go with your eyes?'

'Blue would be lovely, Edie. What colour dress would *you* like?' she'd ask.

Today I made a special pet of perky little Petronella. When she was finished I sat her beside me on the work table and we chatted together. She seemed familiar. Perhaps I'd had a little doll like this once as well as the wax beauty? And I had kept her in . . . a little cabinet? Played with her alongside a friend who had another little doll like this one? We would make the dolls act our little stories for us, make up words for them, and my friend sometimes sang a song too . . . I tried hard to remember but it was too difficult. Memories came to me like little wisps of smoke, but then they vanished.

Mum, Dad, Alex, Peter, Gordon . . .

These names were important somehow. I whispered the names over and over, knowing I mustn't ever forget them. Had they forgotten me, the way I kept forgetting them? I was sure there was a way to be with them again. I knew I had to say something. But what was it? I shook my head in despair, while the little doll watched me silently with her blank glass eyes.

Chapter Eight

I must have fallen asleep over my sewing. Someone was shaking me. But these hands were rough, the smell sour. It was Missus.

I cowered away from her. I had no idea how long I'd been sleeping. It seemed like hours. I must be desperately behind on my quota of dolls, the day's length of calico stretched right across the table. It was stained red across one corner. The blood had seeped out of my makeshift bandages!

I started crying in fear.

'What is it?' Missus said, looking alarmed.

'The pain!' I said, wringing my hands. It didn't hurt any

more than usual but I hoped she might feel sorry for me. She saw the bloodstain too.

'Oh Lord, what have you gone and done to yourself, you silly girl?' she said.

She undid the bandages and shook her head. The little cuts and sores looked much the same to me, but she seemed anxious.

'It's because you've got the hands of a little lady. They should have hardened up by now. I'm going to have to try the salt treatment,' she said.

'The what?' I asked fearfully.

'It's what the sweeps do with their boys, the little ones that scramble up the chimneys. They bleed something terrible at first so they rub salt into the sores. It takes a week or so but they say it works a treat,' she said.

'Doesn't it hurt a lot?' I said.

'Nothing to make a fuss about,' she said quickly, but I knew she was lying.

She hustled me downstairs into the kitchen, and reached in the larder for the salt jar.

'Please don't!' I begged.

'It's for your own good,' she insisted.

She held me down on a chair, scooped out some salt and rubbed it into the deepest cut. I screamed.

'Stop that racket! Folk will think I'm murdering you!' she said, dabbing at another sore.

'I hope they do! I hope the police come and lock you up for ever, you wicked witch!' I yelled, the pain so bad I didn't care what I was saying.

'Ooh, not quite so ladylike now!' she said. 'Now hold still and let me do the other hand. I'm trying to help you. It's to make you better, see?'

'You just want to make me better so that I can go on working for you, sewing all day by myself! If anyone found out how you treat me, you'd get into terrible trouble!' I sobbed, as she attacked my other hand.

'I treat you really good!' she said, sounding genuinely surprised now. 'Fresh porridge in the morning. Meat every day – and a roast on a Sunday! When I was a girl I lived on stale bread and bacon scraps, I'll have you know.'

'That's no reason for half starving me,' I said. 'Ooh! It stings so!'

'Nonsense,' she said, but she put the salt jar down and wiped my face with her own handkerchief. 'Calm down now.

Your hands will be as right as rain in no time. Now, I'd better see to the stew since you say you're starving!'

She gave me a big plateful, almost as generous as her own helping. I'd have usually eaten it up in a matter of minutes, but my hands hurt so much now I couldn't bear to hold my fork and knife. I wondered if I should bend over the plate and lap it up like an animal, but I was too proud.

Missus watched me and then took a spoon out of the kitchen drawer. 'Here,' she said, loading my spoon and holding it to my lips.

I hated her so much I wanted to spit the mouthful right into her face but I was scared she might beat me. I sat like a toddler, opening my mouth every time the spoon approached, and then swallowed the food down.

'That's the ticket,' she said. She fed me steadily until my plate was empty and held a cup of water to my lips.

'There now. Are we friends again? Do you want to come on my lap for a cuddle?' she wheedled.

I sat on her lap, lolling my head on her shoulder.

'Silly girl to make such a fuss,' she said, patting me. 'And such a little spitfire too! You don't really want to get poor Missus locked up, do you?'

Yes, yes, yes! I cried inside my head, but I needed her to keep being kind to me. 'No, not really. It's just that it really does hurt – and I get so lonely locked up all by myself.'

'But I has to lock you up, dear. Otherwise you might take it into your head to run away like that last wretched girl,' she murmured, half to herself.

'She ran away?' I asked, hoping I might hear how she'd managed it.

'She was an ungrateful little hussy,' Missus said, frowning. 'I took her off the streets, saved her from a life of sin, taught her how to sew – and then she abandoned me. Still, her loss. She was never as neat a stitcher as you, dear. And you're so quick!'

I wasn't neat and quick the next day. My hands were so sore and stiff I couldn't even hold the needle. Missus took a close look at them and tutted.

'I suppose they've got to get worse before they get better,' she said. 'There's a bitter wind today. Folk won't want to linger at the market shopping for trinkets. We might as well go to Hoxton and buy some more stock.'

'We?' I said.

'Wouldn't you like that?' she asked, her head on one side.

'Oh, yes please!' I said eagerly. Here was my chance! As

soon as we were several streets away I could make a run for it! But she was way ahead of me. She took the old rope she used for hanging out washing in the yard and tied it tightly round my waist, knotting it many times. She tied a shawl around me so that I couldn't pick at the knots, though my hands were so sore I could barely move them.

I stumbled along beside her, finding it hard at first because I wasn't used to walking any distance after being locked up in the house. I gulped fresh air into my lungs – though it wasn't actually fresh at all. I smelled the horse dung in the streets, the filth in the gutters, the smoke in the air – and then the stench of the river as we walked along the bank.

There were mudlarks wading in the low-tide shallows, bending to peer in the murky water. I looked for Boy, but there were many similar boys as we walked on, each one dressed in rags, some practically naked.

There were adults walking along the riverbank, gentlemen in high hats crossing the bridge, but no one gave the children toiling below them a second glance. When we turned along a busy street with carriages rattling past, I saw a boy with a broom sweeping the dung away so that ladies could cross to the other side without staining their long skirts. He held out his dirty hand for a tip each

time. Some folk gave him a penny. Most ignored him. One lady was annoyed when he timidly tugged at her skirts, and hit him hard about the head. No one interfered. No one cared.

I heard a little flower seller calling out 'penny a posy', and I called out to her, hoping she might be Jenny. The girl turned round and stared at me blankly; not my Jenny at all. Missus gave me a tug at the rope.

'Now now!' she warned me.

'I thought I knew her,' I said. 'She was my friend at the market, remember?'

'Well, you don't need no friend now. You've got me,' she said. 'It was your lucky day when I found you.'

She thought I was *lucky* to be made to sew from morning to night and have salt rubbed into my sores? The children around me had hard lives but at least they weren't locked up.

It was a long, long way to Hoxton. Missus stopped on the way to buy a cup of tea from a pavement stall, and gave me a few sips, holding the cup to my mouth.

'Here dear, it will warm you up,' she said.

The man at the tea urn smiled. He looked a little like the potato man in the market. 'You've got a kind ma, popsy,' he said to me.

Missus was distracted for a moment, talking to the woman in the queue behind her.

'She's not my ma,' I whispered urgently. 'She makes me sew dolls until my hands bleed, look!' I scrabbled at my knotted shawl to try to show him.

'Hey, what you doing?' Missus said sharply, and she pulled my shawl tighter.

'Young 'uns, eh?' said the tea man.

He didn't believe me. Or maybe he did and he simply didn't care. I could see there was no point persisting. I walked on with Missus all the way to the doll warehouse in Hoxton, my teeth clenched, determined not to cry.

The doll warehouse was an extraordinary place, long narrow rooms with boxes of dolls and doll parts right up to the ceiling, and a display of dolls in a big glass cabinet. There were little china heads, and whole dolls with arms and legs but totally bald. There were large, grand china dolls with big glass eyes and real hair, and humble wooden dolls with round painted heads. There were tiny china dolls standing stiffly to attention, their arms and legs welded to their bodies.

Missus looked at these little statue dolls, eyes narrowed. Then she nodded at the old man behind the counter. He was

small and thin and had a very pointy nose and whiskers, like a human mouse. I could only see his head and narrow shoulders. The rest of him was obscured by the counter. For all I knew he had a long pink tail.

'I'll have six dozen heads, same as always, and another three dozen of them Frozen Charlottes,' she said.

The man's nose twitched. 'You're taking Charlottes?' he said, surprised.

'If you please,' she said.

'You ain't going to make much profit on them,' he said.

'Well, that ain't none of your business, is it?' she replied tartly. 'Can you fetch 'em, please?'

The little man shrugged, went to a tall pile of boxes, nimbly climbed a ladder, and took the top box. He climbed down one-handed, and repeated the performance at another pile. He didn't have a tail, just a pair of striped trousers and shiny black boots. When he put both boxes on the counter, he clicked his heels together.

'Six dozen heads and three dozen Charlottes,' he said. 'I'll put string around them for ease of carrying. One for you and one for your . . . daughter?'

'My daughter indeed!' said Missus, but she looked

strangely proud that he should think it. 'She's my young apprentice and shaping up nicely. But her hands are troubling her a little, so I'm insisting she rest up for a day or two. I have a kind heart, see.' She nodded at the mouse-man and then at me too.

'What's your name, little miss?' he asked.

I opened my mouth, but Missus interrupted. 'No chit-chat now. We've more purchases to make. Good day,' she said briskly, taking hold of both parcels herself.

'Good day to you both,' said the mouse-man, and his nose twitched at me.

I twitched mine back – and then Missus gave a tug on my rope and I was pulled out of the shop.

'Horrid little man,' she murmured. 'Gives me the creeps – but his dolls are the cheapest in town. Now, materials.'

This new shop was an Aladdin's cave, hung with silks and damasks in canopies and curtains, headless stuffed dummies swathed in cotton and velvet, and stacks of materials every colour of the rainbow on the shelves. There were big baskets of scraps and end-of-ranges. Missus put the doll boxes on the floor and scrabbled in the baskets, fetching out pinks and blues and yellows and reds – the best colours for doll dresses. Then

she picked up the boxes again and took her selection to the lady behind the counter.

This lady had a vast undivided bosom, as if she had a big cushion stuffed down her bodice, a head like a cottage loaf, and a huge rosy face with a topknot of hair. She was wearing a hyacinth-blue silk dress trimmed with lace, as if she was going to a party, with a blue velvet rose at her neck and another tucked in her topknot. She looked at us with twinkling eyes as blue as her outfit.

'Who's the little poppet?' she asked Missus.

'My apprentice,' said Missus. 'I'll have ten yards of calico, if you please.'

'My my! A little shrimp like that! She should be playing with dolls, not making them,' said the material lady.

'Oh, she loves to sew!' said Missus. 'And I treat her well, don't I, young 'un?'

There was my chance. I took a deep breath, but Missus rushed in first.

'I cosset her with milk porridge and a good meaty stew at night, rub her little hands with mutton fat, even take her on my lap if she's in a mope – don't I?' she said to me.

I supposed that was more or less true.

'But—' I began.

'And today I'm going to buy a length of that good cotton mix to make her a new frock,' Missus said. 'What colour would you like, Girlie?'

'Oh, the sky blue, please!' I asked excitedly, pointing.

'No, that would show the dirt too much,' said Missus. 'We'll have the beige check. Three yards please. No, make it four, so she can have a nice roomy skirt. I'll make it myself, a frock fit for a little lady.'

I watched helplessly as the material lady cut it with swoops and snaps of her silver scissors. She saw my expression.

'It's a bit plain, ain't it, lovie, though it's very kind of your missus to kit you out like that. Tell you what, I'll throw in a length of lace for nothing. You can trim the collar and cuffs with it, even sew some on your petticoats. Us little ladies like to look pretty,' she said.

She was the largest 'little lady' I'd ever seen, but I nodded, smiling back at her. She tucked the generous roll of lace down my shawl.

'You keep it safe, dear,' she said.

I liked her so much. If only I could be *her* apprentice and wear a party dress and cut lengths of material with those big silver scissors.

'Thank you so much!' I said. 'May I give you a kiss?'

Missus tutted but the material lady was charmed. 'Of course you may, you dear little sweetheart,' she said, and she bent over the counter so that I could reach up and kiss her great, plump, peachy cheek.

'Please may I come and live with you?' I whispered urgently into her ear.

She didn't take me seriously. She simply laughed fondly and patted my own cheek. 'Bless you, dearie,' she said.

'Come on now, we've got a long way to walk home,' Missus said sharply, fumbling in her reticule for the money to pay for our material.

She had to carry that parcel too, as well as the two boxes of dolls and doll heads. Perhaps she couldn't keep such a firm hold of my rope?

'What were you up to, kissing that overdressed fool?' Missus grumbled. 'You've never asked to kiss *me*, after all I've done for you! And I've deliberately paid out for Charlottes that hardly make me any profit. They can't be dressed, seeing as their arms won't lift. It's to give you a rest till your hands heal. Aren't you grateful?'

'Yes, I am,' I mumbled.

I knew she was waiting for me to ask to kiss *her* but I couldn't bring myself to do it. She sighed at me but didn't nag any more. It seemed an even longer journey back. Missus had to pause every now and then, putting the parcels down and rubbing her back. I watched her to see if she ever seemed to be losing her tight grip on the rope. She caught my eye and wound the end of the rope round her wrist, tying it tightly, and then gave me a nod to show me that there was no getting away from her.

We walked on in silence. When we got back at last, she supervised my visit to the privy and then locked me back in the workroom, though I couldn't possibly do any work with my hands thoroughly bandaged. I managed to get my shawl unwound and held the roll of lace in my clumsy hands, holding it against my cheek. It smelled of the material shop, so fresh and clean. I worried that Missus would keep it for herself rather than trim my new dress with it. So I hid it on the shelf amongst some scraps of calico, and when Missus came in at last and summoned me down to the kitchen for some bread and dripping, she felt amongst my rewound shawl.

'Where's that lace that fancy fool gave you?' she asked.

I shook my head helplessly. 'It must have fallen out of my shawl on the journey,' I said. 'I'm sorry! Please don't be angry.'

'It's your loss, not mine,' she said. 'Here, do you need me to feed you?'

'I'll manage myself, thank you,' I said.

She gave me treacle on my bread, for being good while she salted my sores, and put fresh bandages on my hands. I hoped it might taste sweet like honey or golden syrup but it was harsh on the tongue. I swallowed it down anyway and she nodded approvingly.

'There's not much point opening up my stall for half a day. We'll keep each other company, you and me, to stop you being so lonely like. I'll make a start on your frock. I'll learn you how to sew proper clothes, not just the dolly scraps,' she said.

I'd sooner have had anyone else's company than hers, but it was quite interesting being measured and then seeing her making paper patterns for the bodice, the sleeves, the waistband, collar and the skirt, pinning them to the material and then cutting them out with her scissors. They didn't make such satisfying sounds as the big silver scissors, but they made a small rasp of their own. I found I was opening and closing my mouth at each snip.

'What are you doing, you silly? You look like a codfish!'

The word struck a chord in my head. *Codfish!* I

remembered someone else saying that word. A man. Someone dear to me. But who could it be? Father died so long ago I could barely remember him. It was *Dad*, in my other life. Dearest Dad. I tried to conjure him up in my mind, but it was so hard. I missed him so. I missed Mum, and Alex, and . . . I couldn't even remember the others. I was forgetting more day by day. I was stuck in this life for ever.

Chapter Nine

I started crying. I sobbed and sobbed. Missus didn't know what to do. She tried shaking me. When that didn't work she took me on her lap to soothe me. There was nothing she could do. In the end she half carried me downstairs and laid me on my makeshift bed near the stove. She busied herself with cooking, but I couldn't eat anything.

She tried to spoon a little gravy down my throat and then gave up. She let me be, wiped my face, and put a hand on my forehead.

'You're burning up!' she said. 'You've given yourself a fever! You must stop this silly sobbing!'

I couldn't, though I tried hard. I cried myself to sleep and when I woke in the night my cheeks were still wet and my head throbbed.

'Dad! Mum! Please come and get me!' I cried.

I waited. I could hear Missus snoring in her bedroom above my head, the *drip drip drip* of the solitary tap. Something scuffled near the pantry, a mouse foraging for food. But no Dad, no Mum. I lay where I was, crying weakly until I went to sleep again.

When I woke up again it was morning. I sat up wearily. I had a throbbing head, my eyelids were swollen, and my throat was sore. I got up and drank straight from the tap, gulping the water down thirstily and then splashing it on my hot face. My hands throbbed inside their bandages.

It was a waste of time crying myself silly. If this was the only life I had now, I had to make the best of it. When I pulled the bandages off with my teeth, my fingers were still a mess of sores – but perhaps the skin wasn't quite as raw. I curved my hands as if I was sewing. They oozed a little but didn't hurt quite as much.

Missus inspected them when she came down to the kitchen and looked triumphant. 'There! I was right, wasn't I?' She reached for the salt pot.

'But they're getting better!' I protested.

'Yes, and we want them better still, don't we?' she said, rubbing the salt in vigorously. It still stung but I clenched my teeth and put up with it. 'I've still got some penny and thruppenny stock – and for the next few days we'll see how the Frozen Charlottes sell. Folk might like the novelty, and they're cheaper, see.'

'So I don't have to sew today?' I asked.

'No, you're going to sell along with me!' Missus said. 'That'll be a lovely treat, won't it? Company!'

It actually *would* be a treat to be allowed outside again. Missus must have sewed on by candlelight last night, because my new frock was finished. She tried it on me and then stepped back, nodding.

'Perfect fit! You look like a real little lady now,' she said.

I peered down at myself. I didn't like it anywhere near as much. It was so plain and I hated the insipid check – but the material was soft and smelled of the Aladdin's cave.

'Well? Don't I get a thank you?' Missus demanded.

'Thank you very much,' I said.

'Plenty of room for growth too,' said Missus. 'I might take

it in a tad at the waist. Didn't realize you were such a skinny thing. Better start building you up. Shame you lost that scrap of lace. It would have been the finishing touch.'

'I'm sorry,' I said, hanging my head, praying she wouldn't search the workroom shelves and find where it was hidden.

'Oh well, it would have got dirty soon enough,' she said. 'Come on then. Get your boots on. We'll have a bite to eat on the way to market.'

I fumbled with the buttons.

'Here, let me do that,' Missus said, bending over.

I stared down at her greasy hair and wondered if I could ever grow to like her now she was trying to be kind to me in her own gruff way. It might be better if I did, but I could hardly bear her touching me, though I tried not to show it.

She insisted on tying me to her again, though I begged her not to do this. 'I swear I won't try to run away,' I said, crossing my sore fingers behind my back.

'I had a little dog once, a brown terrier with one black eye, so I called him Patch. I loved that naughty boy, though he chewed his way through everything and stole my supper when I wasn't looking. I kept him on a lead but he hated it and would never walk to heel. So I let him off once when we was walking

on a patch of grass and he was off like a shot. Disappeared out of sight. Never came back. I learned my lesson.'

'I'm not a dog,' I said.

'And I'm not a fool,' she snapped, so I didn't persist.

She bought us both a mug of tea halfway to the market – and a currant bun. I chewed it slowly, with rapture. It was such a wonderful change after my usual bowl of watery porridge. When we walked on to the market I actually had a spring in my step.

There was the lovely hot potato man! He gave a double take when he saw me, and then gave me a big smile. 'Hello there, little missy! How are you doing, eh?' he asked.

'She's doing very well. She's my apprentice now and coming along nicely,' said Missus.

'Really! An apprentice doll-maker! Well, that's a turn-up for the books. Good for you, girl,' the potato man said, bending down to give me a pat on the back.

'I'd sooner be *your* apprentice!' I dared whisper.

He laughed heartily at that. 'I could only give you a trade – but doll-making's a proper skill,' he whispered back.

'What are you two mumbling about?' Missus asked. 'Come along, girl, we've got the stall to set up!'

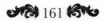

'Pop back at dinner time and you'll get a free potato!' he called after me. 'Two! One for Mrs Dolly too!'

Missus tutted at him, but she went red and simpered like a girl. When we went past the butter market, I remembered sleeping in the corner and someone snatching Mother's pocket watch. I squinted at the stone floor, looking for it, although of course it was gone for ever.

'Don't pull that face!' Missus said sharply. 'Don't you start that crying again neither. I'm not having you make a spectacle of me!'

She set her two carpet bags down and started unpacking the dolls. She'd wrapped each in old newspaper so their china heads wouldn't crack. She set me to unwrapping each one while she arranged the stall, laying them down in rows.

'Wouldn't they look better if you propped them up in some way? They look so sad like that, as if they're dead,' I said.

'Whatever sort of fanciful nonsense is that?' said Missus. 'Hurry up now. Gentlemen sometimes walk through the market on their way to work and buy a little trinket.'

I thought that was a bit fanciful myself, but one elderly man in a smart frock coat and a tall hat did pause at the stall, touching this doll and that with one finger.

'How much are they?' he asked.

Missus rattled through the prices and told him he couldn't do better anywhere else.

'Look at the fine strong stitching, sir,' she said, pulling at a thruppenny's arms and legs. 'They'll never come off. Last a lifetime, no matter how the little one pulls at them.'

'My little grand-daughter's a very careful child,' said the gentleman, sounding offended. 'I think I'd prefer to find her a half-crown doll from the arcade with an outfit of clothes. These are a rather gimcrack affair.'

'Suit yourself, sir,' said Missus, sniffing.

'I think your grand-daughter would have more fun with a shilling's-worth of these little dolls, sir,' I found myself saying. 'She could pretend they were sisters or friends, and if one got dropped and the china head cracked, it could easily be replaced.'

'These heads are made of the strongest china. They don't crack!' Missus protested.

'Sometimes little children get a bit carried away,' I said in a rush. 'And perhaps a nurse or governess or her own kind mama will teach her how to sew, and then she could make her own outfits for them and take great pride in them.'

'I think *you're* a little child who's got carried away!' said the gentleman, but he chuckled as he said it. 'Still, you have a very persuasive tongue. Very well, pick me out four of these thruppenny dolls.'

'Certainly, sir. I'll wrap them in newspaper to protect them, and your grand-daughter will be overjoyed when she sees what's inside, I promise you,' I said.

He went off with his parcel of dolls – and he insisted on paying an extra thruppence for my 'expert salesmanship'!

Missus stared at me, astonished. 'My, my!' she said. 'Where did you learn to come out with that patter?'

'It just came naturally to me,' I said proudly.

'Well, don't get too big for your boots now,' she warned. 'Gentlemen like that are as rare as hen's teeth. Try that game on someone else and they'll likely give you a clip round the ear.'

I sold three more dolls that morning, and several Frozen Charlottes to mothers with toddlers, declaring they were as good as a rattle any day, and would be a little friend to keep them happy. I had a sudden flash of memory that those two lovely men – what were their names now? – had told me about lead paint and I hoped the babies wouldn't use the little china dolls as teething rings.

Missus seemed in awe of my skill as a salesperson. She still didn't trust me though. She kept all the money in her own leather purse strung round her waist, even the pennies people gave me for my cheek. When we had to use the horrible facilities at the back of the market, she insisted we go together, keeping me tied to her. But she was pleased when the lovely hot potato man gave us both a free lunch, and the lady on the

fruit stall next to us gave me a red apple too.

'You've got a little treasure here,' she said to Missus. 'Are you going to bring her every day?'

'Someone's got to stay at home and sew,' Missus said gruffly.

'Well, maybe it should be you!' said the apple lady. 'Them dolls are walking off the stalls on their own little legs because of her silver tongue.'

Jenny came wandering along with her basket of flowers in the afternoon, and grinned when she saw me. 'How do, Edie!' she said. 'I see you're set up now! I wish my ma had a doll stall. Do you get to play with them dolls ever?'

'I sew them together – I don't get a chance to play with them,' I said.

'You're too big a girl to play!' Missus snapped.

'I've never had a doll,' said Jenny wistfully, fingering the different sorts.

'Here, you, get them grubby paws off my stock!' said Missus.

'Couldn't I have one?' said Jenny. 'Just one of these little ones without clothes? It could go in my pocket and keep me company.'

'Then give us your tuppence and clear off. You're blocking the stall,' said Missus.

'Tuppence!' said Jenny, jingling the coins in her pocket. 'Ma would notice if that much went missing. Couldn't you sell me one for a farthing?'

'Could we?' I asked Missus. 'We've made heaps of money today.'

'And we're taking every penny of it home! I'm not working my fingers to the bone to give it all away to little guttersnipes,' she said, sniffing.

'I ain't no guttersnipe! I'm a respectable girl!' Jenny said indignantly.

'And she was so kind to me when I first came to the market,' I said.

'You hold your tongue. Push off, you! Let this lady see the whole doll display, if you please!' said Missus, turning to a woman standing nearby with a little girl.

Quick as a wink I thrust a Frozen Charlotte into Jenny's hand and she darted away. I held my breath – but Missus hadn't seen.

'Do you like the dolls?' I said to the little girl. She nodded eagerly. She had long golden ringlets, a pale blue dress and a snow-white pinafore, looking so loved and cared for. I felt a pang of envy. My new frock was so humdrum and ugly,

and my hair was matted now because I didn't possess a hairbrush.

'May she have one?' I asked the mother.

'Well, she's certainly been a good girl,' she replied fondly. 'Pick one out, dear.'

The little girl looked from one to another anxiously.

'I can't choose!' she said.

'That doll's my favourite,' I said smoothly, pointing to a thruppenny. 'She's called Evangeline. She's got a very beautiful face, hasn't she? Look, she's smiling at you!'

'Oh, I want Evangeline!' she said at once.

Another doll sold! And one given away, but I hoped Missus wouldn't notice when she added up the takings at the end of the day. There was so much that she bought two chops from the butchers, though we had the remains of the stew still in the pan, and a slice of marzipan cake for a pudding.

'There, see how I treat you! That's a supper fit for the Queen herself!' she said.

She'd taken a chop and a half, and most of the cake, but I didn't argue with her.

'Perhaps I could come to market with you again tomorrow?' I suggested.

She examined my hands and applied more salt. It didn't hurt anywhere near as much now, but I squealed determinedly, hoping to convince her I still couldn't possibly sew.

She gave in grudgingly. 'I suppose you could have another day on the stall. But if we carry on selling at this rate we'll run out of stock. We can't rely on the Charlottes, as we don't make enough profit on them,' she said.

'You make a profit on me instead,' I said.

'Don't you get so full of yourself,' she said. 'You were just a novelty today. Trade will likely go slack tomorrow – you wait and see.'

I waited. I saw. We made five whole shillings on the takings! I seemed to come properly alive at the market, chatting non-stop to the customers. Sometimes we had a big queue at the stall. My voice was hoarse by the end of the afternoon, but I was so exhilarated I sang to myself on the long trudge home. The bread stall lady had thrown some crumbs to an eager flock of sparrows hovering nearby so I sang a song about feeding the birds. I used to sing it when I was little. When I was little in the *other* world.

'Don't stop singing!' said Missus. 'I've never heard that song before. It's a catchy little tune. Go on, sing some more.'

'I can't remember it now,' I said, and realized it was true. 'Missus, can I come to the market again tomorrow, please, please, please?'

'No, you can't! We're nearly out of stock, girl. You need to get sewing again,' she said firmly.

'Couldn't we both sew in the evening and then both sell during the day?' I suggested.

'I'm not staying up half the night again – it makes my head ache; and I can't stand at that stall all day long as well, not with my poor legs,' she complained.

'Then why don't you sit down to sew, and *I'll* go to market and sell,' I said.

'Do you take me for a total noodle? You'd run off with the profits and set yourself up elsewhere!' she said.

Oh my goodness, *she* was the noodle! Maybe I would do just that! I was sure I could do better than Missus too. I'd make the dolls to suit the customers. Some of the richer ones wanted proper dressed dolls from the arcade, so why didn't *I* have a go at making them? I'd seen fine china dolls at the warehouse in Hoxton and beautiful silks at the material shop. I could try making patterns for dresses and mantles and bonnets and petticoats and long drawers trimmed with lace.

I had lace already! I didn't complain the next morning when Missus locked me in the sewing room. I sewed tentatively at first, scared that the sores might start bleeding again, but the salt treatment had really worked. My hands were stiff though, and I was infuriatingly slow and clumsy at first, but after an hour or so they loosened up and I was sewing faster than ever.

I hummed as I worked, planning hard. When the distant church clock struck twelve I ate my bread and dripping, and drank my watery milk in two minutes, and then started sewing again straight away. I'd already made nine dolls. The tenth would be for me. I made a body and two arms and two legs, sewed them together as neatly as I could, attached the head and glued on the wig, adjusting it carefully.

'There now! You are the very first of my own dolls. You're so beautiful! What shall I call you?' A name suddenly popped into my head. 'I shall name you Alexandra! That sounds lovely. Now, my dear, I think it's time we made you a special little outfit.'

I picked the finest material in the scrap bag, a pink silk-cotton patterned with tiny daisies, and fashioned her a proper dress with a bodice and full skirts. I had to unpick it twice because the material bunched, and I started to worry

about the time I was taking – but at last I got it right. I made her a petticoat too, edged with my precious lace, and long drawers with lace trimmings too. Underwear is very important. I wanted her to be perfect in every detail, the best doll I'd ever made, better than any elaborate beauty in the arcade.

I tried to fashion her little boots too, but the material was too flimsy. I'd have to buy the softest, most flexible kind of leather from the Aladdin's cave, and stronger needles and thread. I was so intent on dressing her that I lost all sense of time, and my hands stayed nimble and quick. But then I caught the chimes of the clock again – half past four! Missus would be packing up at the market in an hour or so and I had only nine dolls to show her.

I quickly put Alexandra on the high shelf with my lace, covering them with calico, and then started assembling more dolls for Missus. I worked hastily, my stitches getting bigger and bigger. My fingers were hurting now, the old sores stinging once again, but I didn't dare stop to rub and rest them.

Then I heard Missus coming in the front door and I had six more finished now, but one was still lacking a dress, and one had already lost her wig because I hadn't applied the glue carefully enough.

'Oh dear, oh dear,' said Missus, as soon as she'd unlocked the workroom and peered round. 'What's the matter with you? You've been slacking!' She picked up one of the dolls between two disdainful fingers. 'Look at the size of those stitches! A child could rip it apart in five seconds! And the legs aren't even – any fool can see that!'

'I'm sorry, Missus, truly. I tried and tried, but my hands have grown so clumsy now, and hurt all over,' I said.

'Don't give me that story! You're just in a sulk because I wouldn't take you to market again. You're a lazy, deceitful girl. You deserve a good beating!' she said, grabbing hold of me.

I cowered away from her. She was so much bigger and stronger than me. I could try to fight her back but she would easily overpower me. I could scream for help but no one would come.

'Mum!' I shouted, scarcely knowing what I was saying. My mother here was dead, the other mother an increasingly hazy memory, but I blurted it out anyway.

It stopped Missus in her tracks. She stared down at me and her face crumpled. 'What was that you called me?' she asked shakily.

I suddenly understood.

'Mum. Mumma. Mama,' I said, looking up at her. 'Please
don't be so angry with me! I did try – I swear I did, Mama.'

'So you think of me as your mama?' she said. 'You soppy
ha'porth,' she went on, but she said it softly. Then she pulled
me to her and held me close. I was stifled by the musty wool
of her frock and longed to wriggle free, but I let her cling to
me.

'I had a little girl like you once,' she murmured. 'She didn't
thrive, poor little scrap. But I couldn't help fancying how she'd
look as she grew up. I reckon she'd have looked a lot like you,
Girlie.'

I felt a mixture of revulsion and pity. But I couldn't feel too
sorry for her. She was still wicked to keep me a prisoner here. I
had to get away from her. I'd worked out how I was going to
earn my own living now.

Chapter Ten

I had to take my time. I couldn't risk working on more than one doll a day in case Missus noticed that some of her stock had gone missing. I was getting through the scrap basket too quickly. I concentrated on clothing the penny dolls instead and used a long length of soft white cotton as christening robes for the Charlottes, with a little cape tied round their shoulders to hide the fact that their outfits didn't have sleeves.

I was proud of the outfits I was making now, considering I was so slow to learn to sew neatly. Or was that the other Edie? It was getting hard to remember.

I worked steadily on the dolls for Missus to sell, and although my hands still ached and my eyes burned, peering at small stitches in the dim light, I didn't care so much. I planned everything in my head, thrilled at the thought of freedom.

Missus was kinder to me too and took me to market with her a couple of times as a special treat. The potato man greeted me like an old friend and Jenny was pleased to see me too.

'Look, I've still got her safe!' she whispered, showing me the little doll in her pocket. 'She sleeps in the flower basket at night. She says it smells lovely!'

'Where did you get that basket you use for your flowers?' I asked her, when Missus was deep in conversation with the woman on the next stall.

'You buys them up Covent Garden,' she says.

'How much are they?'

'Thruppence, I think. Why, do you want one? We've got several old 'uns tucked under our stall. I could get you one,' she said.

'Oh, please!' I said.

She went skipping off and returned with the basket.

'Here you are, Edie! Present!' she said triumphantly.

'What do you want that old thing for?' Missus asked me. 'It's battered out of shape!'

'I can patch it up a bit,' I said. I thought hard. 'I wanted to have one to be like Little Red Riding Hood when she sets off to visit her grandma.'

'You're such a girl for fancy!' said Missus, though she looked tickled. 'You don't want to be like that Riding Hood girl and get eaten by a wolf, do you?'

She laughed, and I laughed along with her. She didn't guess I had a much more practical use for the basket. I was sure she had no inkling I was plotting my escape. She was actually starting to trust me. The last time she took me to market she didn't bother with the rope. She simply took my hand. She had a firm grip but I was pretty sure I could pull away from her. Another time she didn't lock the sewing room. That *was* tempting, but I'd only completed a handful of my own dolls.

I didn't make a bolt for it. I waited, sewing calmly. After ten minutes or so I heard her heavy tread on the stairs and the sound of the key turning in the lock. Perhaps it had been a test? Perhaps she had simply forgotten and had come rushing back. She seemed very pleased with me that night when she returned from market and gave me a slice of fruit

pie from the baker's. Apple and sultana pie, my favourite. No – wasn't my favourite pudding frozen berries with white chocolate sauce?

'Have you ever made frozen berries with white chocolate sauce, Missus?' I asked.

She stared at me. 'Frozen berries?' she said.

'Berries frozen in ice?' I said. 'And then you pour hot chocolate on them.'

'Never heard of it,' she said. 'It sounds too fancy anyways. Can't beat a good pie, in my opinion.'

'Perhaps you're right,' I said, because the baker's pie was delicious. I rubbed my finger round my plate to scoop up the last of the crumbs.

Missus did the same, winking at me. I started to wonder if I really wanted to escape. She was trying hard to be good to me now. But after supper she got out her accounts book and started adding up the figures by candlelight. She checked the coins in her cash box, and counted the payments for stock all over again.

'It still don't match!' she shouted, banging her fist on the table. 'I'm always so careful. It must be you, Girlie! What have you been up to?' she demanded.

I was so scared I thought I'd bring up my pie before it had properly reached my stomach. What would she do if she searched the sewing room and found the fine clothed dolls hidden under the calico on the top shelf? There would be no idle threats then. She'd beat me till I was black and blue.

'I haven't been up to anything, Missus,' I said, doing my best to look wide-eyed and innocent.

'Have you been giving them dolls away to that little pal of yours?' she asked, taking me by the shoulder and shouting into my face.

'No! Course I haven't!' I said.

'I don't believe you! There are always nippers crowding round my stall now,' she said.

'Well, maybe it's them. If there's a crowd of them, one could easily grab hold of a doll,' I said. 'Maybe you don't see as well as you used to, Missus?'

Thank goodness that hit home. She'd been complaining of misty eyes recently and often rubbed them.

'It's all those years of sewing,' I added quickly. 'Look at the way you've been frowning over your accounts book. I bet it's hard to keep those figures in focus now.'

She blinked hard. 'I can see proper,' she said, though her eyes were red with strain.

'Anyway, you've got me to sew for us now, Mama,' I said.

Her face softened. 'That's right,' she said. She loosened her grip on my shoulders and patted me instead. 'You're a good girlie, really. You wouldn't play tricks on your old ma, would you?'

'Of course I wouldn't,' I said, though my heart was thumping.

I felt bad then, wondering if I could really go through with my plan, but I was resolute again by the next morning. I worked extra hard, knowing I hadn't got much time left. She'd be checking her accounts regularly now. I'd not be able to bluff another time.

She kept me locked in the next day and the next. I thought about getting everything ready and then waiting behind the door of the sewing room. The moment she opened it I could give her a shove and make a bolt for it.

I wasn't sure it would work though. I was livelier now she was feeding me treats, and she was old and tired, but she was still surprisingly strong, especially if she was in a temper. If she managed to shove back and block my escape, I'd never get

another chance. She'd watch me like a hawk and keep me locked up in the sewing room for ever.

She brought home a big meat pie in the middle of the afternoon, and was in a surprisingly good mood. Thank goodness I was stitching away at the plain dolls, looking demure, though I had two more dressed beauties in the pile under the calico.

'A fine lady came by, picking up her skirts and threading her way through the cabbage leaves, a servant girl puffing along behind,' she said, chuckling. 'She's a governor at some children's hospital and she'd got it into her head that she wanted to give the sick little souls a dolly each to play with in their beds. *My* dolls! Mad idea if you ask me, because not many of those children last long, but I wasn't arguing. She took the lot! Every single one of them, and wants more still, would you believe!'

'Well, that's wonderful,' I said.

'So we'd better *both* get sewing or I'll look a fool in the market tomorrow with an empty stall!' she said.

She sat in the sewing room with me. She had the chair, I sat cross-legged on the floor, and we sewed together. I kept looking at the calico on the table, praying that we wouldn't use

it all up. I would be done for if she reached up to the top shelf
for another length of it!

Luckily she decided to concentrate on the tiny penny dolls
as we sold far more of them. Fine ladies and gentlemen with
fat purses were still a rarity at the market, but most ordinary
folk could afford a doll the price of a currant bun. I reckoned
the calico on the table would just about last, even if we went
on sewing by candlelight.

After Missus had made several dolls she stopped to flex her
fingers and then gave them a good rub. 'My, they've stiffened
up,' she said. 'It's a while since I've had to sew myself! How are
your own hands now, Girlie?'

'They don't hurt too badly now,' I said.

'So the salt cure worked?' she asked.

'I suppose so,' I replied. 'But it really, really hurt when you
rubbed it in.'

'It was for your own good,' she said. 'Still, I suppose I have
been a bit hard on you. You act so quaint that I forget you're
really quite a little girl. Mama's baby!'

'Yes . . . Mama,' I said reluctantly.

'I'm good to you really, ain't I?' she said.

I nodded, sewing hard, going *prick prick prick* with my

needle, secretly pretending I was pricking *her*. It made me squirm when she went so soft and sentimental, but I needed her to stay in a good mood with me.

She left me sewing when she went to heat up the pie and served it with gravy from the stew.

'This is a real treat, eh?' she said, when we sat down together at the kitchen table. She'd poured me a glass of small beer too and clinked her tankard against my glass. 'Here's to us!' she said.

'Here's to the future!' I said. I sipped at the beer cautiously, knowing I would need a clear head if I was going to follow through with my plan. Luckily it didn't seem very strong at all, though I didn't care for the taste.

I ate my portion of pie with gusto, and when she saw my cleared plate she let me have another slice.

'We'll build you up for the winter, eh!' she said. 'Still, you've got your fine new frock to keep you warm, and we'll find you a good thick shawl. You're a lucky girl, I reckon.'

'Yes, I am,' I said, rubbing my full stomach. 'I'm so full my tummy hurts.'

'What, you've got a bellyache now?' she said, laughing. 'You'd better take to your bed early and sleep it off.'

I hardly slept at all I was so pent up. The rich meat pie had

given me a perfect way of executing my plan. I had to give it a try now. But if I failed it would mean the end of this new cosiness and cosseting. Missus would feel betrayed and make my life a misery.

Perhaps it was just as well I'd lain awake all night fretting. Missus saw there was something wrong with me the moment she came down into the kitchen.

'What's the matter with you?' she asked, as I struggled up from my makeshift bed and stood before her, shivering in my shift.

'I don't feel well,' I mumbled, hanging my head.

She put her hand under my chin and tilted my head so she could peer properly.

'You're very pale,' she acknowledged. 'And you've got great dark circles under your eyes.'

'And my tummy hurts so. Please, Mama, I need to dash to the privy!' I said, clutching myself.

She unlocked the back door and I dashed out to the dark little privy. I actually did have a slight stomach upset because I wasn't used to eating so much. She was waiting in the yard for me when I staggered out again, many minutes later.

'Oh Lordy, you have got the bellyache, haven't you? No more meat pies, eh!' she said.

'Ooh!' I groaned and rushed back into the privy. I stuck my fingers down my throat. I couldn't quite manage to make myself properly sick, but I was sure she heard me heaving.

When I emerged this second time she was still standing there, arms folded, looking worried.

'Now what am I going to do with you?' she said. 'Am I going to have to stay home and act nurse?'

'No, Mama!' I said urgently. 'You need to go to market and sell the dolls we made last night. I'll stay here and sew fast. But . . . but . . . but . . .'

'That's more buts than a billy goat!' said Missus. 'But *what*?'

'But could you not lock me in today? I fear I'm going to be in need of the privy many times,' I said.

'You've got the bucket,' she said.

'But it will be so awful if I have to keep using it,' I wailed, shuddering. 'Please, Mama.'

'This isn't a trick, is it?' she asked sharply. 'You're not planning to run away after all this time together?'

She suspected me already! It was easy to start crying. I let the tears roll down my cheeks unchecked.

'How could you think such a thing?' I sobbed. 'I'd never try to leave you. You're my own mama now.'

I hated saying it – but it worked.

'And you're my girlie and I'm a bad mama for doubting you,' she said, softening. 'All right. I won't lock you in this time.' She opened the kitchen door and checked the little yard one more time, looking around. 'Anyways, you ain't a spider, and that's the only creature that could climb them walls. Bye bye then. If you really keep being taken poorly then never mind the sewing for today. Just take to your bed. I'll see if I can buy some eggs at the market. They'll settle that poor old stomach,' she said.

She was acting so motherly now it made me feel worse than ever.

'Goodbye,' I said. 'And – and thank you.'

She left me in the sewing room and she didn't lock the door. She didn't even come back to check on me. I waited a good hour, to make sure. I made one little doll as a gesture and propped her up on the sewing table. I raised her arm, as if she was saying goodbye too.

I crept out of the room to check that Missus wasn't lurking anywhere, though I'd heard her go out the front door. I tried that first, but she'd made sure of locking it from the outside, so I couldn't simply step out into the street. But the back door

from the kitchen opened easily enough. I used the privy again, my tummy in such a turmoil of fear and excitement that I genuinely needed to go.

Then I went back into the house, up the uneven stairs, back into the sewing room, and reached up to the top shelf. I brought the special dolls down onto the table. They looked splendid, even the little Frozen Charlottes in their long gowns. I took Jenny's basket and did my best to straighten it out. It was wearing thin at the bottom, but I padded it with calico, making sure that not even the tiniest doll could fall through. Then I set them all out prettily in the basket, wedging them in tightly. I mixed them up so the finely dressed stood proudly in the middle and the little dolls peeped over the edge of the basket.

I covered them with the old shawl Missus had given me. I felt bad about taking it. I felt bad about taking the dolls too. I supposed it was stealing – but she hadn't given me a penny in wages, and she'd made a big profit since I'd started sewing for her. I couldn't linger guiltily or I'd lose my resolve. I had to go now. *Now now now!*

I hurried downstairs, the basket over my arm, and went into the kitchen. There was the rope hanging from a hook on the door. I grabbed it and then went out into the little yard and stood

by the wall in the shade of the tree. I set the basket down, unwound the rope, knotted it at one end and threw the other end up in the air with all my strength. I hoped it would soar upwards, right over the branch, and then fall down so that I could haul myself up it, bracing my feet against the wall as I climbed.

I'd pictured it half the night – but it didn't work the way I wanted it to. The rope flailed around in the air and then landed with a thump, falling far short of the tree. I tried again. And again. And again.

I was useless at throwing and yet I had dim memories of games in a playground when I could set a ball flying with one flick of my wrist. I tried taking a running jump and throwing, though I could only manage three paces in the tiny yard. I tried throwing overarm and underarm. I tried throwing as I leaped in the air.

After many attempts I got the rope higher, and several times the knotted end bounced against the trunk of the tree, but never enough to wind itself up and over the branch. My arm ached, my neck ached, my shoulders ached, I'd wrenched my whole back – and yet I couldn't manage it.

It was no use. I couldn't do it. I'd have to trail back indoors, put the rope on the peg, hide my basket full of dolls and give

up. I sank to the floor in despair. But then a snatch of song echoed in my head. Something about picking yourself up and starting all over again? So I picked myself up and started throwing the rope. I was so nearly managing to throw it right over the branch. If only I could grow a bit bigger!

I looked around. There was nothing I could stand on in the yard. Then I suddenly ran back into the kitchen and seized a chair. I manoeuvred it out of the narrow door and propped it hard against the brick wall, so it wouldn't tip. Then I clambered up onto it, clutching the rope. I threw it as hard as I could, and it sailed up and over the branch in a perfect loop! It hung there, both ends dangling, ready for me to climb up!

I jumped down from the chair, grabbed my packed basket of dolls, and put the handle over my shoulder so I still had both hands free. Then I got back on the chair, clasped both lengths of rope and started climbing up the wall, step by step. It was tough supporting my weight with my hands, but the salt treatment had hardened them up. I pulled and stepped, pulled and stepped, until I finally reached the branch. The basket was banging on my back, my hands were stinging, and I was boiling hot with effort, but I was there!

I still had to get over the wall and down the other side of it, but I still had the rope to cling to and it was easier sliding down. I jumped the last few feet and felt a sudden throb in my ankle as I landed. I was terrified I might have twisted it in my haste, but after taking a few tentative steps it seemed all right. I'd made it! I was free at last!

I didn't know where I was standing here behind the cottage, but I had a vague idea in which direction the market was – so I started walking rapidly in the opposite direction. I had to get as far away as I possibly could, further than Missus would ever walk. I couldn't risk her spotting me. I had a new life now!

Chapter Eleven

I walked and walked and walked. I didn't get tired. Jenny's boots seemed to have springs. I bounced along, my basket on my arm. It grew heavy but it just meant I had lots of stock. Many little painted mouths were smiling up at me under the shawl, ready to pop out when I found the right trading place.

I found another street market but they had a doll seller already there. He was a smiley little man with a bent back and black hair as glossy as his own Dutch dolls. He nodded at me kindly, thinking me a customer. I wasn't sure the smile would stay on his face if he realized I was a doll seller too, competing for customers. And although it felt as if I'd been walking to the

edge of the earth, I reckoned it was only about three or four miles from the market where Missus plied her wares. He might know her and tell her about me. I couldn't risk it.

'You have very pretty dolls, sir,' I said, and then walked on. I felt a little thrill. *My* dolls were the prettiest in their little outfits.

I lingered hopefully at a hot potato stall, hoping the man selling them would be as friendly as the lovely man in the other market, but he flapped his hand at me.

'Don't stand there looking hungry, child. Either buy one or move on!' he said irritably.

So I moved on. A lady at a fruit stall didn't seem to mind when I timidly knelt to pick up an apple that had rolled off her stall onto the ground. I offered it to her but she shook her head.

'You can eat it if you want, lovie, but it'll probably be bruised,' she said cheerily.

It *was* a little bruised but still tasted sweet and juicy and I crunched away at it, slaking my thirst as well as my hunger. I had another flash of memory – a fruit bowl piled high and Mother – no, *Mum* – telling me I should eat more fruit. I felt such a sharp longing for her that I doubled over, my basket nearly spilling.

'What's up, my dear?' the apple lady asked, concerned.

'Just – just a pang,' I said, blinking hard to stop myself crying.

'Hunger?' she said. 'Here, have another.' She picked out the biggest apple on her display, rubbed it on her apron and handed it to me.

I thanked her fervently and she insisted on giving me a penny too. I cheered up and bought myself two halfpenny rock cakes from a baker's shop. They weren't as soft as the currant buns, but they lasted longer and filled my stomach properly.

I went on my way well fortified and walked another hour or so. Then at last I found the right place. It wasn't another market – it was a busy street of small shops, some with stalls outside. They sold any number of wares: old books with leather covers, new boots with their tongues lolling, aprons plain or fancy, a flock of hats with feathers, clocks chiming randomly, umbrellas and walking sticks standing to attention, ships in glass bottles sailing nowhere, and spinning tops humming as they whirled.

I didn't need to hire a stall. I could walk up and down showing them off in my basket, calling my wares. There were several child sellers with baskets wandering around already, selling flowers, oranges, watercress, gingerbread – but no dolls!

So I took a deep breath and uncovered my precious wares. They had tumbled about a little during their long journey, but I soon rearranged them.

'What are *they*?' said the big boy selling watercress.

'What do they look like?' I answered. 'They're dolls.'

'You can't eat 'em,' he said.

'Well, you can if you want – but they wouldn't half stick in your throat,' I said.

He chuckled, but the orange-selling girl scowled. 'Less of the lip, kid. So, did your ma set up a new doll stall?' she asked.

'I haven't got a new stall. Or a ma. I look after myself,' I said.

They looked at me with new respect. The littlest girl selling gingerbread peered at my dolls closely, poking each one with her sticky finger.

'Like little people,' she murmured. 'Can I have one?'

'Only if you give me a penny,' I said.

'Easy,' she said, fumbling with the purse tied round her waist.

'Don't, Lizzie,' said the oranges girl. 'That's your gingerbread money. Your pa will give you what-for if you spend it on knick-knacks.'

'I'll do a swap if you like,' I said. 'I'll give you a lovely little dolly to be your friend, Lizzie. And you give me a piece of gingerbread. It's a real bargain, because I won't have anything left but a few crumbs after I've eaten it – but you'll still have the doll, won't you?'

I held out the penny doll with the brightest dress. Lizzie snatched it and thrust a square of gingerbread at me. It was too sticky to store in my basket so I ate it straight away, chewing fast in case she changed her mind. It tasted so good. My stomach was full to bursting now, which was just as well, as I wasn't sure what I'd do about supper. Or a bed for the night.

'Can I have a doll too?' asked the flower girl, looking enviously at Lizzie. 'I'll swap a penny nosegay,'

Her flowers were drooping already, tight rosebuds that looked as if they'd never actually open, but I needed to make friends with these children, so I handed over another penny doll, and she pinned a nosegay to my chest.

'Mmm, what a lovely scent,' I said politely, though the withered little buds didn't smell of anything at all.

I looked at the oranges girl. 'Would you like a doll too?' I asked.

She pulled a face. 'I'm twelve years old, you ninny,' she said.

The watercress boy laughed.

'Then what about you, sir?' I said. 'I'm sure you're secretly hankering after a dolly to play with?'

'Cheeky little git,' he said, giving me a push, though not hard enough to make me lose my footing.

'Only joking,' I said quickly. 'Well, I'd best start selling.'

'Did Big Joe say you could?' he asked.

'Big Joe?' I repeated.

'He's boss of this street. Keeps an eye on things. Runs the Coach and Horses on the corner,' he said, pointing.

I looked round for an actual coach with horses, but saw it was a public house with that name in gold letters on a sign above the door.

'I'll go and ask him,' I said determinedly.

'I'd better go with you,' said the watercress boy, sighing. 'You don't want to go in there by yourself.'

'I'll be fine,' I said, trying to sound bold and confident. I seemed to remember I'd been in pubs before and thought them happy places where I had snacks and lemonade in the garden.

The Coach and Horses was very different. It was dark and gloomy, and so thick with smoke my eyes watered. I could see clusters of men at tables discussing business with glasses of whisky, and solitary men slumped over their tankards of beer, some in a stupor. There were women too, a couple of them overly painted with bright tawdry dresses. Others were thin and ragged, some with babies in their arms, all looking wretched. I could see this wasn't a place for children in spite of the babies.

I approached the woman behind the bar, clutching my basket tightly.

'What are you doing here, missy? Looking for your pa, are you?' she asked, her head on one side. 'Has he had a drop too much?'

She sounded sympathetic but I felt cross. I'm sure my papa hadn't been the sort of man to get drunk in pubs, and my own dear dad only had the odd drink of beer. What would he think if he could see me now? What was happening in that life if I was stuck here? Was I asleep? Or was I . . . dead?

I shivered.

'I'd like to speak to Mr Joe, if you please,' I said.

'Oh, hoity toity!' said the bar woman, sniggering. 'Here, Big Joe, Little Lady Guttersnipe wants a word in your ear.'

One of the men at the table stood up, glass in hand. He was well over six foot and broad with it. His shirt sleeves were rolled up, showing thick muscle. He was scowling.

'What do you want with me, child?' he asked gruffly.

I swallowed. 'I've come to see you to ask if I can sell dolls in the nearby streets,' I said timidly.

Big Joe cupped his ear with one hand. 'What was that?' he said, though I was pretty sure he'd heard me the first time. The men with him were all agog now.

'I'd like to sell these dolls, sir,' I said – and I held out my basket. 'Perhaps you'd like one?' I meant for one of his children but he chose to misunderstand.

'You think I'd like a little dolly to play with?' said Big Joe, and the men burst out laughing.

I hated being made to feel a fool. I lost any sense of caution. 'If you feel the need, sir, I'm sure a doll would be very comforting,' I said.

The men choked back their laughter, their eyes swivelling to Big Joe. They waited tensely. Big Joe slammed his glass down on the table and took several giant steps towards me.

'Oh, so you're a pert little miss, are you?' he said. He raised his big brawny arm and I thought he was going to hit me – but

he just ruffled my hair instead. 'Enough of the cheek, if you please. You can sell your wares all over my patch, so long as you pay your dues. I charge the stallholders a down payment initially and then a monthly rent, plus ten per cent of their profits, and woe betide them if they don't pay up. Don't you think that's fair?'

I took a deep breath, very aware that I had no pennies in my purse and had yet to sell a doll and make the smallest profit.

'I can see you think that's fair, sir. But I wonder if you could make an exception for me, as I don't have a stall, only a basket, and I'm only at the start of my trading days. As soon as I'm making a profit, I promise I will pay my ten per cent though,' I said. 'I can't say fairer than that.'

The gentlemen still held their breath but Big Joe smiled.

'Then it's a deal, Miss Pipsqueak,' he said, and held out his huge hand.

I shook it as firmly as I could, though I was trembling.

'Now run away and stop interrupting my meeting,' said Big Joe.

'Certainly, sir,' I said, and ran right out of the public house, the dolls dancing a jig in my basket.

The watercress boy was lurking in the doorway. 'You were taking a risk, Dolly girl!' he said. 'Folk don't mess with Big Joe!'

'He doesn't scare me one bit,' I lied.

'He don't scare me neither,' the boy said hastily. 'Still, you're pretty feisty for a girl. Don't get carried away. Try that cheek on some of the other big fellows round here and you'll regret it. See that ugly bloke with the bashed-in bowler, selling kettles? He'll give you a thump as soon as look at you, old Kettler will. But don't worry, I'll look after you.'

I wasn't too sure I wanted this cocky boy to look after me, and the girl selling oranges didn't look too happy about it either, but I could see it would be good to have a friend here so I nodded. Then I took a deep breath and started crying my wares before I lost courage.

'Come and look at my dolls! Little beauties, all of them, dressed in their finery. Give your little girls a treat! Present your sweethearts with a token of your love! Penny dolls, tuppenny dolls, and golden thruppenny dolls, each one stitched to last a lifetime!' I sang out.

The watercress boy stared at me. 'You don't have to call out that gubbins! I just call "fresh watercress". You needs call "dolls for sale!"' he said.

'You do it your way, I'll do it mine,' I said.

I acted cheery confidence as I marched up and down the street singing my song, but my heart was beating fast. I was attracting a lot of attention, but people were just nudging each other and pointing at me. People came out of the shops to peer at me. A lot of the stallholders were sniggering. They were thinking me a figure of fun. A stray dog ran circles round me, barking, and everyone started laughing. Big Joe was standing in the doorway of the Coach and Horses, shaking his head at me.

I very nearly ran right away, but sheer cussedness made me hold my ground. I kept on singing, holding out my prettiest doll for all to see. Big Joe whispered to one of the fancy ladies in his pub, and she came waltzing over to me, holding her satin skirts above her ankles.

'My, she's a lovely dolly,' she said, straight-faced. 'I always wanted a doll when I was a little girl. In fact, I want her right now! I'll stick her on my windowsill like an ornament. How much is she?'

'She's thruppence, ma'am,' I said warily. I was sure she was trying to make a fool of me, egged on by Big Joe.

'Thruppence!' she repeated, feigning surprise.

'Yes, and she's an absolute bargain,' I said. 'I don't think you'd find a finer dressed doll in an arcade, and they charge five shillings!'

'I daresay I agree. She is a bargain.' She felt in the little hidden pocket in her skirts and I heard a jingle of coins. She brought out a handful of pennies, a gold thruppenny bit and a silver sixpence, and then rejected them all but one coin. The sixpence!

'I'd charge at least sixpence for the bigger dolls, dear,' she said. 'Take a little tip from me. Always charge as much as you can get away with.'

She pressed the sixpence into my palm, folded my fingers
over it and then walked off, holding the doll up for everyone to
see. The crowd gawped and giggled. I didn't care if this was
still an elaborate game. I had the money tight in my hand –
enough to keep me fed for a couple of days.

I held my head high, and sauntered off with my basket.

'Come and look at my dolls! Little beauties, all of them,
stitched to last a lifetime. Penny dolls, tuppenny dolls, golden
thrupenny dolls, sixpence specialities, and shilling dolls to order!'

The lady turned and laughed, and Big Joe did too, and I
realized they were on my side. The watercress boy was watching
and he grinned at me too. I marched up the street and down
the street, and when I eventually got tired I leaned against a
wall or sat on a step, still alert to every possibility of a sale. And
people did begin to buy my dolls. By the end of the day my
pocket was heavy with coins and my basket much lighter.

I bought myself a small meat pie and sat on the step eating
it, marvelling that it was only yesterday that Missus had brought
a pie home for both of us. She'd be discovering I'd run away
right this moment. I shivered at the thought. Perhaps I should
have walked much further away, just to be safe.

I could start walking again now. There was another couple

of hours of light left – and if I kept to the streets I could walk in the dark too. I should try – but I was feeling so tired now, the elation of the day draining out of me. Where was I going to sleep tonight, and all the other nights of this new life of mine? If I was out selling every day how could I make enough new dolls and sew their outfits? And where was I going to get the dolls and material? I only knew of the one place – but Missus went there too. What if I bumped into her?

It was clear I should go elsewhere – and yet it had gone so well on this little patch. Even Big Joe was on my side. And the watercress boy had been kind to me in his own way.

He came up to me and sat on the step beside me. 'You all right, Dolly?' he asked.

'I'm perfectly fine, Cressy,' I said.

'Cressy! I like that. My real name's Algie,' he said.

I was so used to being called Girlie now, but I knew that wasn't my name. 'Well, I'm Edie, but you can call me Dolly if you like,' I offered.

'Suits you,' he agreed.

The other children had gone off home now their parents or masters had shut down their stalls, but the watercress boy seemed to be by himself, like me.

'Why aren't you off home?' he asked.

'Haven't got a home,' I said, trying to sound as if it didn't matter in the slightest.

'Thought as much,' said the boy.

'What about you?' I asked.

'Ain't got one neither,' he said. 'So where are you going to bed down for the night?'

I shrugged. 'Maybe in one of the shop doorways?'

'Bad idea,' he said. 'Some fools stay late at the Coach and then take it into their heads to pelt rough sleepers with rubbish – or worse. And others steal the very boots off your feet.'

'You've got a point,' I said, remembering Mother's pocket watch.

'And then there's the rats,' he said. 'They don't bother me, but you might be fussed by them.'

'They don't bother me either,' I lied. 'Though I wouldn't want to be bitten.'

'I know where you can get a bed for the night for two pennies,' he said. 'In a proper gaff indoors. And if the lady what owns the house takes a shine to you, she might throw in a bit of supper too. She fair spoils me. Says I need feeding up.' He grinned complacently.

He *was* very thin, his cheekbones so sharp they looked as if they might start poking through his skin. He was pretty grimy too, and his hair stuck out about his head like a sweep's brush, but I could see why this lady liked him. He had a lovely smile, though one of his teeth was missing.

'Shall we see if she'll take you too?' he said.

'All right. Thank you!' I said.

'It's a bit of a walk and you look tired,' he said. 'I'll carry your basket if you want.'

I hesitated. I wondered if this could be a trick. Might he run off with it? He'd seen how much money I'd made selling my dolls.

'Do you think I'm going to steal it?' he said incredulously, reading my expression. 'As if I'd go mincing down the street selling dollies! I'm only trying to help you.' He sounded genuinely upset.

'I'm sorry. It's just I can't get used to the way life is here,' I said, without thinking.

'What do you mean "here"?' he said. 'You from a different country then? You speak a bit strange.'

I knew there wasn't any point trying to explain that I wasn't

from a different country, but deep down I knew I was from a very different *time*. I didn't understand it myself. My head hurt whenever I tried to work it out, and every day it was growing harder to remember the other Edie. I was starting to wonder whether *that* life was simply a dream, and this life was real and the only one I'd ever had.

He was looking at me closely. 'It's all right, you don't have to talk about it if you don't want. Come on then.' He held out his hand and pulled me up. When he slung my basket over his shoulder, his shirt got caught and was pulled up, exposing his back. He tugged it down quickly, but I had a glimpse of long raised scars. He'd obviously once been severely beaten. I wondered who had done it to him – a master, a father, a random stranger?

He knew I'd seen them.

'I was caught stealing bread when I was in the workhouse,' he said matter-of-factly. 'It weren't even for me – it was for my little brother.'

'How awful! They *beat* you for taking some bread?' I hesitated, hardly liking to ask. 'Where's your little brother now?'

'Up there,' he said, staring up at the clouds. 'Well, so they say.'

'I'm so sorry,' I said.

'Still, that's life, isn't it?' he said. 'Or rather, that's death!'

It seemed a terrible thing to make a joke of it, but I supposed it was his way of coping with it.

'Are workhouses really terrible places?' I asked timidly.

'The worst,' he said. 'But I made a bolt for it. And now look at me! I'm doing fine, ain't I?'

'I suppose so,' I said.

'I've got a full belly, I've got boots on my feet, I've got a bed for the night, I've got friends and I've got a good speciality, watercress. Of course, it's seasonal, so I fall back on selling matches, but I can't make as much profit on them. I goes and picks the watercress myself, at crack of dawn before anyone's around, down them water meadows. It's good quality too. Here, try some.'

He offered me one of his leftover bunches. I wasn't very keen on green salad stuff, but I tried a tentative nibble.

'Ugh! It's horrible!' I said. 'It's so strong it's stinging my tongue!'

'It's the iron in it, silly. Do you good,' he said, munching on a bunch himself. 'Try another bite. You'll get used to the taste.'

'No, thank you,' I said.

'Suit yourself. Mrs Lazenby loves my watercress. She's the lady who runs the lodging house,' he explained.

'Is she kind-hearted?' I asked.

'So long as you pays up prompt,' he said.

'Do children really have to *pay* for a bed?' I asked.

'Of course they do,' he said, sounding surprised.

'Even very small ones, too little to work?'

'Well, they have to rely on their family. Their big brothers,' he said.

'It's like that for all children?' I persisted.

'Unless they're stinking rich!'

'But it's so unfair!' I cried.

'Course it is. But there's rich folks and poor folks and that's the way it is,' he said. 'There's nothing you can do about it.'

I wasn't so sure. Perhaps when I was older I'd find a way to make it fairer for everyone.

Chapter Twelve

Mrs Lazenby took a shine to me too, which was a great relief.

'Who's this dear little creature, Algie?' she asked.

'She's Dolly,' he said. 'Because she sells them, look. Ain't they pretty?'

'Oh my! And who makes them, dear?' she asked me.

'*I* make them,' I said proudly. 'And I made a good profit today, so I have two pennies for my bed tonight, if that's all right with you, ma'am?'

'Don't she speak sweet, Algie? Like a little lady! Of course you can have a bed, my precious. I'll find you a lovely bed all to yourself!' she said, as if it was a big treat.

The other lodgers had to share, two to a bed. The men had one room, where they topped and tailed, with a pillow at either end for their heads. The women had another room, but they mostly slept curled round each other for comfort. There was a special children's room too. The watercress boy shared his bed with another younger boy. He was very gentle with him, letting him huddle under most of the blanket.

My bed was squashed into a corner. It was very small, just a lumpy mattress with a rough blanket. It made me itch and my neck ached without a proper pillow, but I was used to roughing it now and at least it seemed relatively clean. My stomach was full too, with Mrs Lazenby's boiled beef and carrots, and I couldn't feel lonely in a room of people snoring and sighing.

I woke in the middle of the night to find Algie crouching beside me.

'Just checking you're all right, Dolly,' he whispered.

'Yes, I'm fine, Cressy,' I mumbled and went straight back to sleep.

He was gone when I woke up, though it was still that silvery pre-dawn light. I got out of my small bed, stretched my poor

cramped body, picked up my basket, and then threaded my way carefully through the crowded room of sleepers.

Mrs Lazenby was already up, fully dressed in a print frock and pinafore, bustling about her kitchen making an apple pie.

'Morning, little lady. How did you sleep?' she asked.

'Very well, thank you. Where's Cressy? I mean, Algie?'

'He's off to the meadows for his watercress, bless him,' she said. 'He's a good lad.'

'Yes, he is,' I agreed.

I went out into the backyard to use the privy. It was as dank and disgusting as the one where Missus lived, but I was getting used to it now. There was a pump too, even a sliver of soap balanced on a brick, so I got as clean as I could. When I went back into the kitchen, Mrs Lazenby had made me a cup of tea and buttered a slice of bread for me.

'Thank you so much,' I said, sitting down at her table. 'What do I owe you for the food?'

'Bless you, dear. If I started charging a half-starved child for a few scraps, I couldn't live with myself,' she replied.

'You're a very good woman,' I said. 'I wonder, might I ask another favour?'

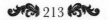

'And what's that, eh?'

'Could I possibly sit here and sew until it's time to go out selling my dolls? I'll take care not to get in your way,' I promised her.

'Of course you can sit here, you quaint little thing. I'll be glad of your company,' she said.

'And I'll be glad of yours,' I said.

She chuckled as she rolled out her pastry, taking care not to sprinkle flour too near my calico. She watched as I sewed little arms and legs and bodies into shape, stuffed them with sawdust and attached the china heads.

'My, my, you've got nimble fingers!' she said. 'Did your mother teach you to sew?'

I murmured something vague because I didn't really know the answer. I remember Mother being ill and giving her medicine, but I couldn't remember much before that. Did I once make a cross-stitch sampler with my name and age, and the date, and every letter in the alphabet? I didn't think my other mother sewed with me, though her fingers were nimble enough. I thought of her tapping away on her . . . what was that device she held in her hand?

I was forgetting the past, forgetting the future. I was stuck

here, in what was now the present. My eyes blurred and I couldn't see to sew any more.

'So sorry, my love. Why won't I learn to hold my tongue? You'd think I'd have learned by now. Pry, pry, pry, that's me. I even reduced young Algie to tears, and he's such a proud young lad. Here, have a little chew on this. It's hard to eat and cry at the same time,' she said, holding out a long curl of apple peel.

I nibbled on it and found she was right.

'Cheer up now, chickie. I'll make sure you get a big slice of my pie when you get home today,' Mrs Lazenby said.

I wiped my face and hands on her dish towel and then resumed my sewing, my needle flying now. We worked on in companionable silence. I started on another doll, and Mrs Lazenby crimped her pastry, fashioning fancy leaves in the middle, and put it in the oven. I made a little frock from scraps, while Mrs Lazenby started chopping fat and gristle from a mound of meat and feeding chunks of it into her grinder to make mince. I started on a nightdress and tiny bonnet for a Frozen Charlotte, as Mrs Lazenby began a suet pudding. It was a sweet one, and she gave me a teaspoon of raspberry jam that stayed tasty on my tongue.

The lodgers who worked in the factory appeared bleary-eyed in the kitchen ready to leave for their six o'clock shift. She made them a cup of tea and gave them each a buttered slice so they started the day well. There was one young man who came down late, pale and dishevelled, still reeking of the ale he'd drunk last night. She gave him tea and a sharp telling-off, but refused him any bread, even though he begged for a slice.

'No point feeding you when you look as if you'll throw it up again the moment it's gone down. Away with you!' she said crossly. 'And come back in that state another time and you'll be out on your ear! I'm not having drunks in my house.'

Yet she was soft with a bedraggled woman with tangled hair and a torn dress who was in a similar state.

'There now, dearie. Sit yourself down a moment with little Dolly here and drink your tea,' Mrs Lazenby said, stirring in two spoonfuls of sugar for her. 'Maybe she'll sew up that tear in your frock for you. What happened, Maudie? Did you fall on your way home?'

She shrugged her thin shoulders. 'Can't remember,' she murmured in a hoarse voice.

Mrs Lazenby tutted but didn't say anything further. The woman pulled her dress over her head and silently handed it to

me. She stood shivering in her ragged petticoat, her head drooping, while I stitched the tear as quickly as I could. She didn't flinch when a couple of boys blundered into the kitchen and stared at her. She didn't even try to drink her tea. It was as if she wasn't really there at all, though when I handed the dress back to her she murmured thanks.

'Well done, Dolly,' said Mrs Lazenby. She held out the teacup to the sad lady. 'Drink it down and then get off to that sweatshop.'

The woman's hands were shaking so that she spilled some of her tea, but she managed to swallow most of it and then nodded thanks at both of us. When she'd trailed off I turned to Mrs Lazenby.

'Is Maudie very ill?' I asked.

'Ill from drinking herself senseless with cheap gin,' said Mrs Lazenby. 'But who can blame her, poor dear. Her husband beat her, so she left him and took her children with her, but he came after her and said they were his by right and he got custody of them, even the baby. He won't let her see them. Her heart's broken. She works in the match factory, and everyone knows it's a bad place and you get ill from working there, but she don't care now.'

'That's so awful,' I murmured. 'Why don't they arrest that horrible husband and give her her children back?'

'Why indeed?' said Mrs Lazenby. 'It's the law, my dear.'

'Well, they should change it!' I said indignantly.

'You're a little firecracker, aren't you, though you look so demure sitting there sewing,' said Mrs Lazenby. 'You're a sight for sore eyes. No wonder young Algie's taken a shine to you!'

'He's a very kind boy,' I said.

It was such a relief to have found a friend already – but I wasn't Algie's only friend. Nan the orange seller clearly felt he was *her* special friend. She ran up to him in the street when he arrived with a basket of freshly picked watercress, crying 'Algie, Algie, Algie!' as if she hadn't seen him for months. She stood telling him some silly tale, tossing her long hair about and smiling to show off her dimples. Her expression changed dramatically when he came over to me and admired the way I'd arranged the dolls in my basket.

She sat down on a step and peeled one of her own oranges and beckoned Algie over. 'Come and share my orange, Algie,' she called.

It was a hot day and the orange looked very fresh and juicy. 'Yes please!' he said. He sat beside her, breaking his half into

segments – and then held a couple out to me. 'Come and have a bit of orange, Dolly!'

'It's for you, Algie, not that stuck-up doll girl,' she said crossly.

'Dolly's not stuck-up. She's a sweet kid,' he said.

'Look at her with her airs and graces, mincing along like she's a little princess!' she said.

'Ah, stop being a little cat, Nan,' he said, laughing, and he gave me his whole half of orange.

'Meow, meow, meow!' she said, trying to turn it into a joke, but she was certainly looking as if she'd like to scratch me.

I didn't really care. I was thrilled that Algie liked me. I palled up with little Lizzie, the gingerbread girl, too. I pretended that the doll I'd given her was real and had long conversations with her, answering myself in a little squeaky voice. Lizzie thought this extraordinary and laughed in delight. She had a mother selling bread and cakes in the bakery down the road, and several older siblings, but it seemed no one had ever played with her before.

I sold seven dolls that day and skipped back to Mrs Lazenby's for supper. Algie imitated me, laughing at my antics. Nan had wanted him to go for a walk with her after the shops

closed, but he'd said he had done enough walking for one day – but he danced along beside me, swinging his empty basket.

We ate the mince and mash potatoes that Mrs Lazenby made for everyone, but we were the only ones who got to share her apple pie. She offered a slice to Maudie too, but she shook her head, wound a thin shawl round herself, and disappeared outside. One of the factory workers tried to sweet talk Mrs Lazenby into giving him some pie too, telling her she had lovely skilled hands that made delicious pastry, and if it wasn't for Mr Lazenby away at sea, he'd pluck up the courage to want to put a ring on her fine finger.

She batted him away, laughing at his cheek.

'Is Mr Lazenby a sailor, Mrs Lazenby?' I asked, when he'd given up and ambled off.

She chuckled at that. 'If he is, he's gone on a very long voyage,' she said.

'There ain't no Mr Lazenby, is there, Mrs Lazenby?' said Algie.

'Well, there might have been once – though I was never actually his missus. He was a real gent though, and I was fond of him. He must have been fond of me too, because when he

popped off I discovered he'd left me a considerable sum of money, bless him. That's how I came to start off my boarding house. I'm a respectable woman now,' she said happily.

'Don't you ever fancy taking another husband, Mrs Lazenby?' Algie asked. 'Or are you waiting patiently till *I* grow up?'

'You cheeky young monkey!' said Mrs Lazenby. 'Still, I reckon you'll make some young girl very happy one day.'

'Nan would have you,' I said.

'Nan! She's just like a sister,' said Algie. 'We've known each other years. She can be a bit sharp at times, but that's only her way. She'll be a good friend to you when she gets to know you, Dolly.'

I wasn't at all sure about that. Nan barely spoke to me, though I tried hard to get on with her, and I heard her calling me names to some of the other children.

'Stuck-up scheming minx!' she said. 'Even her little nose is stuck-up!'

So I thumbed my little nose at her and decided she was the last person in the world I wanted for a friend. I knew I'd had a very special friend once, with a funny nickname I couldn't quite remember now. We had played together ever since we

were little. It must have been long ago in the past . . . in my other life. Or was that the future?

I gave up trying to puzzle it out. I had another more pressing worry. I only had half a dozen doll's heads left and was running out of calico. I had to go to Hoxton and buy more with my earnings. Big Joe was happy enough with what I'd given him so far – but I had to keep on selling or I didn't know *what* he would do!

I wasn't sure how to get there but I had a tongue in my head and could easily ask the way. The thing that was worrying me the most was bumping into Missus when I was there. She hadn't gone on a particular day – she just waited until supplies were low and then set off. She made the journey in the morning, so I could try going in the afternoon – but maybe she'd change her timing to try to catch me. She knew I'd taken the dolls, the calico and material, the needles and thread and scissors, so it was obvious I was intent on selling dolls. She'd work out that I was running out of everything so she might be lurking there all day long.

Did it really matter? I hadn't signed any contract to say I'd work for her. She had no right to keep me locked up every day and keep me on a lead like a dog the rare times she let me out.

I was getting stronger every day now. Surely if she tried to take hold of me I could give her a shove and run away?

I wasn't sure I would dare to. I was still frightened of her – and I felt guilty that I'd left her. I knew she'd become fond of me. I thought of the way she'd dandled me on her lap and shuddered.

'What's up, Dolly?' Algie had been watching me closely as we went up the stairs to the crowded bedrooms.

'I don't know how I'm going to get more doll things. I have to go to Hoxton to buy them,' I said, kicking off my boots and lying down on my small bed. No one took their clothes off when they went to sleep. I was used to my frock becoming more and more crumpled and making do with a quick splash at the pump instead of a proper wash. It was uncomfortable sleeping in a cumbersome dress but I was so tired I slept soundly.

'Hoxton's only an hour or so from here. It's an easy walk – but I'll take you if you're scared of getting lost, Dolly,' said Algie, sprawling on his own bed.

'Oh Algie, you wouldn't go instead of me, would you?' I wheedled.

'What? You want me to go and buy a lot of little dollies?' Algie sounded appalled.

'I could write you a list of the exact things I need,' I said.

'That wouldn't be no use, because I can't read,' he said cheerfully. 'Never learned.'

'Didn't they teach you at the workhouse?' I asked.

'There was too many of us,' he said, pulling a face. 'There was this one pauper woman tried to learn us, A is for apple, B is for bird – that kind of malarkey, but it didn't mean much. I've no time for reading anyways.'

'Well, I could tell you over and over until you remembered. I need two dozen little penny heads, two dozen Frozen Charlottes, and a dozen of the thruppenny specials; then a whole bolt of calico from the material shop and—'

'I can't get all that fancy stuff!' Algie interrupted. 'And how would I carry it back?'

'I'd lend you my basket, of course,' I said.

'I'm not prancing about with a blooming basket full of dollies,' said Algie. 'I told you, I'll go with you, but I'm not going on my own. I'd look a laughing stock. If any lads saw me, they'd jeer and throw stones.'

'I can't go! I'm scared Missus would see me. I think she'll be looking out for me,' I said anxiously. I'd told Algie about how I'd had to work for Missus, locked in the little room day after day.

'No she won't!' said Algie. 'Well, maybe she might be, but she can't hang about there all day, every day! What are the odds of you meeting up with her, eh? Just go there, buy your stuff, and come back. Run hard if you see her. You're a nippy little thing. She couldn't possibly catch you. There's nothing to be afraid of, honest.'

I wasn't so sure. I had a terrible dream that night where Missus spotted me, threw a shawl over my head, bound me up and bundled me into her carpet bag. She dragged me through the streets back to her cottage, banging me deliberately against brick walls, and then locked me back in the sewing room. It had shrunk in my dream to a cell with slime on the walls and alley rats running over my bare feet. She had me manacled by the ankles, leaving my hands free to sew. I tried screaming for help, but then she gagged me so tightly with rags I could scarcely draw breath and was sure I was suffocating. I tried clawing at them but I couldn't tear them away. '*Help, help, help!*' I sobbed.

'Hey, Dolly, wake up! What is it? Stop fighting! It's me, Algie!'

I opened my eyes and flung my arms round his neck. 'Don't let her get me!' I cried.

There were murmurs and protests all around me.

'Shh, now! You've woken everyone up! You poor girl, you were obviously having a nightmare,' said Algie, hugging me.

'Missus isn't really here, is she? And the rats?' I gasped.

'There's no Missus here – and if there are rats, Mrs Lazenby's cat will sort them out in no time!' Algie said. 'You're in a right state, little Doll. Calm down now. I've got you safe. No Missus is going to catch you, I promise.'

'So will you go to Hoxton for me tomorrow and buy my things?' I begged.

'No I won't, you artful little minx!' he said. 'Do you think you can wind me round your little finger?'

I hoped I might, but though he still held me tight and soothed me back to sleepiness, he remained firm. I was very quiet in the kitchen at breakfast.

'What's up with our little princess?' Mrs Lazenby asked. 'Look at that sad little face! Who's upset you, dear?'

'No one,' I mumbled.

'You haven't fallen out with Algie, have you? He seemed in a bit of a mood too when he went off this morning,' she said, spreading my bread with honey as well as butter.

'I wanted him to go and buy my doll heads and material

for me, but he won't,' I said. 'He said he'd feel foolish buying such things.'

'Silly boy,' said Mrs Lazenby. 'Still, you know what these young lads are like. They've got their pride. He'd be scared of his pals making fun of him. Why can't you go and buy your stuff yourself?'

'I'm scared I might bump into this horrid lady I used to work for,' I mumbled. 'I know it's silly but I can't help it.'

'Well, tell me what you need, young Dolly, and I'll fetch it for you myself,' said Mrs Lazenby.

My spirits rose for an instant, but when she heard that the specialist shops were in Hoxton she shook her head regretfully.

'I couldn't possibly hobble all that way, dearie. My bunions are giving me gyp as it is. Here, have some more bread and honey!'

It was very kind of her, but I couldn't stop fretting. I set off with my half-full basket of dolls with a heavy heart. I didn't make any effort to sell them, but people flocked round me of their own accord, and I found I sold five in the first hour. Lizzie trotted round with me, chatting all the while, and I made an effort to talk to her *and* her little doll.

'You watch out your ma don't see you,' Nan said, walking past. 'You should be selling, not going *natter natter natter* with that Dolly girl. You haven't sold a single piece of gingerbread yet.'

'Yes, she has,' I said, thrusting a couple of coins into Lizzie's pocket and selecting a slice of gingerbread for myself, though I was already full of bread and honey.

Lizzie laughed and Nan scowled. 'You think you're so clever, sucking up to everyone in the street and turning folk against me,' she said.

I knew who she meant by 'folk'. Yet when Algie came back from the water meadows with his basket of watercress, he went up to Nan, not me. He chatted to her earnestly, and they went off together.

'Look! Algie's got his arm round Nan now!' said Lizzie, giving me a nudge.

'Who cares?' I said. But *I* cared, terribly.

Chapter Thirteen

Algie and Nan were gone quite a while. When they came back Nan was smiling – and she had a string of bright blue beads around her neck.

'See Nan's beads!' said Lizzie, who didn't miss anything. 'I'll wager Algie's bought them for her from that pedlar round the corner. Does that means she's his sweetheart now?'

'I don't know,' I said. It seemed obvious Lizzie was right. Nan's eyes were shining as blue as her beads, and Algie looked pleased too, a big smile over his face. I turned my back on them both, telling myself it was ridiculous to care so much. I was only a little girl compared with Nan. Of course Algie was

keen on her. He had been a friend to me, not a sweetheart. He'd done his best to look after me, that was all. And now he'd lost patience with me because I'd been so demanding.

Well, I'd learned my lesson. I didn't need him to sort out my worries. I'd just have to brave it out and take my chances going to Hoxton by myself.

'Dolly? Hey, Dolly!'

'Algie's calling you,' said Lizzie.

I shrugged. 'Doesn't mean I have to answer,' I said.

'You gone deaf, Dolly?' said Algie, taking hold of my arm and pulling me round to face him. Nan was by his side, smirking.

'You're hurting me,' I said, trying to wriggle away from his grip.

'I'm barely touching you, noodle,' said Algie. 'What's up with you? Listen, I've got good news!'

'I'm not interested,' I said, pretending to yawn. Was he going to announce that he and Nan were sweethearts now?

'Well, you jolly well should be! We've solved your problem, haven't we, Nan?' said Algie.

'Yep. You're going to owe me a favour, Dolly,' said Nan, setting down her basket and fingering her beads.

'What do you mean?' I asked sharply.

'Nan's going to go to Hoxton for you!' said Algie. 'You tell her what you want and she'll fetch it for you. She's got a good memory.'

'Or you can write it down for me. You're not the only one who's had some schooling,' said Nan.

I borrowed a stub of pencil and wrote a list on a scrap of cardboard, using big print. She had to spell it out slowly, mispronouncing some of the words, but she managed it all.

'There now! Give me the money then and I'll go now,' said Nan.

I hesitated. She was Algie's friend, but I knew she hated me. 'Do you really know the way to Hoxton? And how will you find the right shops? I don't even know the name of the street,' I said to her.

'Course I know the way. I've got an aunt who lives over that way. And I know where that doll place is – I've seen the heads peering out at you from the window, fit to give you the creeps. The material place is nearby; it's where my aunt gets the stuff for her frocks. So there, miss!' said Nan, nodding her head at me.

'Yes, there you are, Dolly!' said Algie. 'Say thank you then and give her the money, and she'll be on her way.'

'Thank you,' I said reluctantly, and pressed the exact change into her hand.

Her sharp nails dug into my palm as she snatched the money. She flounced off.

'Good for you, Nan! You're a star!' Algie called after her.

She looked round and gave him a dazzling smile. He grinned back, going pink.

'There now, Dolly. Take that scowl off your face. I thought you'd be thrilled to bits for Nan to be doing you a big favour like that,' said Algie.

'She's not doing it for me, she's doing it for you,' I said. 'Because you bribed her with that necklace. Think I'm stupid?'

'I think you're blooming ungrateful! I did it for *you*, to stop you fretting,' said Algie.

I felt instantly sorry. 'It was very nice of you,' I said meekly.

'And now I've got to hoick Nan's oranges around as well as my watercress till she gets back,' said Algie, rubbing it in.

'You're the kindest boy in the whole world,' I said – but I still wished *he* had made the trip for me.

The morning seemed to go on for ever. Algie thought Hoxton an hour or so away, and Nan might be ten or fifteen minutes making my purchases, so I figured she'd be two and a quarter hours. When there was no sign of her by twelve noon I started to panic, becoming convinced that Nan had skipped off with my money and Algie's beads and was now laughing at both of us for being such fools.

'Calm down, Dolly! Nan's a good 'un, I keep telling you,' said Algie.

'You might have known her all your life but you don't see what she's really like. You only like her because she keeps fluttering her eyelashes at you,' I said crossly.

'I do not!' Algie said hotly.

'Then why did you buy her those blue beads!' I said.

'I bought her the beads to bribe her into fetching them things from Hoxton. I was doing it for *you*,' said Algie. 'You know that!'

'I'm sorry. I just don't know who to trust any more. It's so strange and horrid here in the past,' I said.

Algie stared at me. 'What do you mean, *"here in the past"*? That doesn't make sense.'

'I – I don't know. It came out wrong,' I stammered. I wasn't

sure what I meant myself. I held my head, struggling to make sense of it all.

'Dolly? Don't take on so! I didn't mean to upset you,' said Algie. 'Nan's going to turn up any minute with your new things and I'll treat you both to a pie or a cake and we'll celebrate, all friends together. You wait and see.'

Algie busied himself selling watercress and oranges. I sold another couple of dolls without my usual patter. It really did look as if my suspicions about Nan were justified.

Then at half past four I suddenly saw Nan strolling along, swinging several brown paper parcels tied up with string.

'Nan!' I cried, rushing towards her.

Algie got to her before me, looking tremendously relieved. He'd obviously been worrying too, though he kept denying it.

'Where have you *been*, Nan? We was worried sick!' he said.

'I've been to Hoxton. Isn't that where I was meant to go? And I've brought everything on your list, Princess Dolly, and you worked the money out wrong – you were three farthings short – so I put in the spare penny I keep in my shoe. So you owes me, see!'

'Oh Nan, thank you so much!' I said, feeling dreadful for doubting her. 'Here, have thruppence for your trouble!'

'And I'll go and buy you a pie *and* a cake!' said Algie.

'Don't want none. I had a slap-up dinner at my aunty's,' said Nan, but she took the thruppence.

'There! It was good of you to help out a pal, Nan, and good of you to reward her with thruppence, Dolly,' said Algie, doing his best to praise both of us.

'It wasn't quite thruppence though, was it, because I had to fork out my penny from my shoe,' Nan said. 'And actually I was expecting at least sixpence, as it's taken me all day to get her stuff.'

'All right, it was tuppenny farthing, and I know you've been gone all day, but weren't you mostly visiting your aunty?' I said.

'Dolly! Try to be grateful,' said Algie, though he couldn't help adding, 'And at least you're not down on your takings, Nan, because I did my best with your oranges and sold every one apart from a few soft ones already past it.'

'Aw, bless you, Algie,' said Nan. She handed over the string parcels. 'See how heavy they are, Dolly! Now, you go and sort them all out – make sure I haven't cheated you, ha ha! Maybe I'd like a cake, now I come to think of it. Let's you and me go off to the baker's shop, Algie.'

'And Dolly,' said Algie.

'No, I think I'll go back to Mrs Lazenby's and start sewing more dolls straight away,' I said. And I *did* badly want to check every single item to make sure Nan had kept to my list. There was just one more question first though.

'Nan, you didn't see an old woman hanging around – stout, with a stick?' I asked.

'Yes, I saw an old woman exactly like that,' said Nan.

'Really?' I said, my heart beating fast.

'I saw at least two dozen of them on my journey, silly,' she said.

'But none of them stopped and asked you about me?' I persisted.

'No. Not one of them. The only one who asked after you was the daft old dame done up to the nines in the material shop,' said Nan.

'What did she say?'

'Said she'd heard you'd run away and was worried about you. Asked if I knew you,' said Nan. 'Come on, Algie.' She tucked her hand in his arm.

'No, wait! You didn't tell her you knew me, did you?' I asked desperately.

'Course not! I'd never tell tales on anyone, not even you. Said I needed the doll stuff because I was swapping trades, and now I was off to meet my aunty. See?'

'But does she know who your aunt is?' I felt sick with fear again.

'Well, course she does, she's a good customer,' said Nan. 'For goodness' sake, drop it!'

'What if Missus finds out another girl has started up in the doll trade, and the material lady says she's got an aunt nearby – she might go round to find her and ask where her niece trades, and then she might track me down!' I said, panicking.

'Yes, and she might be crouching in a doorway right this minute, ready to get you!' said Nan.

I gasped, peering round fearfully.

'She's joking, Doll,' said Algie, putting his arm round me. 'Hey, you're trembling! It's all right. It's hardly likely that Missus of yours would do that. She'll have got some other poor little girl slaving for her by now. You mustn't worry so.'

Of course I worried. I went back to Mrs Lazenby's clutching my parcels, swivelling my head round at practically every step, making sure Missus wasn't creeping up on me. I wished now I hadn't risked Nan going to fetch things for me.

And when I got back to my new home I discovered she'd got mixed up with the amounts and bought too many thruppenny heads and not enough penny dolls or Charlottes, my steady sellers. She'd bought calico, a tub of sawdust and a mixture of material scraps, mostly in garish or dull colours, though roughly the right amount.

I laid everything out on my small bed and held a little doll head in each hand. 'Do you think Missus will come and catch me?' I whispered to them.

'Yes!' said the little penny doll. 'Grab your things and run run run!'

'But you're happy here,' said her big thruppenny sister. 'And Algie told you not to worry.'

'Algie isn't always right,' said the tiny head.

'But he looks after you. And so does Mrs Lazenby,' said Thruppenny.

'You must look after yourself! Run!' said Penny.

'You can't keep running for ever,' said Thruppenny.

'Then I won't run now,' I said, cradling her head and thrusting tiny Penny back in the basket. 'But I will look after myself. I will be very, very cautious.' I looked towards the basket. 'And if Missus *does* come after me, then I will run.'

It seemed the best plan. The stuffy room smelled of stale bedding but at least I had it to myself right now. I sat there, cutting and stitching and stuffing until I had four little bodies, and then I gave each one a head.

'Now, my pretties, let's choose your clothes,' I said.

I laid out the materials. They groaned when they saw the grey, the brown and the navy scraps.

'We want pink and blue and scarlet and purple and bright green and yellow!' they insisted.

'They are not really suitable colours for little girl dolls,' I told them.

They didn't care. They kept clamouring until I'd cut out a little frock for each one. Mrs Lazenby brought me a mug of tea and I held it tight, warming my stiff fingers, and then I sewed on. I was still stitching when Algie poked his head around the door.

'There you are! Oh my, have you made all those dolls already? You're like an entire toy factory rolled into one little girl,' he said. He came and sat on my bed. 'Are we proper friends again?'

'Of course we are,' I said, stretching and smiling.

'And you'll be friends with Nan too now?'

I wrinkled my nose.

'Don't pull that face!' said Algie sternly.

'It's my face. I can do what I like with it,' I said. 'But I will try to like Nan if I must. Though I rather think it will be impossible.'

I was still very scared that she'd betrayed me, even if it was unwittingly. I felt sick at the market the next day, jumping whenever anyone came near me, forever peering at the faces in the crowd – but there was no sign of Missus. I didn't see her the next day or the next day or the next. The tight knot in my stomach eased. I started to take deep breaths again. I even managed to chat to my customers and enjoyed helping the little girls choose a special dolly playmate.

Algie grinned at me every time he passed by with his watercress basket. Nan and I kept our distance but we stopped glaring at each other. I sold dolls until four o'clock each day and then skipped back to Mrs Lazenby's to get in at least two hours' sewing time before anyone else came home. I stopped thinking about Missus – she was just a scary sad person from my past, best forgotten.

I kept up steady sales during a long sunny spell, but then we had several days of wind and rain. Few people came out

shopping. Some of the traders didn't even bother to set up their stalls. Algie and Nan and Lizzie and I wandered around with our baskets but sold very little. I wondered about going back to Mrs Lazenby's earlier in the afternoon, but I was getting desperate to make some money by the fourth day of bad weather. I still had a little saved, but if I didn't earn any more soon I'd not even have enough for my tuppenny bed, let alone any food. Mrs Lazenby was generous and she seemed to have a particularly soft spot for me, but I couldn't rely on her good will for ever.

So I stayed in the street with my basket when Nan and Lizzie both went home with their mothers. Algie stayed with me for another hour, because the rain was actually good for his watercress, keeping it fresh and bright green.

'But your little dollies are getting soaking wet!' he said. 'Let's pack it in for the day.'

I'd done my best to cover them up but they were starting to droop, their carefully sewn frocks turning into sodden rags. I knew Algie was talking sense, but I thought the heavy grey clouds might be starting to lift at last. There was a chance of making a few sales if the drizzle stopped as folk started drifting home from work.

The word *drizzle* hung about in my head, repeating itself. I had a weird kind of flashback – or flash*forward*? Had I known someone called Drizzle? No, not exactly Drizzle. Dreezel? It seemed an unlikely name and yet I felt sure she was my special friend. I tried my hardest to remember, knowing it was important.

'Dolly! Stop your daydreaming!' said Algie.

'Shush!' I said impatiently. I'd nearly remembered. I could conjure up a face, a peal of laughter, a singing voice . . .

'Don't you shush me, little moppet!' said Algie. 'Just look at you, with your hair plastered to your scalp and your frock clinging to you. You're like a little drowned rat! You'll catch your death if you don't come home with me and get warm and dry.'

'I'll wait until I sell *one* doll,' I said. 'A thruppenny one, hopefully. I've only got a penny savings left!'

'I've got more. I'll lend you some,' Algie offered. 'Come *on*!'

'No, I'm staying,' I said obstinately, standing my ground.

'All right then. Suit yourself. But don't blame me if you get a streaming cold,' said Algie. He shook his head at me in exasperation and then marched off, his wet boots squeaking.

I stared after him, wondering about giving up after all . . . but the rain really was stopping now.

'I'll sell just one doll,' I murmured to myself.

I stood in the middle of the street, uncovering my poor sodden dolls.

'Come buy my dolls!' I called. 'Penny dolls, tuppenny Frozen Charlottes, and thruppenny specials, finer than any you'll find in an arcade. Come buy my—'

Then someone pushed me violently, knocking me right off my feet and scattering my dolls into the gutter! Someone forced their heavy knee into the small of my back, leaving me helpless and squirming. I felt a rope going round my neck and being tied tightly, almost strangling me. I screamed, getting a mouthful of gravel. My head was pushed forward.

'Shut that little rosebud mouth, do you hear me!'

It was Missus, it was Missus, it was Missus!

She jerked me upwards by the rope, so I had to clutch at it to stop it flattening my windpipe. There she was, her face flushed crimson with triumph and fury.

'Thought you'd got away from me, didn't you?' she spat at me. 'I'm going to teach you a lesson you'll never forget!'

'Algie!' I gasped, half-choked. Then I filled my lungs as best I could and screamed, 'Algie! *Algie! ALGIE!*'

But Algie wasn't there. He was back at Mrs Lazenby's. None of my friends were there. They'd given up and gone home. But there were still a few passers-by trudging back from work.

'Help me! This wicked woman is trying to kill me!' I yelled desperately.

Most ignored me – but I caught hold of one woman by her skirts. 'Please! Please rescue me! Look, she has me by the neck, like a dog!'

The woman looked at both of us worriedly. 'Here, what are you doing with that kiddie? That's no way to treat a child!' she said.

'I'll treat her any way I want. She's my own daughter and she's run away from me and gone to the bad!' Missus panted, pulling me tight to her.

'I'm not your daughter!' I shouted, and I clenched my fists and started pummelling her big chest.

She took off her shawl and trapped me tightly in it, binding my arms so I couldn't move them.

'May God strike you for denying your own mother!' Missus cried, giving me a shake. She turned to the gawping woman. 'I loved her with my heart and soul, giving her the food off my plate, learning her my own trade, and this is the way she repays me!'

The woman shifted her weight from one foot to the other, not knowing which of us to believe.

'She's not my mother! My mother is . . . My mother is . . .' I couldn't remember! Was my mother the poor wretched woman in her sick bed? No, she wasn't my real mother, and I knew she was dead anyway. My own mother was lost in time and I couldn't reach her!

I burst into tears. '*Mum!*' I cried.

A man came out of his shop at the end, peering at me. It was the baker, Lizzie's father!

'Oh please, Mr Baker, help me! This wicked woman is trying to drag me away! I'm Dolly, Lizzie's friend! You know me!' I called.

He stared at me uncertainly. 'My Lizzie has lots of friends – I can't tell one from another!' he said.

'I'm the girl who sells dolls!' I cried.

'So you are,' he said, scratching his head under his big white hat. He walked over to us. 'What are you doing to this poor girl?'

'I'm taking her back with me where she belongs!' Missus panted, hanging onto me with terrifying strength.

The baker was a large man who loomed over both of us, but he looked at her warily. He reached out to grab me from her, but then seemed to have second thoughts. 'Your daughter, you say?' he asked.

'The love of my life, but now she's broken my heart!' Missus cried hoarsely. There were real tears running down her reddened face, as if it was really true.

'She's *not* my mother!' I repeated, but my voice sounded

reedy and uncertain, as if I was telling a childish lie.

The baker shook his head vigorously, almost dislodging his tall hat. 'I can't interfere in family troubles,' he said, and backed away.

'Come back!' I cried.

His wife was watching from her doorway, and several of her children. I saw Lizzie, her eyes nearly popping out of her head.

'Run for a policeman, Lizzie!' I called.

'You can't do that!' said the baker, but Lizzie dodged under her mother's arm and was off like a shot, her arms pumping, her legs pounding.

'Police! Police!' she yelled. She knew where to go – the Coach and Horses public house! She darted inside – and came out with two burly men in navy uniform, police helmets askew and ale tankards still in their hands. Big Joe was with them too, in his shirt sleeves with a leather apron round his waist.

Missus saw them advancing and panicked for a moment. She lost her tight grip on me. I pulled away from her, almost tearing my arm from its socket, and ran to Big Joe. He bent and lifted me up. I clung to him, sobbing.

'Save me, Big Joe! Don't let her drag me off with her!' I cried.

'Don't take on so, little 'un. I've got you safe now,' he said.

The two constables had hold of Missus, while she cried too.

'She's my child! I've a mother's right to take her back, even though she's a scheming little thief! Look at them dolls she's been selling!' she shouted, nodding at the little bodies scattered over the pavement. 'She stole them! And my scissors and threads and scraps – all my valuable property – my trade!'

'You stole them, little Dolly?' said Big Joe, sounding more amused than shocked.

But the policemen were taking it more seriously. 'You stole from your own mother?' one said, and the other shook his head and tutted.

'*I* made the dolls, every single one, and all their clothes, everything! She locked me up all day long and forced me to sew for her! She's not, not, *not* my mother, she's telling wicked lies,' I insisted.

More people came out of their shops, a crowd gathering around us. Some started egging us both on, as if we were street entertainers.

'Let's take 'em both down the station and get the truth out of 'em there,' one policeman said to the other.

'You take the mad old woman. I'll keep hold of the child here,' said Big Joe.

'No, we'll take her in too. Sounds like she's a bad 'un, treating her mother like that!' said the first policeman.

'Big Joe, please! Keep me here!' I begged.

But the police stood firm. 'Now then, Joe! We turn a blind eye and let you run your business your way – but you have to let us run our business *our* way,' one said.

'You don't want a charge of child abduction, do you?' said the other.

Big Joe hesitated – and then handed me over. 'Sorry, Dolly. Can't be helped,' he said, sighing.

The policeman carried me under his arm while the other dragged Missus along, both of us screaming.

Chapter Fourteen

People gawped as I was carried along. Women shook their heads, looking horrified.

'Poor little lamb! What are they doing to her? Shame!'

Others shook their heads at *me*.

'Dirty little wretch! What's she been thieving then? I hope she's locked up good and proper!'

Boys jeered and jostled to get a better look at me.

'Squealing like a little pig! Hey, I can see right up her skirts!'

And one boy came running, calling out frantically, 'Dolly! Oh Dolly, I'm coming! Set her down, you brute! She ain't done nothing!' It was Algie, desperate to save me.

He tried to pull me away, but the policeman had me tight. Algie tried hitting and kicking him, but with his free hand the policeman took his truncheon and hit him hard about the head. Algie fell to the floor, stunned. I screamed harder, reaching up to get at the policeman's face.

'How dare you hit Algie!' I shouted, and I scratched as hard as I could.

'You little varmint! You'll have my eyes out!' The policeman deliberately ran at the wall, hitting my head hard.

I was stunned for a moment, blood trickling into my eyes. I managed to twist my neck to see Nan cradling Algie's head. She was looking at me with the oddest expression. She looked concerned – and yet triumphant. Perhaps she *did* betray me. Perhaps she was just pleased to get Algie to herself.

'Algie!' I cried.

He struggled to get up, reaching his hand out to me helplessly.

I closed my eyes, feeling dizzy as the blood seeped from my head. The policeman twisted me round at an angle so that my head was hanging down. I thought it might be to stop the blood flowing so fast – or he might have wanted to stop it splashing on his uniform.

I could see the other policeman struggling with Missus, who was still shouting furiously, calling for her so-called daughter.

'She's not my mother!' I murmured as the buildings started swaying and the shouting echoed in my ears.

Then everything went black as night and I was flailing in the dark, feeling as if I was falling right out of myself – and suddenly a memory flicked through me like an electric shock. Was I leaving this old Edie Trimmer and rushing through time and space to my real self?

Mum! Dad! I cried as loud as I could, but no sound came out of my open mouth. Then I felt a jolt and the swaying stopped and I was lying down. I hoped with my whole heart and soul that I was back – forward? – in my own bed in my real home. But there was no soft pillow, no scent of fresh sheets. I opened my eyes. I was lying on a thin tick mattress that reeked of some former occupant – and the policeman was peering at me, his face horribly close to mine.

'That'll learn you not to try to scratch my eyes out!' he blustered.

I wriggled away from him, sitting up. I was in a dismal cell, the only window high up and barred.

'Am I in prison?' I whispered.

'Not yet – but you will be soon!' he said. 'Little spitfire, that's what you are!'

'I haven't done anything, I swear to you! It was Missus who attacked me. Look, I've still got the rope round my neck!' I said, tugging at it.

'Well, how else was your poor ma to get you back home?' he said. He was parting my hair gingerly, though it was slippery with blood.

'Don't! That hurts!' I said, ducking away.

'It's only a scratch,' he said quickly. 'And it's your own fault. You banged your head against that wall in a raging temper, that's what you did.'

'No I didn't! *You* banged it! You're only saying I did it because you're scared you'll get into trouble for hurting me so,' I said, putting my own hand up to my head. It came away covered in scarlet, which frightened me.

'See, you're just trying to make it worse,' the policeman said. 'Look, I'll bring you some water and you can mop yourself up a bit before the sergeant interviews you.'

He went out of the cell. I heard the sound of the key clicking into place, locking me in. I was terrified. What if I was left here by myself in the gloom, bleeding fast?

I thought of poor dear Algie. He had been so valiant trying to rescue me. I hoped his head didn't hurt as badly as mine. I groaned and clutched my head. I knew I had to staunch the blood somehow. I lifted the hem of my frock and pressed it hard against my wound.

'Pull that frock down, you brazen minx!' said the hateful policeman, coming back into the cell. He had a basin of water and shoved it towards me, spilling some of it. The basin was greasy and the water had scum on it, but I supposed it was better than nothing. When the policeman went out again I took my stained frock off, removed my shift altogether, hurriedly pulled my frock on again, and then used my shift as a combination flannel and bandage.

The pain was so bad that I felt faint again, but I managed to keep my hands up in the air, pressing the cloth to my head. I could feel a throbbing beneath my fingers, which frightened me even more, but I pressed tighter and at last the blood stopped flowing. I sat in that horribly uncomfortable position until I heard the sound of the key in the lock again.

'Right, you! Sergeant needs to see you now. Up you get! And don't come out with any lies, do you hear? Say any

nonsense about me bashing your head and you'll get worse than that afterwards,' he said. He looked as if he meant it too.

I staggered when I stood up and he did his best to steady me.

'Now then, now then. No play-acting! And take that rag off your head. You're just trying to make out your head's really hurt,' he said.

'It is,' I said groggily. 'And if I let go of it, the blood will start seeping again.'

He sighed as if I was being totally unreasonable, but he didn't try to pull my shift away. He led me down a dank corridor to another bigger room containing an older man in smart uniform, the other policeman – and Missus! She gave a cry when she saw me and tried to take hold of me.

'Uh-uh!' said the older man quickly, as if commanding a dog. 'I'll have no argy-bargies in my office. Take the mother out to the front office while I interview the child.'

'She's not my mother,' I said.

'Ungrateful, unnatural child!' Missus wept, knuckling her eyes as she hustled away.

'What have you done to your head, little girl?' the older man asked, narrowing his eyes and peering at it.

I glanced at the policeman. 'I – I hurt it trying to set myself free,' I mumbled.

'Well, that only shows you how foolish it is to run away. Now, let us commence our chat. You'd better sit down before you fall down,' he said, pointing to the chair beside his desk. 'Off you go, Constable.'

'Had I not better stay, Sergeant, to keep an eye on her? She might be small but she can cut up rough,' he said, clearly not wanting to leave me alone with him in case I told tales.

'I think I can look after myself!' said the sergeant. 'Off with you, quick sharp!'

The policeman marched off, looking back at me warningly as he went out the door. I looked at the sergeant, trying to work out if he was equally violent and unpredictable. He looked at me, maybe pondering the same about me. The room was very quiet, though far away I could hear someone start screaming.

The sergeant saw my eyes blink in shock. 'No need to worry. That's just a wicked thief being locked up!' he said. 'Are you a wicked thief, child?'

'No, sir!' I said quickly.

'You've never stolen something that belonged to another?' he continued.

'No, sir,' I said again, but I couldn't stop my voice wavering.

'Are you quite sure?' he said. 'Tell me the exact truth. I will know if you are lying.' He started buffing the silver buttons on his tunic with his handkerchief while he waited.

'Well, I suppose my scissors did belong to Missus,' I mumbled. 'And she paid for the first few dolls, but I made them for her. But the second lot were bought entirely from my earnings, I swear.'

'So you did steal from your own mother!' he said, gazing at the shine on this buttons with satisfaction.

'She is not my mother! She did not give birth to me, and that's the absolute truth, I swear it!' I said.

'I am inclined to believe you,' he said, to my huge relief. He paused. 'However, I daresay she treated you like a mother, giving you little treats and letting you climb on her lap for comfort?'

'No! Well, she did sit me on her lap sometimes, but I didn't want to,' I said.

'And she gave you the choicest cuts of meat when she could spare the money?' he enquired.

'That was just a bribe to make me work faster,' I said.

'So you didn't always work as hard as you could to please her?'

'I *did* work hard! So hard that my fingers bled – they were so sore I cried. And then she put *salt* on them, which stung till I wanted to tear my fingers right off!'

'Salt is a very good remedy for sores,' said the sergeant. He suddenly took hold of my hand, making me jump. I shrank away from him as he held my fingers in front of his face. 'They look fully healed to me,' he announced.

'And she kept me locked up by myself all day long! What mother would lock her own child in a horrid little garret day after day?' I said.

'A mother who feared her wilful child might run away?' he countered. 'And you did exactly that at the first opportunity, though she hasn't figured out how you managed to rise ten foot in the air without a ladder. She believes it was witchcraft! Do you practise the black arts, child?'

I stared at him, wondering if he was having a grim joke at my expense.

'You don't really think I'm a witch, do you?' I said. 'You must be mad!'

'And you must be the most impertinent wretch I've ever

had brought before me!' he said, his face flushing with rage. 'How dare you take that tone with me! I've a good mind to have you whipped for impertinence!'

He didn't seem to be joking. My heart started thumping hard and I felt the blood oozing from my temple again.

'I'm very sorry, sir,' I said. 'Please don't whip me! It wasn't anything to do with witchcraft. I threw a rope up in a tree beside the wall and climbed up it.'

'Aha! So you confess you ran away!' he said.

'Yes, because she was horrible and made me work so hard.'

'Sitting sewing in a daylit room isn't my idea of hard work,' he said, giving his buttons yet another polish. 'Little children crawl in darkness through the mine tunnels, risking life and limb. They climb up inside black chimneys and frequently take a tumble. They work twelve-hour shifts in factories and are so tired they fall into the whirring machines. *That's* my idea of toil. Perhaps you would prefer this kind of occupation?'

'No, sir. I am quite content to work hard and sew, but please couldn't you let me work for myself? I am fair and honest, I promise you. Ask Algie!' I cried.

'Algie? Might he be the street urchin who attacked one of my fine upstanding officers? A very fine fellow to speak up for you!' the sergeant said scornfully.

'Well, ask Big Joe! He runs the public house where your officers like to drink,' I said.

'I am very well acquainted with the gentleman you call Big Joe. We might have a little arrangement with him, but he is still a blackguard of the first degree,' he argued.

'Then ask Mrs Lazenby to speak up for me! She's a lovely lady who runs a fine lodging house nearby,' I said. 'Now *she's* like a real mother to me!'

'I know Mrs Lazenby of old,' said the sergeant. 'She's not a proper missus, and she's certainly no lady, and not a mother figure either, so hold your tongue, you ignorant child.'

I didn't dare say any more. I drooped on my hard wooden chair, my hands clenched in my pockets. I pricked myself on a stray needle but hardly noticed the sharp little pain. I wished I had a little doll secreted away to hold for comfort. The faraway howling started up again and I shivered. It looked as if it would be my turn next.

The sergeant sat busily polishing his buttons down his

front. Too busily. The one strained across his large stomach suddenly broke its thread and jerked loose, rolling across the table.

'Botheration!' he said, frowning. He caught hold of the button and matched it back in place as if it would magically sew itself fast again.

I swallowed hard. 'If you please, I could sew it on for you,' I said in a tiny voice, bringing out my needle. It had a scrap of navy thread in it, though it was too fine to hold a silver button in place for long.

He looked at me. He looked at the button. Then he shrugged. 'Very well,' he said, and gestured to his front.

'I think you will have to remove your fine tunic, sir, so I can sew the button on at the right angle,' I said.

He sighed but unbuttoned the rest of his tunic and shrugged it off. He looked less alarming in his white vest and his commonplace braces. I held it over my knees and sewed for dear life. The length of thread was luckily just long enough to double for strength. I had no scissors now so I had to bite off the tiny scrap of thread left.

'Are you *eating* my jacket?' he asked.

I guessed he didn't mean it seriously, because he was

smirking. He put it back on and buttoned it slowly. He gave the just-sewn button a hard tug, testing it, but it stayed in place.

He nodded. 'Not bad!' he said. 'No wonder your mother wants you back again!'

'She's *not* my mother!'

'So you keep saying, till my head hurts,' he said.

'I'm the one with the hurt head,' I dared reply. The blood seemed to have stopped again, but the pain was worse, sharp and throbbing.

'Yes, you should get that seen to,' he said, as if I could somehow bathe and bandage my head whilst stuck here in his police station. He leaned back in his chair, hands on his stomach now, eyeing me up and down.

'So what am I going to do with you?' he asked.

'Please, please, please don't send me back to Missus,' I said.

'But what is the alternative? Shall I send you to the magistrate tomorrow so that he can sentence you to a prison sentence for theft?' he threatened.

'They don't send children to prison,' I said. 'Not for taking a pair of scissors and some doll stuff.'

'Well, certainly, that would be unusual. But let me see . . . I've heard of a child being given seven years' hard labour for stealing a loaf of bread before now. Is that what you'd sooner?' he said.

'You're only trying to frighten me,' I said, but I couldn't be sure. I supposed seven years with Missus might be better than seven years' hard labour, whatever that was. I imagined myself on a giant treadmill or wielding a pick-axe or hauling rubble, with a terrifying man in charge whipping me to go faster and kicking me whenever I fell down. It couldn't really happen, could it?

I held my throbbing head, dizzy again.

'Now you're playing for sympathy,' said the sergeant, but he walked round his desk and pulled my shift to one side to look at the wound. 'It doesn't look too bad,' he said, but he was clearly lying.

'If you send me to court they will ask me how I hurt my head and I shall tell them that a policeman rammed it against a brick wall,' I said, trying to tuck my shift back into place. 'Then maybe *he* will get sent to prison instead of me.'

'My, my, am *I* meant to be frightened now?' he said. 'I shall add blackmail to my list of your crimes.' His large stomach

rumbled, and he consulted his pocket watch. 'Time I went home to my supper,' he said. 'So what am I going to do with you?' He pondered, then said, 'I'll be a good Christian man and send you where they'll bring you up proper and give you a good training. How about that?'

'To an orphanage?' I asked warily.

'Something of the kind,' he said. He rang a bell. 'Officer! Here, Officer! Take this girl to the workhouse!'

'No! Not the workhouse!' I said. I thought of the savage scars on Algie's back, the nameless little mudlark shivering as he said the very word 'workhouse'. I didn't know what happened there, but it was obviously dreadful in the extreme.

'Maybe – maybe I'd sooner go back to Missus!'

'Too late to change your mind now. I'm getting tired of your babbling.' He took a deep breath. 'Officer! Take this child to the workhouse!' he shouted.

It was the brutal policeman who had hurt my head that came for me. I shrank from him.

'Come on, you!' he said. 'And no biting or scratching or you'll know what you'll get, don't you?'

He tied my hands tightly behind my back to make sure, and then dragged me down the long, dim corridor, past the cell

where some poor soul was still howling, and then out the heavy door into the street.

I looked round desperately, hoping against hope that Algie might somehow be there waiting to rescue me, but I only saw strangers. Some looked at me with pity as I was dragged along, others winced in disgust and looked the other way. Then we turned a corner – and I stood still, my knees buckling so I could barely keep upright. An old woman was sitting there on the pavement, tumbled in a heap, wailing furiously. She had her apron over her head to hide herself from stares, but I knew her instantly.

'Missus!' I cried. I tugged at the policeman. 'Am I going back with her after all?'

'You're not going back with that old biddy. Didn't you hear what the sergeant said? You're off to the workhouse!' said the policeman.

Missus clambered to her knees, pulling her apron down. She stared at me, tears still seeping down her cheeks.

'Oh Missus! I'll come back to you!' I said.

'I don't want you no more!' she cried. 'The lies you've told! I treated you so good too! You fair broke my heart when you ran off like that. I've been searching for you for so long. And

then when I find you at last, you turn against me, you scheming wretch. So they're taking you to the workhouse, are they? Good riddance! It's where all the liars and the cheats and the vile and the addled end up! It's where you belong!'

'I'll second that,' said the policeman, pushing me along. 'You be on your way, mother, or I'll arrest you for causing a disturbance on my way back to the station!'

Missus screamed abuse at both of us, while I was dragged onwards. I tried to memorize each side street and passageway so that I might be able to find my way back to Mrs Lazenby, but I was soon hopelessly lost. There were tall buildings around me, seeming to close in on me till they blocked out the sky. A factory siren went off and a flock of startled pigeons flew up towards the clouds. I stared at them, wishing I had wings too.

We were approaching a bleak grey-brick building with an archway over the entrance.

'This is it: your lovely new home!' said the policeman, baring his teeth in a horrible grin. 'The Bonham Street Workhouse. Most popular lodging house in the district.'

There was a queue of people outside, all of them pale and dirty, their clothes unwashed. Surely they weren't queueing to

get *in*? They weren't being prodded along by a hateful policeman. They were standing there, swaying and muttering.

The policeman kept his firm grip on me and dragged me to the front of the queue. People started complaining bitterly.

'She's not here just to doss down for the night. This is going to be her brand-new home,' the policeman said. 'I'm taking her to the relieving officer.'

I didn't know what that meant. Was this officer going to give me some kind of relief? It didn't seem likely by the reaction of the crowd.

'God help the poor little mite,' said an old lady wearing a dirty white cap to hide the sparseness of her hair. She reached out to my head, still swathed in my shift. 'Have you hurt yourself, dear?'

'Don't you say a word!' said the policeman to me, and marched me past her.

We went to the lodge in front of the grim workhouse. This relieving officer wore a scarlet coat and a peaked cap, and had a brisk, soldierly appearance. Everything about him was clipped: his white hair cut to the top of his ears, his nails snipped into stubs, his beard exactly one inch all over. Even his voice was clipped.

'Another waif and stray, Officer?' he said. 'Committed any crimes?'

'Theft. Assault. Insubordination, Mr Hamlin,' said the policeman. 'Lucky not to be doing a seven stretch. Sergeant's too soft if you ask me.'

The relieving officer clicked his tongue against his teeth and issued small tuts of disapproval. 'Leave it with me, sir,' he said.

Oh dear Lord, I wasn't even a girl any more. I was simply an *it*.

'With pleasure. By the way, add "lying" to the list. Comes out with all kinds of gory nonsense. Even tried to make accusations against me, would you believe!' said the policeman.

He released me so abruptly I staggered, nearly falling. If I'd had my wits about me I might have run for it then, when the door was still open – but I simply stood swaying, wondering how much bleaker this nightmare could get. *Was* it a nightmare – or was it my new reality?

Mr Hamlin dipped his pen into a bottle of brown ink, and waited, nib poised, to fill in a form. 'Name?' he enquired.

'Dolly,' I said, because it was Algie's name for me.

'Dolly what?'

'Just Dolly,' I said, not wanting to leave any other record that I'd been in such a shameful place.

I watched him write in a neat, sloping copperplate: *Dolly Blank.*

'Age?'

I wasn't sure how to answer. I didn't know how old I was now.

'Age?' he repeated impatiently.

I was very small. So was I eight, nine, ten? But I seemed much older now I'd been fending for myself. Was I already in my teens?

Mr Hamlin wrote *Unknown* before I could suggest an age.

'Creed?' he barked.

I blinked.

'Sorry?'

'Yes, you'll be sorry if you keep messing me about, girl. *Creed?*'

'I'm afraid I don't know what that means,' I said.

Mr Hamlin tutted irritably. 'Another heathen,' he muttered.

'No, I'm not!' I said.

'Haven't you ever heard of the Lord Jesus?' he asked.

I suddenly remembered playing Mary and rocking a baby doll Jesus in my arms. 'Yes, I have!' I insisted. 'Mary, Joseph and Jesus, the Holy Family.'

He sighed in acknowledgement and wrote *Christian* on the form.

'Occupation?' he asked next.

It seemed bizarre to be asking my occupation when I was a child. Still, I really did have an occupation now.

'I make dolls, dressed dolls. And then I sell them from a basket in the street,' I said proudly, holding up my head. It was only a small movement, but I felt my wound opening again. I pressed on my makeshift bandage to stop the blood flowing.

'Single, married or widowed?' Mr Hamlin enquired ridiculously.

'Well, I'm single, obviously,' I said.

'Less of the lip. I didn't compose this form. I just have to fill it in. Now stop wasting my time. I daresay there are many folk out there waiting for a chance to get in,' he said sternly. 'Last residence?'

'Mrs Lazenby's,' I said.

He tutted like the sergeant and wrote *Bawdy House*.

'Why have you put *Bawdy House*?' I asked. Was it because I boarded there, and his spelling had let him down?

'Indecent house,' he muttered, with a curled lip.

'No it's not. It's a lovely house,' I said.

'Whether in W H before?' he went on. '*Workhouse*,' he said, slowly and deliberately, as if I was lamentably stupid.

'No. Never. And I don't want to be here now. Can't you please let me go back to Mrs Lazenby's?'

'You've been delivered here by an officer of the police, so here you stays,' he said.

'For how long?'

'For as long as it takes,' he snapped. 'Cause of admission is next. And we know that, don't we? What was it the officer said? Theft, assault and insubordination. And a liar! Shocking!'

'That officer was the liar,' I said. 'Look what he did to my head!'

'Don't start,' he said. 'Last question. Nearest relative?'

I stood there silently. I had relatives somewhere, a dear mother and father . . . though it was harder and harder to remember them now. I knew it was pointless trying to explain to him. He would think I was raving.

'Could I say a friend instead of a relative?' I asked.

'Of course not. Anyone can make a friend. It's a relative what's important. And if you ain't got none then you belong here,' he said. 'Orphans are two a penny in the workhouse.'

He wrote *Orphan* with a flourish. 'Consider yourself lucky, Dolly Blank. I am the official relieving officer of Bonham Street Workhouse and I am hereby admitting you to our charitable institution.'

He stamped my admission form.

Then I was led away by another burly man in uniform into the workhouse itself.

Chapter Fifteen

I held my breath. I'd never smelled such a stench in my whole life. It was as if I'd tumbled into a sewer. I put my hand over my mouth, choking.

'What is that awful smell?' I gasped.

The burly man looked down at me. He'd seemed fierce, like a great bulldog, but he eased his grip on me and gave me a pat on the back. 'The sanitation isn't what it could be,' he said. 'And the windows are nailed shut. But don't worry, little girl. You'll get used to it.'

I knew I'd never get used to it if I lived here all my life. And that seemed a terrible possibility. We turned right, along

a corridor which seemed full of very elderly ladies in grubby mob caps and long coarse grey frocks stumbling along, some blind, some bent over, some lame. Had they once been small girls like me? And this was a *work*house. How could such elderly women possibly still work? They were being herded along by a younger woman in the same outfit, but with a big badge sewn onto her dress. It was red with a yellow O in the middle.

'Is she a matron? And what does the O mean?' I asked the burly man.

'She's one of the paupers, but she's been made an officer. O is for officer,' he said, perhaps assuming I couldn't read.

'Is everyone here an old woman?' I asked.

'We're in the right wing. Females here. Except me,' he said, chuckling. 'They have to have a big chap like me, who'll stand no nonsense.'

'Where are they all going?'

'To have their supper in the dining room. That's why they're stepping out in such sprightly fashion,' he said, laughing at his own grim joke.

'Should I be going to supper too?' I asked. I wasn't sure I'd ever be able to eat a morsel in this terrible place.

'Nah, you have to go to the Female Receiving Room for further assessment,' he said.

We walked on down yet another corridor. I heard screaming, high and piercing. 'Is someone being beaten?' I cried. I remembered the terrible scars on Algie's back.

'I doubt it,' said the burly man. 'Don't fret, child. No one's going to beat a little girl like you.'

When we turned the corner we saw a woman being dragged along the floor by two women with the yellow O badges on their chest. She was arching up, trying to look back – and far down the corridor two boys, one about Algie's age, the other much younger – were being frogmarched in the other direction. The elder boy was fighting wildly with male officers, and the younger one was screaming, saying one word over and over again: 'Ma, Ma, Ma!'

'What's happening? Why is he being taken away from his mother?' I said.

'Questions, questions! Why do you think? The boys are going to the male wards, the mother is going to the female,' the burly man said.

'But why do they have to be split up? They're a family!' I said.

'Rules is rules. We don't allow families here. It's tidier to divide everyone up, males to the left, females to the right,' he said, as if it was a simple matter.

'So when will that mother be able to see her boys?' I asked.

'Well, she won't. She'll mope for a bit, but she'll get over it. Most do,' he said.

I stared up at him. 'But *why* can't she see them if they're under the same roof?'

'It's not convenient,' he said. It was such an extraordinary answer that I was stunned into silence.

He'd told me that rules were rules, but this terrible place had rules that didn't make any kind of sense. I trotted along beside him dumbly to the Receiving Room. I'd thought it would be a large office with hard chairs and orderly rows, like an enormous doctor's waiting room, but it had no furniture at all, and females were crowded in together, old and young. Some women looked very ill, others muttered restlessly, and babies wailed hungrily in their mothers' arms.

'So mothers can keep their babies?' I asked the burly man.

'Until they're two. If the baby's mother dies, we try to feed 'em cow's milk, but they seldom thrive,' he said matter-of-factly. 'Here, child, take your form and wait your turn.'

There was a woman swaying beside me, reeking of drink, her eyes barely focusing. 'Yeah, take your turn, take your turn,' she said, elbowing me out of the way. 'Had a thump on the head? Well, stop pushing in or I'll give you another one!'

I held on tight to the burly man. 'Can't you stay a little while?' I whispered.

'Can't stay, I've got to fetch the next inmate – and the next, and the next, till we lock the gates for the night,' he said.

'But there's no one to look after me!' I said desperately.

'That's why you're here! So chin up, chicken. Don't look so sad. You'll get used to it in time,' he said, and went on his way.

I couldn't stop the tears rolling down my face.

'Ooh, poor little girlie!' said the drunk woman, mocking me.

'Why are you being so horrible to me?' I said, knuckling my eyes.

'Cause I feels like it,' she said, and she gave me a hard poke in the chest.

'Stop that!' said someone behind me. It was the poor woman who had been torn away from her boys. She was crying too, but she poked the drunk woman in turn. 'Touch that child again and you'll bitterly regret it, I'm warning you!'

'I ain't afeared of you!' said the drunkard, but she seemed taken aback. She staggered, bumping into someone else, and then slid slowly to the floor. She sank into a heap, her eyes closed.

I gasped, staring down at her. 'Is she *dead*?' I asked.

'No, she's just passed out,' said the woman. 'No wonder, the state she's in. I'm surprised Mr Hamlin let her in.' Her voice was hoarse from crying. She wiped her streaming eyes with the back of her hand. 'They took my boys away!' she explained.

'I saw it. I can't believe they could be so cruel. It's so awful for you,' I said, and I timidly put my arm round her thin shoulders.

'I'll get them back!' she said, clutching me. She started coughing. I could feel her whole body shaking with the effort. 'I'll get rid of this cough and get strong again. I'll work and work. They'll send me out on licence and then I'll get my boys back!'

'Yes, you will,' I said, holding her tight, but I saw the dark lines under her eyes, her hollow cheeks, and her chalk-white face, and knew she didn't have much chance of getting better.

'What about you, child? Have you been cruelly separated from your family?' she asked, scarcely able to get the words out for coughing.

'I've been separated from everyone,' I said.

'You poor little thing,' she said, and she patted me on the back. 'What's your name, child?'

I remembered my new name. 'Dolly,' I said.

'And I'm Margaret.'

We held onto each other. It felt so good to have a friend standing beside me in this crowded stuffy room. We had nowhere to rest our legs, unless we lay down like the drunken woman. We weren't given any food or drink, not even the crying children were. We had nowhere to relieve ourselves. We stood swaying with exhaustion while slowly, slowly, slowly we shuffled forward towards the big desk at the end, where a sharp-faced woman in an elaborate cap and apron assessed each newcomer.

Everyone had their form stamped, even the babies, and then they were dispatched through a big door.

'What's through there?' I asked my new friend Margaret.

'The place where we sleep, I suppose,' she said.

An old woman in front of us turned round, shaking her head. 'Nah, nah, no sleeping yet. It's the bath-house,' she said. 'You have to strip right off too, and it's a wonder we don't catch our death of cold.'

'I don't need a bath! I keep myself clean – and so do my boys!' Margaret said indignantly.

'Don't matter. They don't care whether you're clean or not. They got to make sure you ain't got no creepy-crawlies,' said the old woman.

I wasn't quite sure what she meant. Did she mean nits? I'd had them once – didn't half our class catch them when we were in the Infants? At school!

'Do children go to school now?' I asked Margaret.

'Well, my boys went to a dame school when they were little, and we could afford it. They can both read and write and figure,' she said proudly. 'But then my husband went off and we fell on hard times—'

'We're all here because we've fallen on hard times,' said the old woman. 'And it can't get no harder than the workhouse. Still, I'm banking on a proper bed tonight, and that's luxury to me.'

'Do we sleep together in one great big dormitory?' I asked. 'It must be a terrible squash.'

'Bless you, dearie. We're divided up. I goes in the vagrants' ward. It's for folk like me, the in-and-outers. I stay here a night or two, and then I'm off a-wandering once more,' she said. 'I like my independence, see – but I also like a good rest and a bit of meat to have a good chew on.' She cackled and opened her mouth, showing us she was completely toothless.

'So we can leave the workhouse whenever we want?' I said. It seemed almost too good to be true. And it was.

'*I* can, because I'm a vagrant, no fixed abode,' she said, sounding proud of it.

'Then I am too! I live with Mrs Lazenby, but it's just a lodging house.'

'But was you brought in by the police?' she asked, eyes narrowing.

'Yes, but I hadn't really done anything wrong,' I said.

'Don't matter. If you're brought in then you have to stay here, ducks,' said the old woman, scratching herself.

'I wasn't brought in,' said Margaret, wiping her eyes. 'And neither were my boys. I shall fetch them in the morning and we'll go out. I'd sooner us starve on the streets than be separated in this hell-hole. We're decent folk, not drunks or vagrants!'

'Ooh, hark at Miss hoity-toity!' said the old woman, cackling again, but not taking offence. 'Doubt you'll be let out anyways. You're sick, aren't you? You'll be put in the sick ward.'

'But that will be good, because they'll give you special medicine and that will ease the cough and make you feel better,' I said. 'They'll put me in the sick ward too because of my cut head, so we'll be together.'

'Ah, ain't that sweet!' said the old woman, scratching again. Then she caught herself and smacked her own hand. 'Better stop that or I'll be put in the itch ward!'

I laughed uncertainly, thinking she was joking. 'An itch ward! You're making that up, aren't you?'

'No I'm not. And you don't want to end up in the itch ward because if you haven't got them nasty little mites when you goes in, you certainly will have within a day, as sure as eggs are eggs,' she said, unable to resist giving herself another good scratch.

'So have you got them then?' I said, trying to back away from her, though it was too crowded to move far.

'Nah, mine are just fleas, and you can't help them, not when you're a vagrant,' she said cheerfully.

Margaret gave a groan and coughed again, covering her mouth to try to stifle the sound. I saw little beads of sweat on her forehead and knew she must have a fever. I felt so sad for her – and yet worried too. We had been hugging each other close. What if I caught the fever too? I would hate to catch fleas from the old woman but it would be even worse to catch the fever when I knew my mother here had died of it.

I started to feel dizzy again. I knew it was from the blow on my head, and the stuffy room, and not having had food or

water for a while – and yet I couldn't help fearing that I'd caught the fever already.

Margaret was coughing helplessly now, great racking coughs that shook her whole body. I pushed my way through the crowd, right to the desk where the sharp woman with the strange cap was writing in the register book. 'Please can I have a glass of water for the lady back there? She can't stop coughing,' I said.

The grim woman at the desk looked astonished. 'How dare you address me directly! I am the matron! Now go and wait your turn!' she said, making little flapping gestures at me.

'Yes, you can't push in here!' said the woman she was dealing with, looking indignant.

'I'm not trying to push in. I simply need some water for the lady who's coughing,' I persisted, as politely as I could.

'Did you not hear me? Get back at once!' said the matron. The frills on her white cap emphasized the sharpness of her nose and chin.

'But—'

'If you say another word I will have you sent straight to Punishment!' she snapped.

I shut my mouth and did as I was told. I didn't know what Punishment entailed, but I knew from the gasp of the nearby people that it would be terrible. I wriggled my way back through the crowd, where Margaret was still coughing.

'I'm so sorry – they won't give me any water for you,' I said miserably.

'It will . . . stop soon,' she gasped, pressing an old rag against her mouth. She gave one more explosive cough, swayed a little, but then stopped. She quickly wiped her mouth and stashed the rag in the pocket of her frock, but I saw it was now stained red with blood.

'I'm so sorry,' I said. 'Let's hope they hurry up and then

we'll have this bath. Afterwards we'll both be in the sick ward, and the nurses will give you water and medicine and see to the cut on my head.'

'And give you both a nice chop for your supper and tuck you up in silk sheets in a feather bed?' said the old woman, and she cackled with laughter, mocking us.

We waited and waited and waited. When at last it was our turn, the old woman pushed in front of us, showed her form, and was marched off to the bath-house. She gurned at us as she went, holding her ears and sticking her tongue out the side of her mouth in a horrible grimace.

The matron frowned forbiddingly when she saw we were next. I had to support Margaret because she was so weak from her coughing fit she could scarcely stand.

'One at a time!' the matron snapped.

'My friend is feeling very weak,' I explained.

'No I'm not,' said Margaret determinedly. 'I have a slight cough, that's all. I'd like to be put in the general women's ward, if you please. I will work with a will in the hope I can be trained up to be a domestic servant or some such, and then I can be reunited with my sons.' She spoke without pause, and then closed her mouth so tightly her lips disappeared. She didn't

make a sound, but she shook with a suppressed cough, her veins standing out on her forehead.

The matron copied Margaret's name and age into her register book, and then wrote on her form. I read the words scrawled at the bottom:

Pronounced cough and fever. Sick ward.

Margaret read them too. 'No, no, please! If you put me there I'll never get out of here! For pity's sake, let me work!' she cried, but she couldn't suppress the cough any more. She doubled up with it.

The matron sighed and held a handkerchief to her own face. 'Winnie!' she called.

A very old lady in pauper's cap and gown came shuffling forward. 'Yes, Matron?' she said, eager to please.

'Take this poor wretch to the sick ward,' the matron commanded.

'Yes, matron,' said old Winnie, and she took hold of Margaret and steered her towards the door.

Margaret wailed and struggled weakly, while Winnie pushed her feebly to go the other way. It would have been

comical if it hadn't been so sad.

'I know she's sick, but she's desperate to help her boys. I know it's against the rules, but couldn't you let her see them?' I said.

The matron glared at me. 'Speak when you're spoken to, missy!'

She glanced at my form and copied my new name into the register. It was a large marbled manuscript book that looked strangely familiar. I tried to remember where I'd seen that sort of stationery before. Then I was distracted by the words she was writing on my form.

'*Mother and Children ward*!' I read. 'Well, if there is such a ward, why on earth couldn't you let poor Margaret be there?'

'It's for young girl children and newly birthed women,' she said, beckoning to another ancient woman waiting eagerly.

'But I'm sick. Look at my head! *I* need to be in the sick ward,' I said. I tried to unwind my makeshift bandage, even though my stained shift stuck to my temple and started the wound bleeding again.

The matron looked disgusted. 'Stop that! I don't want to see your nasty sores, thank you very much. I've had enough of you.' She clicked her fingers at another old lady with an O on her pauper's gown. 'This child needs to be taught a severe

lesson. Take her down to Punishment.'

'Oh no! Please don't punish me! I haven't done anything wrong!' I cried.

The old lady shuffled forward, her eyes gleaming. 'Leave her to me, Matron!' she said.

She caught hold of me. I tried to struggle free, but the ancient granny held on, surprisingly strong, and dragged me along with her, through the door and out of the crowded room.

'You's going to Darky!' she said, almost singing it. 'You won't like it there!'

'What is Darky?' I asked, struggling harder.

'It's where the bad ones go,' she said with relish, opening a door and pulling me down slippery winding steps to a cellar. It was pitch black. I could hear muffled groans and smell unwashed bodies. She stumbled her way amongst them, dragging me with her. A hand clutched at my ankle and I screamed.

'Stop that noise now!' the old lady hissed. 'You don't want to annoy any of these folk or they might silence you for good.'

I put my hand over my mouth to stop any more screams coming out. I held onto her willingly now, desperate for her protection.

'Here's your bed, your ladyship!' she said.

She pushed me downwards to the floor. I couldn't feel any bed or blanket. There was just a narrow plank on the greasy floor.

I thought she was playing a trick on me.

'I know there's no bed there! It's only a plank,' I mumbled.

'That's yer bed! What did you expect, a bloomin' four-poster?' She cackled and then pushed my hands away. 'Settle down then! Nighty-night!'

Then she was off, moving swiftly for such an old woman. I didn't dare try to stumble after her for fear one of these terrifying unseen people would clutch at me again. I lay down on the hard plank, curling my legs up and wrapping my arms around myself.

My cut head throbbed horribly. I trembled every time someone groaned. Whenever anyone turned over I feared they'd come creeping over to get me. I scarcely slept that long, terrible night. I just had a few snatches of dream-time when I seemed back in my own warm, clean bed light years in the future, where I had a mother and a father and I was truly loved.

Chapter Sixteen

I couldn't tell how long I'd been kept down in that terrible basement. It felt like a hundred years but it might have been only a night. There was no way of telling whether it was dawn or dusk, day or endless night. But at long last someone came into the dank basement holding a lamp. There was a general stirring and a desperate murmur.

'Take me out, sir!'

'Pick me, pick me!'

'I've done my time in Darky! Let me out before I die!'

'For pity's sake, I'm sick, can't you see? I need my medicine!'

'I can't breathe, I can't breathe!'

I saw by the dim lamplight that the ogres I'd been imagining were simply whey-faced people, as shivering and frightened as myself. There were even other children. One boy looked even younger than me. He was crying, though he tried to hide his face when he saw me staring at him.

The officer stepped over him, coming towards me. The boy cast himself down on his plank, clearly sobbing now. Another older boy came out with a mouthful of abuse when he was rejected too, and several others joined in.

I could see this wasn't the right way to get out of this terrible place. I gathered all my strength and got to my feet. My head reeled but I managed to stay upright.

'If you please, sir, I have learned my lesson,' I said as humbly as I could. 'I am very sorry.'

The boy raised his head and sneered, and someone else hissed '*Toady*!' But the officer seemed impressed.

'That's the spirit, child. Who put a little girl like you in amongst a crowd of reprobates and vagabonds, eh? You come with me!'

I went with him, feeling ashamed of my penitent act, but desperately relieved it had worked.

'You're a rum little thing,' he said, when he had a proper look at me in the corridor.

I suppose I did look a sight with my head bound in my bloody shift, my dress crumpled from my sleepless night tossing and turning on the hard plank. I felt filthy dirty too.

'I feel I very much need a trip to the bath house, sir,' I said.

'You don't have a bath now! You've been allocated to Mother and Children, haven't you? You're not due for a bath till Tuesday next week!' he said, shaking his head as if I was demanding the moon.

'But I didn't get a bath last night, sir. I was sent straight down to the basement,' I said.

'And you'll find yourself down there again if you keep arguing, little madam,' he said.

I didn't feel I was exactly arguing but I knew enough to keep quiet.

He nodded in acknowledgment. 'Good girl. Little girls should be seen but not heard, didn't your ma teach you that?' he said.

Neither mother had taught me anything of the sort. Poor Mother had liked me talking to her to divert her from her sickness. And my other mother . . . oh, *Mum*! She always told

me to stand up for myself, to put my hand up in class, and to speak up if anything seemed unfair.

The officer was looking at me carefully. 'Lost your ma, have you?' he asked, kindly now.

I nodded miserably.

'Ah well. Maybe you'll find a motherly sort in your ward who'll take you under her wing,' he suggested.

'There's my friend Margaret. She's in the sick ward though. Don't you think I should be in the sick ward too, sir, as I have such a bump on the head?'

'Aha! You're a sharp little minx for all your innocent little face! Someone's said you get more milk on the sick ward, haven't they?'

'No, sir! I don't even like milk,' I said. I wasn't sure that was true. I liked that milky drink that tasted of strawberries – we went somewhere fun where I had meat in a roll and the strawberry milk drink . . . I screwed up my face, trying to remember the name of the place, but the memory was fading now.

'Don't like *milk*?' said the officer. 'Oh well. Gruel and water will suit you marvellously then.'

Gruel? My friend with the funny name sang a song about gruel, didn't she? It was a sort of porridge, wasn't it?

The officer led me into a huge room with long tables and benches, and a strange thick smell like boiling blankets. There were many rows of women and children sitting there, eating from wooden bowls in total silence. It seemed so eerie that even the smallest child was quiet. The horrid smell wasn't putting them off their food. They were all delving quickly into their bowls, shovelling each mouthful down. I thought this gruel must be delicious. My mouth started watering. I realized it was a very long time since I'd last eaten.

There was a small woman in workhouse uniform wearing a vast white apron reaching down to the floor. I didn't see how she could walk without tripping herself up. She stood by some very large pots on a separate table at the front. An imperious person stood next to her, arms folded, clearly in charge. She wore a familiar ridiculous cap and had features as sharp as a knife. Matron!

'This here is Dolly Blank, Matron,' the officer announced.

Her narrow mouth puckered in disgust. 'You look appallingly dishevelled, Blank,' she said. 'And you're late for your meal!'

It wasn't *my* fault I was late. I couldn't dismiss myself from that hellish basement and march myself here, pronto. But I was fast learning that it was better not to argue.

'I'm sorry, Matron,' I said, bending my head. My head ached and I felt sick. It was a struggle to stay reasonably upright.

Not reasonably enough.

'Stand up straight, girl!' she commanded.

I did my best to obey.

'And remove that clownish garment on your head!'

I tried to pluck my shift off but it was stuck fast. The matron strode over to me and gave a vicious tug. I shrieked in pain as the fragile scab opened up and the blood started flowing again.

The matron dropped my shift to the floor. 'Clear that rag away, if you please,' she said, pointing to an inmate on the front bench.

The woman hadn't finished her gruel but scurried to remove my shift from the room.

The rest of the women and children carried on eating, concentrating hard on their bowls, taking no notice. The matron watched as blood started trickling down my forehead, but made no comment. She looked at the diminutive cook. 'Clear those vats away. Breakfast is finished,' she said.

I looked at her imploringly. Was she deliberately going to deprive me of breakfast, even though she must know I'd gone

without supper last night? She waited for my response. I took a deep breath and bowed my head meekly again.

'When you've served this slatternly child,' she said.

I nodded my thanks and stood in front of the cook. The thick blanket smell became overpowering as she ladled a very small serving into a wooden bowl. She gestured to me to sit at a bench right at the back, the gruel flying off the ladle and spattering my frock. She sniggered at me, but I didn't dare respond.

I scuttled to the back and sat down at the bench of children. They looked at me enviously, eyeing the meagre contents of my bowl. It looked awful, grey and gritty, with a slimy sheen. I took a tentative mouthful. It stuck in my dry mouth even though I chewed determinedly. A few lumps slithered down my throat like slugs. I clutched my chest, trying to stop myself heaving.

The children saw my watering eyes and reddening face. The girl next to me held out her hand for the bowl. I gave it to her gratefully and she wolfed it down in seconds while I stared in amazement. There were small metal tankards on the table. I reached for one, feeling that milk was better than nothing at all – but the liquid was water, and it tasted foul too.

The matron clapped her hands. 'All stand! Ablutions. Children first. Then women. Then work.'

'What are ablutions?' I whispered to the girl who'd eaten my breakfast.

'When we . . . you know, pee,' she whispered back.

Another girl heard and snorted with laughter, though she clapped her hand over her mouth.

'Silence!' the matron bellowed. 'Another sound and you will all go without your dinner!'

They took this so seriously that they actually walked on tiptoe in their ill-fitting boots. I hurried along with the girl who'd eaten my breakfast. She didn't need to tell me the way to the privies. I simply had to follow my nose. It was the most terrible place but I was so desperate to go that I hardly cared, though it was terribly embarrassing

'Where do we wash our hands?' I whispered to the breakfast girl.

She stared at me blankly. 'We wash on Tuesdays,' she said.

'No, I mean washing our hands after peeing,' I said.

'Why would we do that?' she asked.

'Because of germs.'

'What are they?'

I gave up. 'I'm Dolly. What's your name?' I asked instead.

'Wilma. Shh! We'll catch it if *she* hears.' She nodded her head at a girl bossily marshalling the littlest children out of the privies whether they'd finished on their pots or not.

'She's not much older than us,' I said.

'Yes, but she's in charge, see,' she hissed.

The girl's head turned. 'Wilma! Was you talking to that new girl? How dare you!' She let go of the very small child she was holding, came over and smacked Wilma hard about the head.

'Oh! Don't hit her! It was my fault, I made her talk!' I gabbled.

'Then you'll get what-for too!' she said, and she aimed another smack at me.

'Stop it! You can't *hit* someone – and my head's really badly cut. You'll just make it worse!' I said.

'Good! Teach you a lesson!' she retorted.

'It will teach *you* a lesson if my head starts bleeding really badly again, and I bleed and bleed until I drop down dead and it'll be your fault!' I said.

She seemed momentarily disconcerted, not used to anyone standing up to her. The other children were staring

open-mouthed. Then she frowned fiercely at me. 'I'll say you was being rude – and you *are!*' she said. 'Right! I sort out the duties here. *You* get to go and help out in the sick ward today, because they're short of staff.'

The other children laughed and jeered and held their noses, though Wilma looked sorry for me.

I was pleased though. It would give me a chance to look for Margaret, and I could find a doctor and see if he could clean and stitch up my wound. I had enough wit to look woebegone though, because I guessed the mean girl in charge would change her mind if she realized she was doing me a favour.

It was puzzling. I wasn't sure children were allowed to visit sick wards, let alone 'help out'. I didn't know what that would entail, though I didn't like the way the children held their noses. Surely there couldn't be any worse smell than these dreadful privies?

'Show her the way, Wilma,' the girl ordered.

Wilma took my hand and led me past the other children and the women clustering impatiently for their turn to relieve themselves.

'Have you ever had to help out in the sick ward, Wilma?' I asked.

'Shh! No talking allowed in the corridors! You've already got me into trouble once – but ta for sticking up for me,' she whispered.

'She's a hateful pig for hitting you like that,' I whispered back.

'Yeah, Daisy's ever so mean,' Wilma mumbled.

'Daisy! She's more like Stinging Nettle!' I said.

Wilma stared and then burst out laughing, though she immediately clutched her mouth in horror, looking round anxiously.

'Sorry! But there's no one around to hear us. Have you got a best friend in this awful place, Wilma?'

She seemed puzzled.

'Don't people ever make friends here?' I asked.

Wilma shrugged. Obviously no one had ever made friends with her.

'Can we be friends?' I asked, squeezing her hand.

Wilma shrugged, her white face flushing pale pink.

'We'll look out for each other, you and me,' I said. 'So where will you be today?'

She nibbled her lip. 'Daisy hasn't said yet. Might be scrubbing. Or washing. Or they might start me on picking oakum like the big girls. Everything hurts your hands though.'

I looked at her hand in mine. It was rubbed red, though the rest of her skinny arm was a dirty white.

'Don't we have to do lessons?' I asked.

'Someone comes in to teach us if there's time. A is for apple, B is for bird, C is for castle, stuff like that,' she said, gabbling the sentence as if it meant nothing to her. But then it didn't look as if she had any chance of eating an apple, seeing birds flying in the sky, or looking at a castle in this grim prison.

'Maybe I could teach you. I can read,' I said.

She looked impressed. 'How come?' she asked.

'My mother taught me,' I said, which was true whichever time I was living in.

'I ain't got no mother. She died when she had me and I was taken here,' Wilma said matter-of-factly.

'So you've been brought up in the workhouse ever since you were a baby?' I asked. 'How awful for you!'

Wilma shrugged again.

'Would you like me to teach you to read?' I asked.

'Can't learn. Daisy says I'm stupid,' said Wilma.

'No you're not! You just don't know very much, and that's entirely different, not at all your fault. Don't worry, I won't let

that horrible Daisy bully you! I'll always stick up for you,'
I declared.

'But then you'll get sent to Darky,' said Wilma.

I shivered. I didn't think I could stand another night in that
terrible basement. Maybe I wouldn't dare stick up for poor
Wilma after all. It seemed dreadful that fear stopped you doing
the kind things you wanted to do.

There was another smell drifting along the endless corridor
now. It was getting stronger and stronger. A terrible smell of
sad sick people and an overpowering stench of used bedpans.
Wilma lifted her institution frock up to her face without any
concerns about modesty.

'It stinks, don't it?' she said. 'You won't like the sick ward
one bit. They're awful, them sick folk.'

'They can't help being sick,' I said. I couldn't understand
why the ward smelled so dreadfully. Weren't hospital wards
supposed to be ultra-clean places with poorly patients lying
between crisp white sheets?

'They're horrid. They smell. They frighten me,' said
Wilma. 'I'm going back. You go in that door down there.' She
pulled her hand free and went tearing down the corridor, her
boots clumping.

'Wilma!' I called after her. For all my resolution, the sick were frightening me too. I breathed deeply to try to calm myself, but that was a big mistake. I very nearly vomited. I leaned against the clammy brown-painted wall. I put my hand to my head, wondering if it was bleeding again.

The wound seemed to be scabbing over now, but a little yellow stuff rubbed off on my fingers. Was it getting infected? I needed to see a doctor quickly. I forced myself to march right up to the door and open it. The smell was overwhelming.

I looked around me. I was in a long narrow room with rows of iron beds up and down its length. Each was occupied. Many were lying crammed two in a bed, so that if one turned over the other was in danger of tumbling out. Ancient old women were lying on their backs, eyes shut, mouths open. Younger women fidgeted, hair tangled, sweat on their brows. Some were disfigured with pox and others so gaunt you could see the bones under their skin. And there was Margaret, in a bed of her own, but her wrists were tied to the bedposts so she could barely move.

I ran to her. She cried out when she saw me, trying to sit up, though it was impossible.

'Oh Margaret, what have they done to you?' I cried.

'I tried to find where they're keeping my boys but they caught me and tied me up,' she wept. 'I haven't even been allowed to use the privy! It's so humiliating!' She began to cough in her agitation, struggling to catch her breath.

'How dare they? Don't you worry, Margaret, I'll set you free!' I said, trying to undo the knots.

There was an angry shout from the other end of the room. A large woman in pauper's uniform came lumbering over, the officer's lurid badge sewn onto her huge chest.

'What do you think you're doing, girl! Leave them ropes alone!' she shouted at me.

'But she's choking, can't you see?' I said, still picking at the knots.

'She's just trying it on, that one. She'll keep escaping if we set her free,' she said, catching hold of me and hauling me away as easily as if I was a rag doll.

'She's *ill*! Listen to that cough. She has a fever! I'm going to go and fetch a nurse, and you shan't stop me!' I said.

'Hold your tongue! *I'm* the nurse,' she said.

'You're not a nurse! You're one of the inmates,' I said.

'Can't you see my badge? I'm the nurse and what I say goes. Your precious friend here says she's got a cough, that's

all, nothing to make a fuss about.'

I saw blood trickling from Margaret's mouth, though she turned her head away as far as she could, trying to hide it.

'There!' I said. 'See! She's coughing up blood. Surely you know that's serious?'

The so-called nurse did look a little disconcerted then. 'I suppose it *could* be the white plague,' she said. 'She's certainly pale enough, I grant you.'

'No!' Margaret gasped. 'I'm not ill! Let me up! Let me work!'

'See!' said the nurse triumphantly.

'She's desperate to work so she can get out of here to be with her boys again,' I said. 'Look, when does the doctor make his rounds?'

The nurse burst out laughing. 'We ain't got a doctor! Mr Greaves the medical officer sometimes looks in during the morning, but you can't depend on it. Now leave that woman be, and come and help. We've got at least ten of these dirty souls to strip and change before we can serve breakfast.'

It was the worst task I'd ever had to perform. I hated having to wash the poor sick people with an inadequate rag and a filthy bucket of water, but I tried not to make too much of a

fuss because I felt so sorry for them. Some just lay there indifferently, as if they barely noticed what I was doing. Others moaned and closed their eyes tight. One frail old woman was so slight and her skin so papery I only dared dab at her in case I hurt her terribly.

'Thank you, dearie,' she murmured. 'Very grateful.'

I was so touched I nearly cried. This was such a bleak place that it was good to remember there were still kind people here too.

I held her hand and her small misshapen fingers clasped mine. 'This is no place for a little girl like you,' she murmured.

'This is no place for a little lady like you,' I said.

She gave me a smile, which made her look so sweet, even though she had no teeth.

'Oi, you! Don't stand there idle! Get on with your job!' the nurse yelled at me.

'Oh dear,' I said. 'I wish I could stay here and have a chat with you.'

'Needs must,' said the old lady, and she unclasped her fingers and crossed her hands on her chest in a disconcerting fashion. She even closed her eyes as if she were dead.

I gave a little gasp and they flickered open again.

'Don't worry,' she said, smiling again. 'I'm only practising!'

I chuckled and went to the next patient, a woman with a heavily lined face and tousled hair a strange shade of orange. She was very short of breath and holding her chest.

'What you got to be so bleeding cheery about?' she gasped furiously.

It was clear she didn't want me to hold *her* hand. I made my way round the beds, trying hard to clean every patient who needed attention. Some had really wet or dirty sheets. I hurried to the nurse.

'Where do we keep the clean sheets, please?' I asked.

'Ain't got none. Them lazy girls in the laundry tippled on the beer last night and have only just got out their beds!' she said. 'They'll have to do without today.'

'But that's awful! Surely there must be some clean bedding somewhere?' I said.

'What do you think this is, a blooming palace? Hurry up, will you? It will be lunchtime before they've had their breakfast at this rate,' she snapped.

Breakfast was appalling – the same gruel that we'd been served, but now stone cold. Some had milk to drink, but it was pale grey rather than white and had obviously been watered

down. If the patients weren't well enough to sit up then the nurse rammed spoonfuls of gruel into their mouths and held their beakers to their lips so carelessly that half the contents spilled over their faces and chests.

I scurried round, making sure I got to help Margaret and the dear old lady, wishing I could look after everyone properly. Before we'd finished, a plump man with an important air and little gold spectacles came marching into the sick ward, his polished boots ringing on the stone flooring. He held a yellow silk handkerchief to his nose.

The nurse stopped what she was doing and dropped a hasty curtsy. 'Morning, Mr Greaves, sir,' she said.

'Morning, morning! Dear goodness, what a stench! Surely it isn't too much to ask you to keep the patients clean and tidy,' he said, shuddering in an exaggerated fashion.

'Beg pardon, sir, but Polly's near broke her back lifting a patient and can't move out her bed for the agony – and all they've sent to help me out is this useless girl,' she said, gesturing at me.

I ran forward and copied the nurse, bobbing a curtsy. 'Good morning, sir,' I said as politely as I could. 'I am trying

very hard to please and be useful, though I've never done this kind of work before.'

I thought he'd be astonished that I was so young and inexperienced, but he barely looked at me.

'Well, do the best you can do, child,' he said dismissively.

He started walking quickly up and down the rows of beds, with the nurse scurrying behind him. He occasionally paused to mutter a command: 'Bed number three, tincture of iodine'; or 'Bed number six, extra milk for nourishment'; or 'Bed number eight, laudanum if agitated'. He prescribed as if he was treating the beds themselves, not the patients in them.

He didn't seem surprised by poor Margaret's bonds. 'Imbecile?' he asked the nurse.

'Keeps trying to escape, sir. She has to be restrained for her own good,' she replied.

I was so horrified I had to speak up. 'If you please, sir, the lady is very ill, with a cough and a fever,' I said.

'No, no, I have caught a cold, that is all!' Margaret mumbled hoarsely.

'She's saying that because she wants to work. She's fretting about her boys. But she's coughing up blood, sir. You've seen it, haven't you, Nurse?' I said.

'Only a little,' she said. She raised her eyebrows enquiringly. 'Perhaps you'd care to advise, sir?'

'A drop or two of laudanum, then, for soothing purposes,' he said, as if he was being incredibly generous. 'But remember supplies are very limited. Well, I think that is all. No more new patients, Nurse?'

'No, sir,' she said, folding her hands in front of her large stomach and nodding.

'I'm not actually a patient, sir, but I wonder if you could just take a look at the wound on my head?' I said, pointing at it.

The medical officer sighed but peered through his little gold spectacles at my matted hair and bloody wound. He seemed mildly surprised. 'Who did this to you?' he asked. 'Another inmate?'

'It was actually a policeman, sir. He had hold of me and when I struggled he struck my head against a brick wall!' I said.

'By accident, no doubt, whilst you were attempting to escape,' said the medical officer.

'It was deliberate, sir!' I said indignantly.

'A likely story! Don't widen those blue eyes and act all

innocent. I know your type!' he said. 'Keep an eye on this child, Nurse. Watch her like a hawk when you dispense the medicine. We don't want her trying to trade it for extra rations,' he said.

'I wouldn't do that, I promise!' I said. 'But I wonder if I could have a little medicine myself, because I think the wound is getting infected. Shouldn't it be stitched up?'

'A mild skin abrasion? Certainly not! Just keep it clean!' he said. He consulted his watch. 'I must be off to the men's ward. I am already lamentably behind. I was detained by some wretched woman giving birth. Yet another infant born in sin!'

'But I haven't been *able* to keep it clean, sir! I missed going to the bath-house yesterday because I was sent straight down to that awful basement,' I said.

'Then you must have been exceptionally wicked, child,' said the medical officer, and swept me aside, marching briskly out of the ward.

I couldn't get to grips with this terrible place. No wonder Algie and poor Boy dreaded being sent to the workhouse. I might be kept here until I lay in one of these awful unclean beds like the little old women in their greying bonnets and

tattered nightgowns.

I leaned against the wall, flakes of aged whitewash prickling my back.

'Here, noodle, don't go all droopy on me! Come and help hand out the medicines,' the nurse commanded.

She took me to a little cupboard, raised a key from the girdle round her waist and opened the door. There were blue bottles, brown bottles, green bottles, round pillboxes in different sizes, each carefully labelled in neat copperplate, plus a pitcher of milk and several small beakers. The milk didn't look or smell very fresh, but that couldn't be helped.

'Shall I pour the milk for the patients that need extra nourishment?' I asked.

'Not necessary,' said the nurse.

'But the medical officer prescribed it for the lady in bed number six, and—'

'I've worked these wards for the last twenty years and so I think I know what I'm doing,' the horrid nurse said.

She knew what she was doing all right. I watched her throughout the morning. Every twenty minutes or so she went to the little cupboard, and when she returned to the main ward she often had a film of white about her thin lips.

She was drinking the patients' milk herself! No wonder she was one of the few plump people amongst the inmates. I hoped the milk was really on the turn and gave her a bad stomachache.

I learned something even more horrifying when we doled out the proper medicine that first morning.

'Laudanum, bed number eight – plus the new patient. One drop each,' she said, handing me the green bottle.

'Tincture of iodine, bed number three,' she said, selecting a brown bottle and handing it to me. But it didn't say *Tincture of Iodine*. The copperplate handwriting clearly said *Essence of Peppermint*.

'Excuse me, Nurse, but I think you might have made a mistake,' I said.

She sighed impatiently. 'Tincture of iodine, that's exactly what Mr Greaves ordered for bed number three.'

'Yes, I know, but it says *Essence of Peppermint* on the label – look!' I said.

She looked, screwing up her eyes. She pointed along the copperplate with her finger. 'Ah yes,' she said breezily. 'Essence of peppermint is almost the same. It aids the digestion, you know. Probably do her more good.'

She couldn't fool me. She was the chief nurse of this ward of very sick patients, in charge of giving them their medicine – and she couldn't read!

Chapter Seventeen

I felt faint with hunger but the nurse made me wait for dinner until after two, when all the patients had been fed.

'I haven't had *my* dinner, have I?' she said. '*I'm* not complaining.'

She wasn't hungry though, because she'd secretly swallowed a pint and a half of the patients' milk, but I held my tongue. I was trying to make her like me a little, because she could be a cruel enemy. I managed to persuade her to untie poor Margaret when she was barely conscious after the dose of laudanum. I cleaned her up and whispered in her ear that I'd do my level best to find out where her boys were and bring her news of

them. Her eyes were closed, but tears slowly seeped from under the lids, and she murmured their names, Ralph and Algernon.

'I have a friend called Algie!' I said. 'But I don't suppose I'll ever see him again.'

I found I was crying too, out of longing and loneliness and fear. If only I could remember the way back to that other life where I was loved and clean and well fed. Margaret reached out and drowsily patted my back. I put my arms round her too.

'You're here to nurse the patients, not to cuddle and cosset them,' said the nurse. 'And if your friend here really has the white plague, you're risking getting it too, you little fool.'

'I don't care,' I said, and I almost meant it.

I cried again when she let me fetch my dinner at last. I'd been told it was meat and potatoes and I'd been fantasizing about a stew with gravy and mash. I suppose the small portion of food I had doled onto my tin plate could just about be described as such. The stew was a runny greyish liquid with small lumps of mutton and yellow fat. The potatoes were grey and watery with black eyes and signs of blight. It was cold, already congealing, with a light film of grease.

I filled my spoon and held it to my lips, my hand trembling. It tasted even worse than it looked but I knew I couldn't keep

going without any food. I forced myself to put tiny spoonfuls in my mouth, chewing until I managed to swallow. I couldn't cope with the fatty lumps even though I tried my hardest, and had to spit them back onto the plate, defeated.

Several of the patients were watching me.

'Are you not wanting that?' one woman asked. 'I'll have it!'

She had some strange malady that made her fidget continually, scratching at her arms and even her face, so that she had marks all over her. She was a strange colour too, yellowish, like a fading tan, though she clearly never saw any sun inside the workhouse.

'I'd give it to you gladly, but it's only fat – and it's been in my mouth,' I said.

'Who cares? Give it here!' she said.

I did so, though I couldn't bear to watch her swallow it down. I wondered if I would ever get to that stage when I'd eat anything at all, no matter how disgusting. The poor woman still clawed at herself as she ate, seeming not to notice what she was doing.

I went over to the nurse, who was tucking into her own dinner. It was very different from the food served up to the rest of us. She had a pie with a golden crust oozing chunks of good

steak and a rich brown gravy, and a mound of creamy mashed potato. She saw me staring at it. She had a tankard of beer to wash it down too.

'Officers' perks,' she said smugly, not the slightest embarrassed.

I knew there was no point commenting. 'There's a poor lady in bed thirteen who keeps scratching terribly,' I said.

'Oh, her. I think she should be sent back to the itch ward where the dirty folk with scabies go, but some young pipsqueak nurse there insists she's got something wrong with her liver, just because she's gone yellow,' said the nurse. 'It gets on your nerves all that scratching, don't it, but Mr Greaves says she's not got long to go.'

'Oh, the poor thing!' I said.

'Well, she's brought it on herself, I reckon. Too much gin,' she said, tutting, and then she took another swig of her beer.

Luckily the beer and her big meal made her sleepy, and before long she was slumped in her easy chair, snoring. I took the opportunity to go and check on Margaret. She was properly awake now, her eyes wide open and staring round in horror at the grim ward. She was trying to climb out of bed, though she

was so weak she could scarcely struggle out of the tightly tucked sheet.

'Please don't try to get up, Margaret. That hateful nurse will only tie you up again. Just lie still and rest a while. It'll help your cough.'

She did lie back quietly then. I held her hand and sang softly to her to try to soothe her. It was a sad song about looking for someone to love. I remembered the tune from a long time ago – or maybe far into the future. It comforted her and she dozed off again.

I wandered up and down the ward, wiping the faces of the patients who had eaten their horrible meals so eagerly, trying to show them I wasn't like the callous nurse and that I really did care about them. Few seemed grateful for the attention, and several swore at me.

'Come over here, dearie,' my old lady called. 'Don't be upset. It's not you they're cross with. Come and sing that pretty song to me now.'

I went to sit on her bed and I sang the song for her.

'That was beautiful! Made my day!' she said, smiling.

'How long have you been living here?' I asked.

'Too long!' she said.

'Since you were my age?'

'Oh good Lord, no! About ten years, I reckon – but it could be longer, it could be shorter. You lose track of time, though I don't suppose you'll understand that yet,' she said.

'Oh, I do!' I said. 'So were you so poor you had to come here?'

'I've never had much money, dear, but I managed comfortably enough. But then my husband died and I became crippled with rheumatism and couldn't manage. It was the sadness of my life that I couldn't have children, so there was no one to help me out. So this is where I ended up,' she said simply.

'But isn't there anywhere else where elderly people can be cared for?' I asked.

'If I knew of it I wouldn't be here!' she said, with a wry chuckle. 'What about you, my lamb?'

I struggled to explain. 'My mother died and I worked for a woman making dolls, but then I ran away and a policeman brought me here,' I said. 'But – but before that – I had this other life, I know I did, though I can't remember it properly now. Oh, I do so wish I could get back to it!'

'Poor dear,' she said, patting my hand. 'It's hardest of all for the children here, especially the ones who have known

nothing else. At least I've had a good life and can lie here remembering it.'

'I'll try harder to do that too,' I said. 'But it's so difficult and I'm so hungry and my head hurts so! *Why* won't they clean it up for me and make it better?'

'It seems dreadful, I know. I daresay they preach that cleanliness is next to godliness in the chapel every Sunday. I don't think they're deliberately cruel. They're just used to the way it works and it's easier not to think of us as human beings. We're only inmates. We don't even have names in here. I'm Bed Seventeen to them. No one knows or cares that I'm Lavinia Mary Martinet.'

'How do you do, Lavinia?' I said.

'I'm as well as can be expected!' she said. 'So what is your name, my dear?'

'Well, I call myself Dolly now, but that's not my real name. My name is—'

'*Girl!*' It was the nurse, furiously emerging from her office. 'How dare you lie down with a patient! You're totally unsuitable for this work! Get out of my ward. I'll be better off by myself.'

I was sent away in disgrace. I was given strict instructions on how to find the girls' room – but after going down that very

long corridor I deliberately turned left instead of right. My heart beat fast when I saw two male officers with red and yellow badges sewn on their shabby jackets, walking towards me. I hunched up, lowering my chin to my chest, keeping close to the wall. They went on chatting to each other, barely noticing me. It seemed I was just an inmate, of no gender and no name and no interest whatsoever.

I scuttled forward, turned a corner, and heard the strange sound of hammering coming from behind a door. My heart beat fast, wondering what on earth was happening. Someone screamed. Was this where the beating happened?

I dared peep round the door and saw a group of young boys sitting at cobblers' lasts, working on the soles of worn-out boots, hammering in the nails. Several boys were too small for this work and were given the task of running backward and forward with the nails for the toiling boys. I noticed one very little child putting a nail in his mouth, and ran towards him anxiously.

'No! No! Spit it out!' I cried.

'Won't hurt him, miss,' said a small boy, not much older. 'He always does it and nothing happens. Reckon he'd jingle if you picked him up and shook him!'

A bigger boy stopped hammering and put his finger to his lips, nodding at the back of an officer, who was stooping over some unfortunate lad who had hammered his hand and started shrieking.

I reckoned there was enough noise going on for me to risk staying a few seconds. 'Do you know boys called Ralph and Algernon?' I asked the big boy.

He shrugged and shook his head.

'They're new here. Only came yesterday. They were very upset,' I persisted.

'Ah, them. The snivellers,' he said, and pointed to a corner.

A dark boy about twelve was sitting at a cobbler's last, trying to bash at a boot with great determination but no skill at all. A smaller one was cowering right in the corner, a fistful of nails in either hand, his face red and blotched with crying.

I scurried over to them. 'Are you Ralph and Algernon?' I hissed.

They stared at me anxiously. Ralph nodded, while Algernon tried to put his thumb in his mouth, but couldn't free it for the nails, so gnawed on his knuckles instead.

'It's all right. It's about your mother,' I said.

They repeated the word 'mother' tearfully.

'She's in the sick ward but they're trying hard to make her better,' I lied, because it seemed kindest to reassure them. 'She sends her love to you. She says you'll be together again one day.' This was an even worse thing to tell them, because it didn't seem likely at all.

Still, it made both boys smile in spite of the tears rolling down their cheeks.

'I'll tell your mother you sent your love back to her, shall I?' I asked, and they both nodded hard.

The officer straightened up, yawning and stretching,

seemingly unconcerned about the child who was still screaming. I didn't dare wait any longer.

'Remember, your mother loves you so much,' I gabbled, and then made a run for the door.

I didn't think the officer had spotted me but I ran as fast as I could down the corridor, until I eventually found my way to the girls' room in the female quarters. There were two women there as well, one feeding a tiny baby who only looked a few days old. The other wore a red and yellow officer badge and was supervising the girls at their work.

Daisy sat at the front, clearly doing more than her fair share of supervising too. She was stitching away like the others, but when she heard the tiniest mouse-whispers between two little girls of six or so, she grabbed the cane by her side. I went cold with horror. She just reached forward and gave each child a little poke – but the threat was there. The officer nodded approvingly at Daisy and she smiled smugly back at her. Then she glared at me.

'What are you doing back here? I said you had to go to the sick ward!' she said crossly.

'The nurse sent me away,' I said. 'You can go and ask her if you like.'

'What did you do? Kill a patient?' Daisy asked.

I wasn't sure if she was joking or not. 'I was too kind to them. She didn't like it,' I said.

'Trust you!' said Daisy. She delved in a big basket and threw a dirty workhouse frock at me. There was a great tear at the back. 'You'd better get stitching then.'

Wilma put her hand up uncertainly. 'Shall I show her how, Daisy?' she said timidly.

'No you can't!' Daisy snapped. 'You've got your own work to do. She'll pick it up soon enough. And woe betide her if she doesn't, eh, Officer Tiptree!'

The officer cackled, thinking this a great joke. But the joke was on them! I selected needle and thread from the communal sewing basket and looked for an empty chair. Daisy immediately put her feet up on it, stopping me sitting on it. Everyone was watching. Wilma looked anxious.

I kept my face as calm as I could. I wasn't going to let hateful Daisy humiliate me! I sat down cross-legged like a tailor, turned the frock inside out and spread it across my lap, then tried to thread my needle. I was usually adept at this, but I couldn't stop my hands shaking, and the coarse thread wouldn't go through the small eye of the needle. I heard

sniggering. I kept my head bent, because I could feel myself blushing and I didn't want them to see. At last, on the sixth or seventh attempt, the needle was threaded.

The room was silent as they watched. Even the baby stopped suckling. I willed my fingers to stop shaking and started sewing. I was Dolly the doll-maker, and I could stitch in my sleep. I was quick and neat. My material didn't pucker. I didn't get knots in my thread. I sewed and sewed, and I heard Wilma's little '*oh!*' of surprise and relief.

When my cheeks had cooled I risked looking up. They were all staring at me. Daisy had her mouth hanging open. She looked as if she'd been poked in the stomach with her own cane.

Officer Tiptree came to stand over me. She smelled sourly unpleasant though perhaps it wasn't her fault. Maybe she had to wait for Tuesdays to get clean too. Her greying cap was pulled too far down so that it skimmed her eyebrows. Her hair was pulled up underneath so that her scraggy neck seemed unusually long and large.

She lowered this impressive neck to peer at my stitches. I'd learned to keep them very small and even.

'Mmm!' she said. That was all. Not a word of praise. When I'd sewn up the long rent in double-quick time,

she actually told me off. 'Don't be too hasty, girl, or you'll make a mistake and have to do it again,' she said. She threw another frock at me from the unwashed clothing, this one unpleasantly stained. The hem had come down. 'Turn it up!' she commanded.

'Certainly, ma'am,' I said, and settled down to sew again, acting as if it was a special treat, just to annoy her.

I was used to sewing for long hours but we didn't stop until seven here, when my neck and arms and back were aching, and my hands kept cramping. The younger children were yawning pitifully, and one little girl fell asleep as she sewed and pricked herself with her needle.

Officer Tiptree consulted her pocket watch and clapped her hands. 'Supper time!'

We still had a long hungry wait because we had to put everything away neatly, and then queue with crossed legs at the privies, then wait in another queue outside the dining room while the working women finished their own meal. As they filed out, a couple of the women sought their children in the queue and gave them a heartfelt hug before being marched off to their dormitories. The officer on duty in the corridor was surprisingly kind and nodded sympathetically.

The children without mothers watched enviously, their eyes big with longing. Wilma looked particularly sad. I dared sidle up to her and put my arm round her.

'I wish I had a mother,' she said.

'I know. I do too,' I said – thinking of my own lost mother in my other life. I must have screwed up my face because Wilma asked, 'Do you have a pain?'

'Only a sad one,' I said.

She looked puzzled. Perhaps she was so used to being sad that she didn't know you could feel anything else.

'Like being hungry?' she asked. 'But we get supper now and that's the best meal.'

'Really?' I said suspiciously.

'We get cheese!' said Wilma.

'Just cheese?'

'With bread,' she said.

I thought of a cheese sandwich – fresh, crusty, buttered bread with thick layers of cheddar. My mouth really watered and little bubbles of spit gathered at a corner of my lips.

'Oh, cheese and bread!' I said.

'And beer!' said Wilma.

'*Beer?*' It seemed a bizarre drink for children. 'Are you teasing me?'

Wilma looked puzzled. She didn't look as if she knew what I meant. 'Beer,' she said again.

Oh well, Missus had given me light beer, and I'd developed quite a taste for it. But workhouse beer proved very different. It had no froth at all and was just like coloured water. The bread and cheese was a bitter disappointment too. The bread was coarse and stale, without even a scraping of butter, and the cheese was thimble size, gone in a mouthful. Wilma was looking at me hopefully, wondering if she was going to get any of my leavings this time, but I was so hungry I gulped it down ravenously. I even copied the other children and licked my finger and ran it round the platter for stray crumbs.

I saw piles of bread and rounds of cheese still on the serving counter.

'Can't we have any more?' I asked Wilma.

'No!' said Wilma. 'They'll save anything that's left for tomorrow.'

'But it's stale already! That officer seems quite nice. Shall I ask him?' I suggested.

'You mustn't! You'll get into terrible trouble! You'll be sent to Darky,' Wilma gabbled in fright.

That shut me up. I'd rather go hungry than risk another night there.

'So what happens now? Do we get to play?' I asked.

Wilma looked baffled again.

'You know, run about and chat to each other and . . . have fun.' My voice died away. She didn't need to answer me. There was obviously no playtime on the workhouse timetable.

'It's privy and then bed,' said Wilma. 'Sleep time is the best because we don't do nothing. Then it's wake up and privy and breakfast, then work and privy and dinner, then work and privy and supper, then privy and bed.'

'What if we need to go to the privy in-between times?' I asked.

'We're not allowed,' said Wilma.

'Supposing we're absolutely bursting? Do we just wet ourselves?'

'We're not allowed,' Wilma repeated. 'You get a hard smack. And if you wet the bed you have a hard smack too.' She looked woebegone. This obviously had happened to her quite often.

'That's nonsense! It's not your fault if you wet the bed. You can't help it,' I said fiercely. 'I can't stand this place. It's so unfair. Doesn't anyone ever complain?'

'They get sent to Matron then,' said Wilma. 'If you've been very bad you get your hair shaved right off your head and you can't even cover it with your cap.'

'She doesn't *actually* do that, does she?' I asked.

'She does, God's honest truth.' Wilma put her hand up under her cap, as if checking her hair was still there. 'She did it to me once because someone shouted a bad word in chapel and Daisy said it was me, but it wasn't, honest.'

'Oh, I hate that Daisy. So you really, truly had your head shaved, you poor thing?' I said.

'It was all scrapes too, and they bled, and then it was bristly and itchy and everyone laughed at me,' said Wilma. 'It took ages and ages to grow back.'

'Well, it's lovely hair now,' I said. It was thin and mousey, like Wilma herself, but I wanted to make her feel better.

I hoped I might be able to sleep next to her at night so we could reach out in the darkness and hold hands, but Daisy put me right at the other end of the large dormitory, sharing with a big rough girl who didn't look at all pleased at the idea. She

had a grey-white face, but her arms and hands were mottled dark red.

'I don't want to share, especially not with a kiddie!' she said.

'Well, you've got to,' said Daisy. 'Do you want me to report you?'

'I've a good mind to report *you*,' the rough girl retorted. 'You do hardly any work. You just order the little kids about like you was the Queen. You should be taking your turn in the laundry with us.'

'You shut your trap and do as you're told!' Daisy snapped.

She only came up to the rough girl's shoulders, but the bigger girl reluctantly gave in.

'Why does everyone have to do what Daisy says?' I whispered, when she'd marched off to remonstrate with some poor little child who was crying.

'Because she's hand in glove with blooming Matron and all the officers,' the rough girl complained. 'Makes me sick. Matron took a shine to her when she was tiny, started making a special fuss of her and calling her Daisy. And Daisy plays up to her, acting sweet as sugar when she's around her, to get favours. Ugh!'

I said 'Ugh' too, though I felt uncomfortable when I remembered the way I'd sometimes acted with Missus. I was prepared to act smarmy with the rough girl too, so she wouldn't kick me out of bed in the middle of the night.

'What's your name? I'm Dolly,' I said.

'I'm Gert. Do you wet the bed, Dolly?' she asked.

'No!' I said. 'I'm not a baby!'

'Last time I shared, the girl peed the bed every night. I felt like strangling her,' said Gert.

I prayed that my bladder wouldn't let me down. The girls and women took off their frocks, laid them at the ends of their beds, and went to bed in their shifts. I didn't know what to do, as I'd used my shift as a bandage, and now it had been thrown away. I felt too shy to climb into bed stark naked apart from my socks, so I kept my frock on.

It was a very narrow bed. When Gert turned over I had to cling to the edge. We had just a sheet over us, but at least it wasn't dirty, and Gert herself smelled freshly of soap. I realized from the state of her arms that it was punishing work pounding dirty linen in the laundry all day, but it must be a joy to keep yourself clean.

I breathed in her smell, longing for Tuesday to come so that

I could get clean again too. Someone started crying in one of the beds, a small despairing wail, and then someone else joined in, then someone else, and someone else. They were muffled sobs underneath the sheets for fear of punishment. It was the saddest sound I'd ever heard. I was sure one of them was Wilma.

I struggled to get up, but Gert grabbed me by the hem of my frock. 'Don't!' she whispered huskily. 'You're not allowed to get up!'

'But they're crying!'

'They always do. It's a habit. They'll sleep after a while. But if Daisy sees you she'll report you and you'll end up sleeping in Darky and *you'll* be the one crying then,' Gert said. 'Now get back under the cover and go to sleep.'

I did as I was told, because I knew she was telling the truth. I didn't think I'd be able to sleep with that sad sobbing around me, but I was so tired I actually fell asleep in moments. I didn't wake up until Officer Tiptree started ringing a loud bell in the morning.

I had to concentrate so hard on not wetting myself queueing for the privy that I didn't dare leave my place to go and find Wilma, but I caught her up as we filed down the corridor towards the dining room.

Her eyelids were swollen and her eyes red, but she smiled when she saw me.

'Hello, Dolly. Can I have your gruel if you don't want it?' she asked.

It wasn't really the warmest greeting of friendship, but I understood. In fact, my own stomach was so horribly empty that I found it an effort to give her even a mouthful of the grey lumpy stuff. It smelled and tasted just as disgusting, but it was food, and I found that was all that mattered.

Wilma thanked me for the scraping I gave her. 'Will you help me thread my needle today?' she asked in the corridor afterwards. 'My hands are always too clumsy.'

My own hands were shaky and I had a splitting headache. I didn't know if it was because of the lack of food, or the wound on my head. It was hurting more than ever now.

'Wilma, could you bear to look at my head and tell me what the wound looks like?' I asked her.

She glanced at it quickly, wrinkling her nose. 'It looks horrid,' she said.

'But what sort of horrid? Is it still red? Or is it going a nasty yellowy colour?'

'Both,' she said.

'Oh dear,' I said weakly. 'That sounds bad.'

'Will you die?' Wilma asked bluntly.

'No!' I said. 'You can't die from a cut on the head, can you?'

'Folk here die of lots of things,' said Wilma. 'But don't you die, Dolly. I like you.'

'I won't,' I promised her. I didn't care if she only liked me because I shared my food with her. She was still my friend.

I couldn't thread her needle for her though, because Daisy sent me to the sick ward again.

'But she's better than any of us at sewing, Daisy,' one of the girls pointed out.

'No she's not. And I'm not having her swanking about it,' Daisy said illogically.

I wondered if the nurse would send me straight back, but she was in a better mood because the other nurse had returned to work in the ward, though she was very slow and stiff. She stopped every five minutes to rub her back and called it all the names under the sun. But, in spite of her swearing, she was cheerier than the other nurse, and treated the patients better too. She seemed to have made a pet of my favourite old lady and they chatted away together.

I was glad to see that Margaret wasn't tied up this time,

though she looked so weak and white I didn't think she'd have had the strength to struggle out of bed. She'd been given a rag to cough into and I saw that it was already stained bright red. Her eyes were closed.

'Just listen one minute before you go to sleep,' I whispered to her. 'I went to see your boys!'

Her eyelids snapped open. 'Ralph and Algernon?' she said.

'Yes, both of them, and I told them how much you love them and they were very cheered,' I said. 'And they send you all the love in the world and say you're the best mother ever and they can't wait until you can be back together again.'

'Truly?' Margaret gasped, between racking coughs.

'Truly!' I lied stoutly.

I hoped with all my heart that she believed me. Her coughing eased a little. Her eyes closed again. I went on whispering reassuringly until I was sure she was asleep. I knew I should be changing her bedding but I couldn't bear to disturb her.

I crept away. The horrid nurse glared at me while she sat another patient up and poked her into a cleanish nightdress as if she had no more feelings than one of the dolls I used to dress.

'What did I tell you about wasting time chatting?' she said.

She sighed and addressed the other nurse, Polly. 'I sent her back early yesterday. She's useless.'

'I think she's rather a dear little thing. And she's got a strong stomach and that's what's needed here,' she said. She looked at me. 'But what's happened to your poor old bonce, child? Did you take a tumble?'

'A policeman rammed it into a wall days ago. And now I think it's going bad. Oh please, could you clean it up for me?' I asked, wondering if someone might help me at last.

'Are you still fussing about that little cut?' said the nurse in charge. 'Stop your whining and get on with the beds!' She turned to her companion. 'Told you, Polly, she's a waste of time.'

But Nurse Polly took hold of me and led me over to one of the windows. She pulled the blind up and peered hard at my head, gently parting my hair to see the wound properly.

'Looks nasty to me,' she said.

'I need . . .'. I knew there was a word for the tablets that cleared up infections but I couldn't think what it was. Perhaps they didn't even exist in this life. I started crying in exasperation.

'Don't take on so, dear,' said kind Nurse Polly. 'I've heard that milk is good for cleaning wounds. Let's try with that.'

'We ain't got any milk going spare!' said the horrid nurse,

though I'd watched her drink it down thirstily yesterday.

'All right. You're in charge, after all,' said Nurse Polly, but she gave me a reassuring wink. Perhaps she was going to help me after all.

I had to wait until after dinner, when the horrid nurse put her feet up and took a nap. Nurse Polly came over to me, where I was still trying to feed Margaret, worried that she was so very thin.

'We'll try this poor soul with some milk,' she whispered. 'And then we'll see about bathing your poor old bonce with the rest. It can't do you any harm, and it might just do you some good.'

Chapter Eighteen

Milk seemed a very odd way of treating a wound but I was prepared to try anything. It was soothing to have Nurse Polly mop my poor head and then gently dab the milk on. The familiar throb eased a little by the time I went to bed, and she was pleased when she inspected it the next day in the ward.

'It looks a lot healthier already,' she whispered, while Nurse Horrid was forcibly spooning medicine into a reluctant patient. 'We'll dab it with milk again when you-know-who is napping.'

I wasn't sure I liked the smell of milk on my head, but there were so many other smells to deal with it seemed a minor

problem, and no one commented. The next day we were woken up extra early and Officer Tiptree passed round a few stiff hairbrushes.

'Tidy your hair and pass it on – and take your Sunday cap from the table as you file out,' she barked.

'What's happening?' I asked Gert.

She groaned, shielding her eyes from the light, not shifting. She smelled of stolen beer as well as clean washing now. She had been unusually jolly going to bed and had snored very heavily all night.

'Gert, get up this second, you lazy wretch!' Officer Tiptree shouted.

'Not well, miss,' Gert moaned.

'That's your own fault. Now get up or I'll kick you out!'

Gert rolled out of bed, and then was immediately sick on the floor. There was a gasp of horror as we all stared.

'I'll report you to Matron!' said Officer Tiptree. 'Now go and get a bucket, dowse your head in it, and then clean up that disgusting mess.'

'Then can I get back in bed?' Gert mumbled.

'No, you cannot! You're going to chapel even if I have to drag you there bodily,' said the officer.

'That's it, miss, you tell her. Everyone knows what she was up to last night,' said hateful Daisy.

Poor Gert struggled to do as she was told, and she looked so ill I hoped she wasn't going to be sick again in chapel. I took a cap for myself and crammed it on. I supposed I looked like a real inmate now. A workhouse waif! I still wore my own frock, though it was more a crumpled rag than a proper dress now.

We had to walk in file to chapel after privy and breakfast.

'Let me guess what it is for breakfast,' I muttered to Wilma. 'Gruel!'

'Wrong!' said Wilma, and she giggled like an ordinary little girl.

I wondered if it might be proper porridge, maybe sweetened with a little honey? But it was an odd mushy meal made from dried peas. It smelled as bad as gruel and it tasted worse if anything, but I ate my four spoonfuls quickly all the same. It was as well I did because the officers were so anxious to get everyone into chapel by eight o'clock that we had to hand our bowls back almost immediately.

Then we marched off down corridors, through a heavy door, and out into the open. We were in a big grey yard under a grey sky, but I felt as if I was in a flower meadow in brilliant

sunshine. Fresh air! I gulped it down, heady with the taste and smell of it. I stared up at the sky at a flock of birds.

'Look! Look!' I cried out, as if they were exotic birds of paradise rather than humble brown sparrows.

Daisy poked me painfully in the back. 'Silence!' she hissed furiously.

She couldn't dampen my excitement at being outside. I felt I'd been imprisoned in the bleak workhouse for years rather than a matter of days. No one else seemed to share my joy. They marched steadily towards the bleak grey building at the end of the yard and disappeared inside.

It wasn't my idea of any chapel or church. It had no decoration whatsoever, and the windows were plain, not coloured glass. It was just as plain inside, with a stark wooden cross at one end, and row after row of benches, and a wide aisle down the middle separating the men from the women.

I gathered we were meant to look straight ahead, but nothing could stop the flicker of eyes. Men looked at women, and women looked at men, and mothers looked longingly for their children. I wished Margaret could attend chapel, but the sick had to stay in their wards. There were many rows of

elderly folk, some lame, some stooped, some slumped. They seemed the saddest of all, their wrinkled faces mostly blank. I couldn't tell if they had lost their minds, or whether they were so worn down by the rigid routine of the workhouse that they had stopped reacting to anything at all.

When everyone was seated, the minister stood in front of the cross, his religious robes of white and gold and purple outrageously gaudy compared with our workhouse garb. He clasped his hands piously.

'Welcome, brethren,' he said, though his high tone showed he thought the workhouse inmates a million miles below him in status. 'Let us give praise to the Lord.'

This seemed a ridiculous request. I was ready to praise God for the sky and the birds and the sweet fresh air – but how could anyone think the workhouse life anything but hell itself? The short service seemed a painful sham from beginning to end, but at least it was a change of routine, and some of the elders looked a little livelier whenever there was a hymn, joining in with quavering voices.

The Master of the workhouse read a lesson. His voice bellowed and he gestured dramatically at times. He was a portly gentleman with jowls like a bulldog. His complexion was

as red as plum wine and his voice was as fruity. The matron
read a lesson too, her voice as sharp as her features.

I thought we might have some recreation afterwards, a
chance to wander in the yard, or maybe just march round and
round in circles, but we were ushered back inside and sent
straight off to our usual tasks. I assumed I'd be going to the sick
ward, and I'd be able to tell Margaret more comforting stories
about Ralph and Algernon, though to be truthful I hadn't
been able to work out which boys they were in the mass of
faces in the chapel. But Daisy caught hold of me by the arm as
I came out of the privy and started going down the corridor.

'Where are you off to?' she demanded.

'The sick ward,' I said.

'Who told you to do that, eh? You've got to wait and see
what I tell you each blooming day, got it? And you're wanted
back with us, sewing, see?' she said.

It turned out that the matron had ordered a special new
uniform because an important visitor was due next week.
Apparently she didn't think her current frock and cap and
apron distinguished enough, and she wanted a lined cloak too.
The officer was in charge of cutting and pinning – but I was to
do the sewing.

'It's because I've got rheumatics in my fingers. And I don't see as well as I used to. So you're to do the sewing, though of course it will be my work, as I'm in charge of the making of the outfit, see?' she said.

In other words, I was to do all the donkey work because I was the neatest stitcher, and if I made a good job of it then she'd get the credit.

'It ain't fair,' Wilma said loyally, as I sat hunched up over my sewing hour after hour.

'Maybe I could leave a few pins in place on purpose and then when Matron gets pricked she'll blame her and not me!' I whispered.

Wilma tittered, though she looked alarmed. 'Better not!' she said. 'She'll know it was you and you'll get royally punished!'

'Don't worry, I was only joking,' I said hurriedly.

Wilma still looked worried. She didn't really understand jokes. And anyway, I didn't really mind too much. I liked sewing and took pride in my neat stitching, though it had been much more fun making tiny dresses with different colours for dolls rather than one royal-blue cotton frock for the mean matron.

I didn't know how I was going to manage when it came to the white cap and long apron because my hands were

distressingly grimy now, and I knew I'd leave grubby fingerprints on the snowy material. But the frock and gown took me all Sunday and Monday – and the next day was Tuesday, wash day!

I knew enough about the workhouse now not to expect a luxury bath with soap and a soft towel to dry myself. But the bath-house was still a savage disappointment. It was a dank room with green mould luridly patterning the walls. There were ten very basic baths with no curtaining or privacy whatsoever. Each person was required to bob in a bath in full view of everyone, lather themselves as best they could with a sliver of carbolic soap, rinse it off again and climb out, making a dash for the door. The water was stone cold and came as an icy shock. There were a few ragged towels in a heap at the end, but they were sopping wet by the time I reached one.

I dried myself as best I could and then I was given clean clothes. I'd been so longing for them, though the undergarments looked very basic and the frock was such a gloomy shade of grey. The shift was too small and tight under my arms. The stockings had been badly darned so it felt I had stones in my boots, and the frock itself was ill-fitting, hanging very loose at the waist like a smock and reaching down to my ankles. I had no looking glass but I knew I must appear a perfect mess.

Wilma barely recognized me. 'You don't look like you any more,' she said. 'You look like one of us.'

I was starting to *feel* like a workhouse child too. I had tried to amuse myself during the long silences of stitching by making up stories in my head, but it was growing harder to invent anything now. I felt dull inside, as if half my brain had been switched off. The milk treatment had worked and my wound no longer oozed. When I touched it gingerly it seemed to be forming a proper scab now. *It* was better – though *I* felt worse.

I felt dizzy frequently, and when I stood up from sitting cross-legged whilst sewing I had to press myself against the wall to stop falling over. This made me remember tumbling down into this past world and I hoped against hope that maybe I was starting to tumble out of it again. But it didn't happen and it didn't happen and it didn't happen.

I was feeling dizzy out of simple hunger. I was ravenous all the time. I swallowed down the disgusting meals as eagerly as everyone else. I even ate the fatty lumps, though it was more of an effort and I often heaved. Wilma watched me hopefully, but I wasn't willing to share any of my food now. We didn't always get cheese with our supper and had to make do with half a slice of bread with a dab of dripping. We went to our beds

hungry and woke in the morning with gnawing pains in our empty stomachs.

We attacked our breakfast gruel with desperate need. Some of the younger children licked out their bowls when they'd finished their food too quickly, even though they knew it meant a clip round the ear from an officer. I was tempted to do it myself. I wasn't even sure I could be trusted if I was sent back to the sick ward. If a patient showed no interest in eating then would I really spoon it patiently into their mouth – or slyly gobble it down myself?

I did still take a pride in my work. I stitched the matron's white cap and apron with my clean hands and managed to make a good job of it, though the cap was a complicated design, and gathering the material evenly to fit the waistband of the apron was a struggle. I even managed the scarlet cloak. I showed it proudly to Officer Tiptree when the outfit was finished.

She looked it over very carefully, examining the seams and hems, and then she marched off with it without saying a single word. I don't know what she said to Matron, but the outfit was obviously considered a success, because Officer Tiptree came back looking flushed and smelling of brandy.

'Did Matron like her new clothes?' I dared ask.

'She thought I'd done an excellent job,' the officer said proudly. 'Now don't sit there idly. There's plenty of sewing work to do. Get a garment from the pile and get on with it!'

'She's so mean,' Wilma muttered. 'I wish you *had* kept pins in Matron's frock.'

'Oh well. Maybe she'll ask for some new underwear next. Then I can leave pins in her drawers and they'll stick in her bottom,' I said, making light of it. I was too proud to show how much I minded. I told myself there was no point in caring. Things were never going to change. Yet the injustice burned inside me so fiercely that it was a wonder I didn't scorch the bodice of my hideous workhouse frock.

There seemed a remarkable increase in clothes to be mended. There were so many shirts and breeches that we wondered if the male ward had deliberately torn their own clothes in some kind of protest. Then I was called upon to make a new shirt for the Master, of finest cambric with a fancy ruffle at the front that was such a nightmare to stitch I had to unpick it three times before I managed it successfully. We were kept working two hours longer every day, until some of the youngest girls were crying with tiredness.

'Stop that nonsense or I really will give you something to cry for!' Officer Tiptree threatened, and when one tiny girl couldn't manage to control her tears, she gave her such a hard smack that she nearly knocked her over.

Even Daisy was outraged. The littlest girl was one of her special pets. 'Please, ma'am, she's doing her best,' she protested.

'Well her best isn't good enough!' Officer Tiptree snapped. 'I'm warning you, if you don't get a move on and get everything finished for when the visitor comes, we'll all be for it, mark my words!'

'Who *is* this visitor, ma'am?' Daisy asked.

'Mind your own business, miss!' said Officer Tiptree.

It was obviously someone very important. The whole workhouse buzzed with rumours. Was there going to be a general inspection? Was it a Member of Parliament? There was such anxiety amongst the officers that some of the inmates thought it might even be the Queen herself, though it seemed a ridiculous idea that she would ever set her daintily shod royal foot in our foul premises.

At least it was exciting to speculate, and even the saddest and most sullen inmates livened up a little because at last

something was happening. But then we found out it was only going to be happening to half of us.

Officer Tiptree took me to one side and asked me if there was any way I could remodel her uniform so that it was a more flattering fit. She was a bulky woman who had obviously drunk her unfair share of stolen ale and had ended up the shape of a beer barrel. I didn't see how I could possibly style her frock to flatter her in any way whatsoever but I said I would do my best.

She actually had the grace to thank me this time, and suggested I come and sit beside her while I sewed. This meant taking Daisy's place, who glared at me ferociously.

Officer Tiptree changed into a spare workhouse frock without an officer badge and sat almost humbly while I stitched diligently at her uniform, unpicking every seam and inserting a dart here and a tuck there. She was called to an officers' meeting the next morning. She was gone a long time. When she came back it was clear she was in a terrible mood.

She slapped the littlest children for nothing at all, and then slapped them again for crying, and she even slapped Wilma for gasping in fear. She snapped at Daisy and snatched her uniform from out of my hands.

'Give that here, girl!' she commanded.

'But, ma'am, I haven't quite finished it yet,' I said.

'It doesn't matter now,' she replied, and looked about to burst into tears.

'What's happened?' I asked.

She was so upset she couldn't keep the news to herself. 'The visitor is only coming to see the male wards and workrooms,' she said. 'The Master felt it indelicate to take a gentleman to our wing. And I was so looking forward to catching a proper glimpse of him. They say he dresses very fancy.'

'Who *is* this gentleman, ma'am?' I asked.

'He's that writer chappie, Charlie Dicker or some such name. He makes a fortune out of his stories. Folk queue for hours to get the next monthly instalment. I'm not one for reading, but you hear the tales, even in here. Oh, the death of little Nell had me in floods, I tell you,' she said. Her eyes watered at the memory, though she clearly didn't care tuppence about the real little girls grizzling in front of her.

'What's up with you, girl?' she asked impatiently. 'Why are you looking so gormless?'

She shook me hard because I'd gone into a weird daydream. I remembered being told about a writer like that when Alex and I went to stage school. Oh *Alex*! How could

I have forgotten her? She was the star of . . . what was it called?

I tried to hang onto the sudden memory, but Officer Tiptree was shouting right in my face. I closed my eyes quickly, trying to blot her out.

'Whatever's the matter with you? Open your eyes!'

'She looks like she might be having a fit, ma'am,' said Daisy.

'Oh Dolly, don't die!' Wilma clutched me desperately. I had to open my eyes to reassure her.

'It's all right, Wilma,' I murmured. 'I just felt funny for a moment.'

'Trust you to make a fuss about nothing,' said Daisy. 'We all feel funny. We don't have enough grub to eat.'

That was true enough. And it was worse on Tuesday. We didn't have a proper cooked dinner with meat. We were just given gruel again, and hardly enough to cover the bottom of our porringer. There were mouth-watering smells coming from the kitchen that made us even more desperately hungry. We were told that the cook was busy practising making a grand dinner for the important visitor tomorrow and didn't have time for our everyday stew.

The officers didn't complain, because they were called back to the kitchen later and allowed to eat the dinner themselves. Daisy was left in charge of us sewing girls – and for once we were all united.

'It's so unfair! We're starving! Look at Violet – she's getting so weak,' said Daisy, reaching out to the poor little scrap and holding her close.

Violet drooped against her wearily, her little bandy legs scarcely able to support her.

'They didn't ought to treat us like this,' Daisy said. 'We're

meant to get six ounces of meat a day – it's the rules.'

'That's it, Daisy, you tell them,' the girls urged her.

'I will,' said Daisy.

'You wouldn't dare,' said Wilma.

'You wait and see,' said Daisy.

When we got served a meagre splash of gruel for supper, we all looked at Daisy – but of course she kept quiet. If she made a fuss, she could easily get a beating – or be sent to Darky for the night. The officers were in a mellow mood because their stomachs were full of roast beef and roast potatoes and carrots and peas. It smelled as if there might even have been a plum pudding for dessert, and various custards and blancmanges as well, putting the workhouse milk ration to good use.

But I knew now that one little hint of rebellion from us would be enough to have them lash out. It was the way the whole system worked. We were kept in a state of fear, even the privileged ones like Daisy. And the officers themselves lived in fear of the matron – and even she knew she had to please the Master at all times. Otherwise, Darky awaited us.

I still had nightmares that I was back there. They made me groan and thrash about, and Gert got angry if I woke her and

threatened to push me right out of bed. But this night she held me tight when I started whimpering in my sleep.

'Hush now, Dolly. Is your stomach hurting bad?' she whispered.

'Yes, it is!' I mumbled.

'Mine too. And my arms and shoulders. And my hands are bleeding from scrubbing at the sheets to try to get them white again, in case this blooming Mr Dicker or whatever wants to cast his beady eye on them. Good job he's not coming near any of us lot. I'd tell him what I think of him, putting us to all this trouble,' she muttered fiercely. 'Who does he think he is?'

'He's a famous author, Gert,' I said.

'I know that. I ain't ignorant! And he wrote a famous book a while ago about a workhouse and it caused a right stink. So now our lot are frightened he'll write about us in one of his journals and they'll lose their jobs,' said Gert.

'Oh, I do hope so!' I said. 'So surely that means he's on our side, wanting things to be better for us?'

'They'll get worse before they get better,' Gert said darkly. 'They say the men have been threatened with a whole month in Darky if they say anything untoward, and the boys have

been beaten today to learn them what will happen, only worse, if they don't behave tomorrow.'

'I do hope that's not true,' I said, thinking of Ralph and little Algernon. It seemed a crazed thing to do, but I was getting used to the twisted logic of the workhouse and anything seemed possible. I nestled closer to Gert. 'Do you think we'll ever get out of here, Gert? Don't you dream of it?'

'Well, I reckon one laundry's much the same as any other, so it's toil all day and ache all night, whether you're in or out the bleeding workhouse,' she said.

'But what would you do if you could choose something else?' I persisted.

'Don't know nothing else. My mam took in washing to help feed us kids when my pa cleared off, and us girls helped her. Then she got sick and we was taken here. One of my sisters is still here, picking oakum every day because she's not strong enough for laundering. The other one died years ago – don't even know what of, they never told me. Don't suppose it matters,' said Gert. She spoke harshly as if she didn't care, but I could feel her start to tremble.

'But supposing you got trained to do something else? Or maybe met some kind man and got married? What would you

wish for most?' I asked. 'A little cottage in the country?'

'No, a huge great house in the town!' said Gert. 'And I'd lounge about in my bed half the day, with my meals served to me on a tray, and I'd send my sheets out to the laundry and some other poor beggar would have to wash them.'

'So what would you have for breakfast?' I said. 'A bowl of grey, gritty, lumpy gruel?'

'I'd have . . . I'd have . . . I'd have a whole loaf of fresh bread all to myself, each slice thickly spread with butter,' said Gert, sighing wistfully.

'And *I'd* have crispy bacon, five whole rashers, on a toasted slice of your crusty bread,' I said. 'Hark at my tummy rumbling!'

'Hark at mine!' said Gert.

We went on inventing ideal meals until our voices wavered and we fell asleep, still salivating.

Chapter Nineteen

We couldn't even have our breakfast at the usual time on Wednesday morning. We had to wait for the men and boys to eat theirs while the important visitor watched. We were all so desperately hungry that there was an angry muttering amongst us, though the officers did their best to threaten us into silence. When at long last word was sent that it was our turn, some of the women even broke up the line and surged forward eagerly, so that the little girls got jostled and pushed.

We had a shock going into the dining room. It was much cleaner than usual, with new religious tracts pinned to the walls. It smelled different too. We breathed it in greedily.

It was the smell of gruel, but a thousand times tastier, so sweet and creamy that we started drooling.

Wilma and I clutched hands. 'Why does it smell so wonderful?' she whispered.

'It's to impress the important gentleman,' I said. 'Oh, if only he came to visit every month! No, every week! Every *day*! I do hope he's staying for dinner. We might even get a roast!'

'Stop talking, you two!' said Daisy, prodding us, though her own mouth was watering.

We lined up like soldiers now, not willing to risk losing out on this wonderful breakfast. We watched the first few women hold out their bowls and get their portion. Then we saw the shock on their faces. We weren't being served with the sweet milky fare we could smell. We were given the usual plain gritty gruel – and a pitifully small amount too, a quarter of a ladleful at most. Three spoonfuls and it was gone. We were so hungry we gulped it down in a frenzy and finished in a single second.

Was that *it*? We peered up and down the long tables. Everyone had been served the same pitiful meal, even the officers. Obviously the men and boys had had the fine breakfast to impress the Important Visitor, using up most of the rations. We were left with this pathetic portion that didn't even take the

edge off our desperate hunger. We stared at each other, hardly able to bear the disappointment.

Then there was a clap of hands and the portly Master strutted into the dining room, with a cluster of senior officers and a strange man who peered at us intently. There was a confused murmur.

'Silence!' the Master shouted – but he looked confused himself, and extremely agitated. 'Stand up, everyone, and bow to our esteemed visitor, Mr Charles Dickens, the extremely famous and distinguished novelist.'

He did indeed look the part. He was a small man, but he held himself well, head up, shoulders back, somehow standing tall in his highly polished boots. He had abundantly wavy, dark hair, parted on one side, and a neat beard that gave him an air of authority. He wore beautiful clothes, a bright silk bow tie, a maroon velvet jacket, an embroidered waistcoat and sharply cut cream trousers, as if he'd just stepped off a stage.

We stood up and bobbed our heads, peering at each other sideways. What was going on? He wasn't supposed to come and inspect *us*!

'Sit down again. Finish your meal,' the Master commanded, in such a fluster that he didn't take in that our

bowls were empty. He glared at Matron. 'Why do these women look so unkempt and slatternly?'

She went very pink. 'We weren't expecting to have the honour of the presence of Mr Dicker this morning,' she gabbled.

'Well, there's been a change of schedule,' the Master spat out, clearly furious about it. 'Mr Dick*ens* has expressly requested a *thorough* inspection of our establishment.'

'I do not wish to cause any trouble, madam,' said Mr Dickens himself. 'Ladies, children, my apologies. Please feel free to talk among yourselves. I see you have already finished your breakfast. I hope everyone is replete.'

I felt dizzier than ever. It was as if I'd already lived this moment. I knew what to say, what to do. I stood up, clutching my bowl, and walked to the front of the dining room. I swallowed hard and opened my mouth.

'Please, sir, I want some more!'

There was a tremendous gasp from the Master, Matron, the senior officers, the cook, and every one of my fellow inmates. Mr Dickens looked astonished too – but his eyes sparkled.

'What did you say?' the Master said quietly, his head on one side.

'I w-want some m-more,' I said, scarcely able to believe I'd said it myself.

'I cannot believe my ears!' the Master gasped. 'How *dare* you!'

'And in front of Mr Dicker!' said Matron. 'A thousand apologies, sir. She will be royally punished!'

'*More?*' the cook exclaimed. 'I've never once, in all my time here, had any inmate ask for *more!*'

'Excuse me, sirs – and esteemed madam – but it does indeed seem a strange request, judging from the substance dripping from that cauldron,' said Mr Dickens. 'Which, by the way, seems considerably inferior to the portions distributed to the male population. But I believe I know the reason!'

They peered at him. He wasn't looking back at them. He was looking straight at me and he was actually smiling.

'I do believe in remarkable coincidences – indeed, there are many examples in my own work – but it is very unlikely that the child could manage to quote a certain book so accurately unless she had actually read it herself,' said Mr Dickens, beckoning me towards him.

'Beg pardon, sir, but there's very few children here who can read,' said Matron. 'We try our best to teach them, but

they come from very inferior stock, and try as we might, any information goes in one ear and out the other.'

'I can read,' I said. 'And I have indeed read *Oliver Twist*.'

I remembered! I remembered everything! Miss Evelyn had suggested we all read the book so we could understand the characters, but it was a long book with tiny print and quite a struggle to read. I gave up after the first three chapters when I was told I wasn't going to play *any* character. I knew every single one of Oliver's lines in the play but I was never going to get a chance to play him. Reading the play of *Oliver Twist* was *almost* the same as reading the book, wasn't it?

'Ah! I knew it! And did you enjoy it, child?' Mr Dickens asked.

'Oh yes, sir! It was splendid,' I said.

He actually clapped me on the back. I think he felt my shoulder blades because he paused then. 'You're a little shrimp of a creature, aren't you, my dear. I daresay you really could do with some more.' He looked round at my sister inmates, who were watching with gaping mouths. 'I wish I could feed you the splendid dinner that I daresay is being prepared for me right this minute. But do not despair, ladies, children. I have a feeling that the winds of change are already starting to

whistle down these reeking corridors. Have courage. Have patience. Have faith. I am going to do my best to change this entire system. I cannot liberate all of you – but I can liberate one child right this minute. Here she is!' He took hold of my hand and held it high. 'Let us leave this sorry establishment forthwith!'

The Master was so taken aback that his plum face darkened to a terrifying purple. 'Mr Dickens, sir! You cannot simply remove that child. She is the property of this parish, a registered inmate of this workhouse.'

'Is that so?' said Mr Dickens. 'Well, we will simply *un*register her. Please be so good as to find me the relevant document, and I will send my solicitor to sort out everything legally. I daresay we can simply cross out her name and write *Now under the care of Mr Charles Dickens*, and you will have one fewer pauper-making demands on your finances. Is that not a good thing?'

The Master's livid face was a picture as he tried to work it out. 'Well, if you insist, sir. But I must make sure that the child will come to no harm. I am officially the guardian of every underage child in the workhouse – and I take great pains with each and every young personage.'

'I'm sure you do, sir. So what is this child's name and age?'
Mr Dickens responded.

The Master was taken aback. 'Well, it's . . . I'm sure
she's . . .' He wavered. He looked at the matron. 'Tell
Mr Dickens, Matron. She's in your charge.'

'The female children are the responsibility of the officer
over there,' she said firmly, pointing.

Officer Tiptree was all of a flutter. She looked up and
down the tables for Daisy. 'Name the child and give her age,'
she said.

Daisy knew – but was so flustered by the bizarre
proceedings that for once in her life she was speechless. She
gargled incoherently, and then pointed at Wilma, gesturing
for her to take over. Wilma stood up and announced, 'She is
Dolly Blank and she is ten years old and she is my friend.'

'So I am, dear Wilma. You're mine too. And if I am taken
away I will never forget you.' I looked up at Mr Dickens. 'I
don't suppose Wilma could come too?' I begged.

'My goodness, I can't take any more! My house is woefully
overrun with children as it is. But I give you my word that I will
make sure that things improve considerably for little Wilma
and everyone else,' he said solemnly – and I believed him

utterly. 'I think we should leave this establishment forthwith,'
Mr Dickens continued, offering me his arm as if I was a lady.
'Allow me to escort you, Miss Blank.'

'Certainly, sir,' I said giggling.

'But – but you haven't finished your planned tour of the
workhouse!' the Master blustered.

'I really think I have seen enough already, sir. I feel in need
of some fresh air. Thank you kindly for your hospitality. I bid
you good-day,' said Mr Dickens. 'Fare you well, good ladies
and little children.'

A few bold ones called out goodbye, and when Mr Dickens
gave them a flamboyant wave, most dared raise their arms and
wave back. We walked down the corridors together, officers
scurrying in front and behind us to show us the way. I couldn't
believe it was happening. It was surely another vivid dream. I
clung heavily to Mr Dickens' arm, feeling the smooth velvet of
his jacket to convince myself that he was real.

'Are you feeling faint, child?' he asked, looking concerned.

'Just a little,' I murmured.

'No wonder, with this terribly noxious aroma,' he said, as
we passed the passage to the privies. 'I am so disappointed that
there's been no improvement whatsoever since the wretched

Poor Law was established. I threw my heart and soul into *Oliver Twist*, hoping that it would shame the government into making ground-breaking changes, but I can see I've failed dismally. I have serious work to do. I shall compose a long article this very evening and see if I can stir things up.'

We reached the end of the last corridor and approached the door. A startled lackey unbolted it and stepped aside to let us out. We walked out into brilliant sunshine. Mr Dickens gave a great flourish, as if he had personally arranged it.

'There, my dear! Freedom!' he cried.

I looked all around me, squinting in the sunlight, my eyes watering.

'Now, now, no weeping allowed! I've reduced too many folk to tears already. Shall we go and seek out a proper breakfast? I promise you it will not be a bowl of gruel!'

I glanced down worriedly at my wretched workhouse frock and battered boots. He was too much of a gentleman to comment, but he took me to a small chop house rather than a grand restaurant, and insisted we sit in a private booth where we would not attract glances.

The waiters clearly knew who he was and fussed around us, but Mr Dickens dealt with them speedily, waving away the

menus. 'We would like two splendid breakfasts, please. Eggs, bacon, kidneys, tomatoes, mushrooms and fried potatoes, with tea and milk,' he said.

'And porridge, sir?' the waiter suggested helpfully.

'No, thank you. It resembles gruel a little too closely. I don't think either of us will fancy gruel ever again,' he said. 'Could you serve our meal very speedily? My young companion is near fainting for lack of nourishment. Is there anything else you fancy, my dear?' he asked me. 'Feel free to order any kind of pudding too! I daresay it didn't occur too frequently in the workhouse.'

I sang a verse of the food song from *Oliver!*, with the chorus about gruel. Mr Dickens peered at me, then shook his head and slapped his thighs in delight.

'Did you hear that?' he said to the waiter. 'If the cook can rustle up a cold jelly and custard I will add a sovereign to my bill!'

When the waiter scurried off Mr Dickens turned to me. 'And *I* am near fainting with curiosity. Don't tell me you made up that marvellously witty song yourself!'

It was very tempting, but I decided to be truthful. 'No, sir. I was once involved in a musical play of *Oliver Twist*,' I said.

'A *musical* play! I didn't know there had been such an inventive adaptation. I have seen several lamentable stage productions, with rather large stout ladies playing my dear Oliver. Fine actresses all, but hardly convincing as a small starving orphan,' said Mr Dickens.

'Well, my friend Alex looked wonderful and was a big success,' I said.

'And what part did you play, child?' he asked.

'I didn't have a proper part. I wasn't even the understudy for Oliver,' I said.

'Well, once we have fed you and washed you and given you a bright, pretty frock, I think we will consider another production of *Oliver!*, with you in the starring role. Do you know who wrote this amazing version?'

'It was a gentleman called Lionel Bart, but I rather think he's dead now,' I said. *And actually won't be born for nearly a hundred years*, I thought, and so many memories came flooding back that I became totally overwhelmed.

'You're looking very peaky, my dear. But two waiters are approaching, juggling immense plates of food. I will let you eat your fill and try to stop plaguing you with questions, though my tongue is tingling to know more,' said Mr Dickens.

The beautiful smell of my breakfast was almost too intense. My hand was shaking as I cut a small sliver of crispy bacon and held it to my mouth. I let it rest against my lips for a moment, and then ate it very slowly. I don't think anything had ever tasted so wonderful in either of my lives.

Mr Dickens smiled at me, but he looked sad too.

'What's the matter, sir?' I asked timidly, wondering if he was already regretting his sudden impulse, and was going to return me to the workhouse as soon as I'd finished my meal.

'I was just realizing that I have written about starving children many times, and yet I've never fully realized how dreadful it must be,' he said. 'That corpulent Master deserves to be roasted on a spit and fed to every poor creature in his workhouse.'

'And perhaps the matron could be sprinkled all over with sugar and baked in an enormous pie,' I suggested. 'Though I think she'd still taste as sharp and sour as a lemon. And perhaps we could cook the horrid nurse in the sick ward. She drinks so much milk we could pulverize her and turn her into a strawberry blancmange!'

'You are a girl after my own heart,' said Mr Dickens. 'Eat up now. I shall eat heartily too in order to encourage you.'

I did my best, but found myself almost uncomfortably full after only a few bites.

'Have a little rest. Your poor shrivelled stomach must be alarmed at the sudden onslaught. Don't worry. There's no rush. Sip some of your tea – and then perhaps you might care to sing me another song from this marvellous musical adaptation.'

I drank several mouthfuls, took a deep breath, and then sang the song I'd sung to Margaret, the Oliver solo where he's looking for love. I knew I couldn't sing anywhere near as sweetly as Alex, but I sang it from my heart, longing for someone to love me too. By the time I'd finished it Mr Dickens had tears rolling down his cheeks.

'Bravo! Wonderful! Magnificent!' He enthused so heartily that the waiters came running to see if they were being summoned.

'Can we be of any help, sir?' the head waiter asked. 'If this is a celebration, perhaps you might care for a glass of champagne?'

'Excellent idea!' said Mr Dickens.

'And a glass for the young lady?'

I looked hopeful. I'd never had champagne before and didn't want to miss this chance.

'Perhaps half a glass,' said Mr Dickens. 'With the plates of cold jelly and custard!'

The waiter looked agonized. 'A thousand apologies, sir, but I'm not quite sure we can manage that. Our chef could start making a jelly but I'm afraid it would be hot rather than cold, and entirely liquid. And likewise the custard. We are only catering for breakfast at the present moment in time.'

'Never mind, good sir, it was only a whim of mine,' said Mr Dickens. 'How about piled peaches and cream?'

'I'm sure we can manage that!' said the waiter. 'I'll send the kitchen boy out to market and see if he can find some ripe, juicy ones, and we have cream a-plenty. I will serve them to you as soon as possible.'

'My little companion and I have all the time in the world,' said Mr Dickens. He looked at me. 'You're looking very thoughtful. Perhaps you don't care for peaches?'

'Oh yes I do,' I said hastily. I was puzzling over *time*. What *was* this present moment in time? And did I have all the time in *this* world, or the one in the future? I rubbed my forehead hard, trying to think clearly.

'Do you have a headache? Most people get their headache *after* consuming champagne, not beforehand,' said Mr Dickens.

'I haven't really got a headache. I just seem in a muddle. I can't think straight,' I said.

'I know that feeling well. I frequently feel as if I have a thousand characters tumbling around my head, waiting for me to pin them to the page and tell their stories. So what is *your* story, little Dolly Blank? A perfect name! Perhaps I've made you up!' he said.

I knew he was joking, but I almost wondered it myself.

'I sometimes think I've made myself up,' I said. 'Because there's so much I can't remember. I wasn't brought up in the workhouse. I had a mother and a father too, but then I was left to fend for myself, and then Missus took me as an apprentice, and she was cruel – and yet puzzling, because she was sometimes kind.'

'Ah! Real-life characters are always more complex than the fictional kind,' said Mr Dickens. 'So what kind of apprentice were you?'

'I learned the art of doll-making, and sewed little dresses for them,' I said.

'A perfect occupation for a small girl with nimble fingers who just happens to be called Dolly!' said Mr Dickens

delightedly. 'Perhaps I shall put a doll-maker in one of my books one day.'

'And then I ran away and sold my own dolls, but Missus found me and said I'd stolen her property – well, I suppose I *had* – and then I was taken to the workhouse,' I said.

'Well, let us drink to your liberation,' said Mr Dickens, as the waiter brought us our drinks.

He raised his glass to me and I raised mine to him and took a sip. It was wonderfully sweet and tasted deliciously fruity, like our promised peaches. I took another gulp and then another.

'Steady!' said Mr Dickens. 'I think that might be enough for now. So tell me, Dolly, at what stage in your life did you audition for this musical play about my young charge, Oliver?'

'Well, it's difficult to explain,' I said, taking one more sip. It tasted so wonderful and Mr Dickens' expression was so kindly and curious that I wondered if I dared try to explain.

'Yes?' he murmured encouragingly.

'I know it sounds ridiculous and impossible but I don't think I have had just this one life,' I said hesitantly. 'It's hard to remember . . . it's all like a hazy dream, but bits keep coming

back to me – and I can remember *Oliver!* because it meant so much to me.'

'Did it, indeed!' said Mr Dickens, looking pleased. 'Remind me to give you a signed copy of my book. So you're saying you became involved in this stage version in *another* life?'

'I told you it was ridiculous. Even I find it hard to believe,' I said, taking yet another sip of champagne.

'Now, now! No more, little Dolly. It will make you dizzy,' said Mr Dickens.

I was feeling dizzy already, trying to remember.

'Are there more *Oliver!* songs from this past life?' Mr Dickens asked.

'Yes, but they're not from the past. They're from my future life.' I shook my head because it sounded so foolish. 'Though I know that can't be possible because the future hasn't happened yet, has it?'

'There are more things in heaven and earth than are dreamt of in most people's philosophy,' said Mr Dickens. 'I'm misquoting Shakespeare, the greatest English writer of all time.'

'Some people say that you are the greatest writer, Mr Dickens,' I said.

'Do they really?' he said, looking immensely pleased. He didn't even notice when I took several more sips of champagne, because it was so refreshing. 'I am so immensely glad I've met you, dear Dolly.'

'And I'm immensely glad I met you!' I replied. 'Perhaps I am actually starting to enjoy this past life of mine! Perhaps this is where I belong. I am the real me.'

'Miss Dolly Blank,' said Mr Dickens, raising his glass to me again.

I raised mine too, though I found I had only one sip left.

'Actually, Dolly Blank is not my real name,' I confided. 'My dear friend Algie called me Dolly because of my doll-making. And the workhouse relieving officer wrote *Blank* when he was registering me because I didn't know my surname. But I remember now! It's . . . Trimmers, or something like that.'

'Ah! A very fine name. I wrote about a good chap called Mr Trimmers in an early novel,' said Mr Dickens.

'And my first name is . . . Edith?'

'I have a most interesting young woman called Edith in another novel. She is a fine spirited character, though a trifle haughty.'

'I think I am called Edie, not Edith. And I don't have an

s on the end of my surname. That's it. *My name is Edie Trimmer!*'

I said it triumphantly – and instantly the room grew dark as night and Mr Dickens disappeared altogether. The chop house disintegrated and the London streets outside erupted into rubble. I was whirling around in thin air, blown further and further and further away into the future.

Chapter Twenty

'She's stirring!'

'Her eyelids are flickering!'

'Oh Edie, Edie, wake up, darling!'

'Oh, thank God, Edie!'

'Where am I?' I muttered – and then I burst out laughing because it was such a stupid, clichéd thing to say. I knew where I was. I could barely believe it. But there were Mum and Dad and Alex and her mum – but actually, where *was* I?

I wasn't in my bedroom at home. I was in a strange, light room with faded green curtains around my bed – a hard high bed with a metal bar at the bottom.

'Nurse! Nurse!' Dad was shouting.

I was in hospital!

'Am I ill?' I asked, trying to sit up.

'You've been ever so ill, in a *coma*!' said Alex.

'Ssh, darling,' said her mum.

'You've not really been ill as such, Edie – just very deeply asleep,' said Mum. 'Don't try to sit up yet, sweetheart.' She settled me back on the pillow and gave me a kiss. Her cheeks were wet. She was smiling but tears were pouring down her cheeks.

I felt awful for making everyone so worried. I shut my eyes so I wouldn't start crying too.

'Edie, please don't go back to sleep!' Dad said urgently. He sounded all choked up too. 'I'll run and find a nurse.'

'I'm not sleeping! I'm wide awake, truly. How long have I been asleep?' I thought back, straining to remember everything – though already it was fading. I remembered Mr Dickens, of course, and the workhouse – oh, the horror of that workhouse! But before that I made the dolls, and knew dear Algie, and then there had been Missus, and then Mother, who was so ill . . .

I reached out and put my arms round Mum's neck. 'Promise me you won't ever die, will you, Mum?' I begged her.

'Of course not,' said Mum, hugging me back. 'Well, not till I'm an old, old, old lady.'

'And you won't die, will you, Edie?' Alex asked. 'We're going to stay best friends for ever, aren't we?'

'Of course we are!' I said.

'Alex has been wonderful today. She's been standing by your bed singing you songs from *Oliver!* to see if you might hear somehow and wake up – and it's worked!' said Mum.

'*You* were singing?' I asked Alex. 'And – and was Mr Dickens here?'

'Charles Dickens?' said Mum. 'You've obviously been dreaming, Edie, while you've been in the coma. We've been so worried. It's been two days now.'

'Only two days! But I've been in the past for weeks and weeks!' I said.

'You're just a bit muddled now, darling. I'm sure it's only to be expected. Oh, thank goodness, here's Dad coming back with a nurse – and a doctor too.'

They took my temperature and my blood pressure and shone a bright light in my eyes and asked me lots of questions. I hesitated when they asked me my name, because if saying it had brought me back to this life then maybe saying it again might somehow return me to the past.

'Well, I'm called Edie – it was my great-grandma's name, wasn't it, Mum? And my surname's Trimmer because that's my dad's name, even though Mum's kept her own name because she's independent,' I said cautiously.

Everyone laughed.

'She's herself again, all right,' said Dad.

'She seems fine in every way. We'll do another scan and keep her here for a few hours to keep an eye on her, but it looks as if you can go home soon, Edie,' said the doctor.

'And you still have no idea what made her go into the coma?' asked Dad.

'It's a mystery. There's no sign of any problem inside her head, and her vitals stayed completely normal. There's a scar from some long-ago bump on the head, but that's long since healed.' The doctor looked at me. 'You baffled us, Edie! I don't suppose you have any explanation, do you?'

I took a deep breath. 'Perhaps – perhaps I went back into a past life,' I said tentatively.

They laughed again.

'No, I mean it,' I said. 'There was another me back in Victorian times.'

'Oh darling, you and your Victorians,' said Mum, smoothing my hair. 'Didn't you say just now you were dreaming about Charles Dickens?'

'That's a very superior dream,' said the doctor. 'I usually dream that I'm walking down the street in my underwear, with my stethoscope round my neck and everyone pointing at me!'

They weren't taking me seriously at all.

'Edie's always had the most vivid imagination,' said Dad. 'She used to play the most elaborate pretend games with you, didn't she, Alex?'

'They were magic,' said Alex. She gave me a hug. 'Oh Edie, I'm so glad you're better now! I was so scared!'

'Gently now, Alex,' said her mum. 'We'd better get you back to the theatre now.'

Alex gave me another cautious hug, and whispered in my ear, 'You don't *really* think you went back into the past, do you?'

'Yes!' I said.

'But . . . how? You were still here,' said Alex.

'I don't know how. But I'm not making it up, honestly,' I said. 'You do believe me, don't you, Alex?'

'Yes, of course I do,' she said, but I knew she was only saying it to comfort me.

Still, she was the best friend in all the world, and perhaps her singing to me had brought me back to the present, where I belonged. Back to Mum and Dad and my own life where I was loved and cherished.

When Alex had gone with her mum and the doctor had gone to see another patient, the nurse poured me a glass of water. I drank it down thirstily.

'I'll see if I can find you something to eat too,' she said. 'Lunch isn't due for ages, but I'm sure I can rustle something up. What do you fancy eating, Edie?'

'Peaches and cream?' I said.

'Mm, I don't think the hospital kitchens go in for that sort of thing,' said the nurse. 'What about jelly?'

'Oh yes please!' I said eagerly. 'And could I possibly have it with custard?'

'Edie!' said Mum. 'You don't even like custard!'

'I could maybe find some yoghurt,' said the nurse. 'I'll see what I can do.'

She bustled off, her shoes squeaking on the polished floor. Mum sat one side of me, Dad the other, both holding my hand.

'Promise never to give us another fright like that ever again,' said Dad. He had tears in his eyes now.

'I promise promise promise!' I said, hanging onto both of them.

I had more tests, and a visit from a senior consultant, but I was allowed to go home at teatime. I felt a bit tearful then, because our house looked so bright and clean and lovely, and smelled of flowers and fresh laundry. Mum insisted I lay down on the sofa, even tucking her old, soft pashmina round me.

'There now – you really look like a Victorian invalid now,' she said, giving me a kiss.

'Are you going to give me that laudanum medicine?' I asked her.

'No I am not! That was opium, wasn't it? Dear goodness, they don't mention it in your Victoria Rose books, do they?' Mum said.

'They don't mention any of the really sad things,' I said.

'I'm glad to hear it,' said Mum.

'And even *Oliver!* made workhouses a little bit funny, when they were really terrible places,' I said.

Mum sat down beside me on the sofa, looking hesitant. 'Edie, tell me, darling, did you feel really terribly upset when Alex got the part and not you?' she asked in a rush.

I blinked at her. 'Well, I wished *I'd* been picked, obviously, but I didn't mind *that* much. Alex is actually better than me at singing anyway.'

'Well, maybe. But it must have been really sad for you too, when you had so much fun together being those Von Trapp children,' Mum persisted. 'No one would blame you for feeling a bit left out and jealous.'

I wriggled uncomfortably. 'I suppose I did feel like that, but only a bit. I was happy for Alex too. Why are you going on about it?'

'One of the doctors at the hospital wondered if you had some kind of psychological problem that you couldn't deal with, and that was why you couldn't wake up,' said Mum.

'That's nonsense!' I said.

'I know,' said Mum. 'But I felt terrible, wondering if I'd not realized you were really unhappy because I was so busy at work.'

'I wasn't unhappy in the slightest,' I said. 'Mum, I went back into the past – I did, truly.'

'Well, it must have felt like it. You're so good at imagining things,' said Mum.

I knew there was no way I could convince her. Then Dad came back from a quick dash to the supermarket, with a whole carton of ripe peaches and another of double cream, and sparkling elderflower juice for me and a bottle of champagne too.

'We have to celebrate your recovery, Edie! And you can have a sip too,' Dad said.

'I've already had a whole glassful,' I said.

'When?' said Mum anxiously.

'At breakfast with Mr Dickens,' I said.

'Oh, in your weird dream!' said Dad.

'But it made me feel a bit funny,' I said.

'I'm not surprised,' said Mum. 'I think you'd better stick to elderflower!'

We celebrated together, and then Mum sat one side of me and Dad the other on the sofa and we watched the entire first series of *Victoria Rose* as a special treat for me. Mum and Dad paid attention at first, and kept making little

comments, but after an hour or so Mum checked her emails on her phone and Dad nodded off to sleep. It was still so cosy though, the three of us together, both of them looking after me.

We had chicken for supper with roast potatoes, cauliflower and sugar snap peas, and every mouthful was delicious, though I could only manage a small portion. Mum cooks chicken with rashers of bacon on the breast. I ate a little crispy bit and it was almost as if I was back with Mr Dickens in the chop house – *almost*. But it made me feel scared that I'd somehow get transported back into the past. I didn't want to go into my bedroom and see my trinkets cabinet, and the pen and inkwell and the manuscript book from the old workhouse.

'Can I stay up really late?' I asked Mum and Dad. 'After all, I've been asleep for days, haven't I?'

'You can stay up all night if you want,' said Dad fondly. 'And we'll stay up too and simply thank our lucky stars that you're better again.'

'I'm not sure about all night,' said Mum. 'I should really go back to work tomorrow. Well, work from home anyway. Oh Edie, it's such a relief that you're wide awake now!'

'What if – what if it happens again?' I asked.

'It won't!' said Mum firmly, though I could see the fear in her eyes.

'The doctors have assured us that there's no reason whatsoever that it will,' said Dad. 'And we're going to keep checking on you too. Don't worry if you see us hanging over you in the night, making sure you're still OK.'

'Remember when we used to do that when she was a baby?' said Mum.

'She's still our baby now,' said Dad.

So we did stay up very late, past midnight, though I think all of us were longing to lie down properly in a comfortable bed. Dad kept falling asleep and then waking himself up when his head jerked backwards. Mum lay awkwardly with her head on a cushion and gave herself a crick in the neck. But they still stayed there, watching over me.

'Why don't you two go to bed?' I suggested at last. 'And I'll stay here on the sofa, stretched out properly. I'll watch a film or read a book. I'll be perfectly happy. But I don't want to go to my bed just yet.'

'No, we'll stay with you,' said Dad, yawning.

'Or why don't you squeeze into our bed with us?' Mum

suggested. 'You used to do that when you had bad dreams when you were little, remember?'

So that's what we did, though it was a bit of a squash. It was very comforting having Mum one side, Dad the other, and after a long while I relaxed enough to start dozing. But being so huddled together reminded me horribly of sharing the bed with Gert in the workhouse. I woke up properly then, though my head was still full of the past.

I thought about Wilma. I hoped she wasn't missing me too much. Maybe she could make friends with one of the other girls? And what about Algie? Would he be missing me too, or was he too friendly with Nan now to think of me? And what about my long-ago self? Did I stay in Mr Dickens' care? Did I remember more songs from *Oliver!*? Did he stage his own musical version – with *me* playing Oliver?

It had been so real. It couldn't possibly have been a dream, could it? I lay there, turning it over and over in my head. I felt so restless and fidgety I could hardly keep still – and I was needing to go to the loo. Mum and Dad were sleeping soundly now, exhausted. It would be so mean to wake them up. I managed to wriggle myself right up against the headboard and slip past Dad's head to get out of bed. I tiptoed across the

room and eased open the door. Dad kept on snoring steadily. Mum murmured something but seemed still asleep. I crept out and went to the bathroom.

It was strange to be creeping around our house as if I was a burglar. I went down to the kitchen again and poured myself a glass of cold milk from the fridge. Then I put my hand up and felt under my fringe. I could feel the scar there, raised and uneven. I'd fallen off my bed and bumped my head long ago when I'd tried to fly like Mary Poppins – but I was sure that little bump couldn't have made such a big scar. I'd had it properly treated at a hospital, but you could tell this scar hadn't healed in a neat stitched line. It had only healed because of the milk the nurse had dabbed on the wound.

I remembered how my head had hurt for days. Surely you couldn't feel such pain in a dream? And then of course there was the sentence in the manuscript book that Peter and Gordon had given me. I hadn't dreamed that. It was there, carefully written on the first page. *I* hadn't written it.

The Edie in the past *must* have written it – though how did she come by such a splendid notebook? The children in the workhouse didn't even have slates to write on. The only person to have access to those registers was the matron herself. Had

I managed to *steal* an unused manuscript book? I didn't remember doing that!

I crept out of the kitchen and up the stairs. I didn't go back to Mum and Dad's bedroom. I went past it and along the corridor to my own room. I opened the door and walked in. I started shivering, though it was a warm night.

The curtains were open and the moonlight bright enough to see the shape of things. I walked over to my cabinet and opened the glass door. I touched the green glass medicine bottle, the pinchbeck pocket watch, the little doll. I picked her up, feeling her hard china head and faded frock and soft calico body. She felt so familiar. I had sewn her together, screwed in her head and made that tiny dress. I'd made her and many dozens more just like her.

I set her back on the shelf, and moved slowly and silently to my desk. I switched on my reading lamp so I could see properly. I blinked in the sudden light. There was the pen, the nib very worn. There was the inkwell.

I lifted the lid of my desk. There was the manuscript book. I reached out for it, though my hand hesitated in the air. What was I doing? I mustn't touch it! I couldn't risk returning to the past – yet I so badly wanted to find out the answers to

everything. I stood transfixed, and then my fingers touched the book and opened it to the first page.

My name is Edie Trimmer. There it was, on the page. And there was my first addition: *I am going to tell you* . . . The writing was similar, written in the same ink, but I could see at a glance that another girl had done it. There was the second addition too: *about my life* . . . The last letter in the word trailed down the page where I'd lost control of the pen. But the rest of the page wasn't empty. It was covered in copperplate handwriting – and the next page and the next and the next, on and on and on.

I rubbed my eyes, angled my lamp differently and bent my head right over the book to see as clearly as possible. The words didn't waver. They were there on the page:

This is my first day in this workhouse – but it is oh so different from the dreadful, pestilent place where I was incarcerated in my childhood. It is clean and fresh and wholesome, and I am determined it shall stay so. I am the new Mistress of Dulcis Workhouse. Mr Dickens and I have given it a new name. Dulcis is the Latin word for pleasant, agreeable, or sweet-smelling, and while I have breath in my body I will make it live up to its title.

Mr Dickens has been so good to me. He is known throughout the

world as a brilliant novelist, but how many know that he is also a passionate social reformer, determined to improve the lot of the poor and wretched? I was certainly a poor and wretched small girl when he came across me that memorable day he came to inspect the old Bonham Street Workhouse. I knew of his great tale, Oliver Twist, and so dared to ask for more gruel when he was inspecting the canteen. He was tickled by my effrontery and took me under his wing there and then.

I do not think Mrs Dickens was particularly pleased about this, feeling it not quite appropriate. Mr Dickens hoped to put on a new production of Oliver Twist with me in the starring role, but sadly he became involved in a stage venture with another young actress, and I did not have my chance after all.

Mr Dickens consulted with his great friend Miss Angela Burdett-Coutts, who recommended a respectable boarding school for girls where I would benefit from a good education. It took me a while to settle there, but it was always a highlight when Mr Dickens visited and made a fuss of me. Miss Burdett-Coutts visited too, but I was always rather shy with her. Still, I am very grateful to her for making sure I had a proper education.

Mr Dickens and Miss Burdett-Coutts conferred together when I reached eighteen, wondering whether I would benefit from a young ladies' finishing school in France or Switzerland, but I had my own ideas.

They were taken aback when I said I wanted to be given a position in a workhouse so that I could learn for myself the management of such establishments and see if I could make them function in a more humane manner. Miss Burdett-Coutts thought this a bizarre idea, not at all suitable employment for an educated young lady. But dear Mr Dickens clapped me on the back and said he thought I showed splendid spirit and promised he would help me however he could.

I have spent the last three years in training at various establishments – all lamentable. It has been hard, unpleasant and exhausting work, and the staff have frequently resented my presence. At times the inmates have mocked and made a fool of me. Sometimes I have been ready to give up altogether, but I have somehow found the strength to grit my teeth and continue. (Maybe because I was very reluctant to admit that Miss Burdett-Coutts had been right!)

It has paid off! For the last six months Mr Dickens has renovated and replumbed and redecorated this entire workhouse, kindly providing the funding. I am in overall charge, but my dear friend and colleague, Mr Algernon Cress, is Master of the men's ward. Miss Wilma Waters is Assistant Matron. We have two sick wards presided over by trained nurses and visited daily by a qualified doctor. The Oliver Ward is for males and the Margaret Ward for females. There are also special facilities for the elderly in the Lavinia Annexe. We also have a male

dormitory and a female dormitory and special married quarters for couples. Parents will have full access to their children. Young persons from four to fourteen will be properly educated. I will personally instruct them in reading, writing and arithmetic, and they will of course learn useful practical skills so they can support themselves in the future.

Every man, woman and child who enters the premises will be treated with respect, clothed decently and given the opportunity to keep clean and tidy at all times. Food will be of good quality and very nourishing. Gruel will never ever be served.

The basement contains the new boiler and pipes for the facilities, and will be used for storage. No one will ever be sent down there as punishment.

If an inmate arrives not knowing their own name then they will be allowed to choose their own new Christian name and surname, and duly registered as such. This is of extreme importance. Oh, I do hope my ideas come to fruition and that Dulcis Workhouse lives up to its own splendid name!

'Edie! Oh Edie, Edie!' Mum and Dad suddenly burst into my bedroom and switched on the main light. They rushed to me, knocking the manuscript to the floor.

'I woke up and found you weren't there!' said Dad.

'Are you all right, darling? What are you doing in your bedroom? You said you didn't want to sleep here tonight!' said Mum.

'I know. But – but I woke up, and – and I came in here – and look, please look!' I snatched the manuscript book from the floor. 'Read it! This proves everything! I really *did* go back into the past and meet Mr Dickens. I've written it down here! Read it – oh, please read it!' I cried, thrusting it at them.

They both peered at it, skimming the words.

'Wow, Edie, this is amazing!' said Dad.

'You've managed to write it exactly as if you *are* a Victorian!' said Mum.

'No, *I* didn't write it,' I said. 'Of course I didn't. The long-ago grown-up Edie wrote it, when she was put in charge of her own workhouse,' I said.

'Come on now, Edie . . . Look, you've used up all the ink in the bottle writing this! And it's so good. I'm so proud of you. Never mind being an actress, I think you're going to become a brilliant, imaginative writer,' said Dad.

'You're so clever,' said Mum. 'But you don't have to keep up this pretence, darling. You're very, very convincing, almost scarily so – but we're not fools. We know no one can *really*

time-travel back into the past.'

That was it. I could see there was no way they would ever believe me. There was no point arguing. I let them lead me back to their bed and cuddle me down with them. I thought I'd stay wide awake, puzzling it over, marvelling at the past-Edie's determination – but I was so exhausted that I fell asleep almost straight away.

When I woke up late the next morning, it all seemed so strange and dreamlike that I started to wonder if I really had sleepwalked into my bedroom and written that account myself. Mum and Dad were surely right. Perhaps the vivid past had really been an extraordinary, hallucinatory dream?

But then Peter and Gordon came to visit me the next morning. They'd heard I'd been ill and in hospital, and were so relieved to see that I was better now.

'Here's your glass bluebird, Edie – as good as new,' said Peter. 'And we've brought you a little get well present too.'

'It's another find from the workhouse trunks,' said Gordon. 'We were working our way through them and we found some old books. Sadly they've got water damage and the bindings are in a dreadful state. They might be worth a fortune if they were in pristine condition, but now they're really only fit for

the scrapheap. But we thought you might like this, Edie, seeing as you were so wrapped up in the musical. It's not a first edition, but there's an inscription that *could* just be valuable.'

It was a copy of *Oliver Twist*. I opened the stained pages. There was the inscription, and a signature with a flamboyant flourish:

To my dear Edie Trimmer –
with love from
Charles Dickens

ALSO AVAILABLE

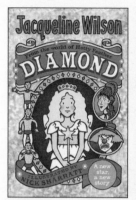

Jacqueline has written lots of other brilliant stories
inspired by history. Have you read them all?

**Find out more about Jacqueline and her books at
www.jacquelinewilson.co.uk**

About the Author

JACQUELINE WILSON wrote her first novel when she was nine years old, and she has been writing ever since. She is now one of Britain's bestselling and most beloved children's authors. She has written over 100 books and is the creator of characters such as Tracy Beaker and Hetty Feather. More than forty million copies of her books have been sold. As well as winning many awards for her books, including the Children's Book of the Year, Jacqueline is a former Children's Laureate, and in 2008 she was appointed a Dame. Jacqueline is also a great reader, and has amassed over twenty thousand books, along with her famous collection of silver rings.

About the Illustrator

RACHAEL DEAN has illustrated numerous books including Aisha Bushby's 'Moonchild' series and 'B is for Ballet', a non-fiction picture book in collaboration with The American Ballet Theatre to mark their 80th anniversary. Rachael works both digitally and traditionally in gouache to create vivid scenes and lively, engaging characters. She is inspired by the natural world, particularly when visiting the gorgeous national park and beach on her doorstep near Liverpool.